GOLDEN VOW

SARAH URQUHART

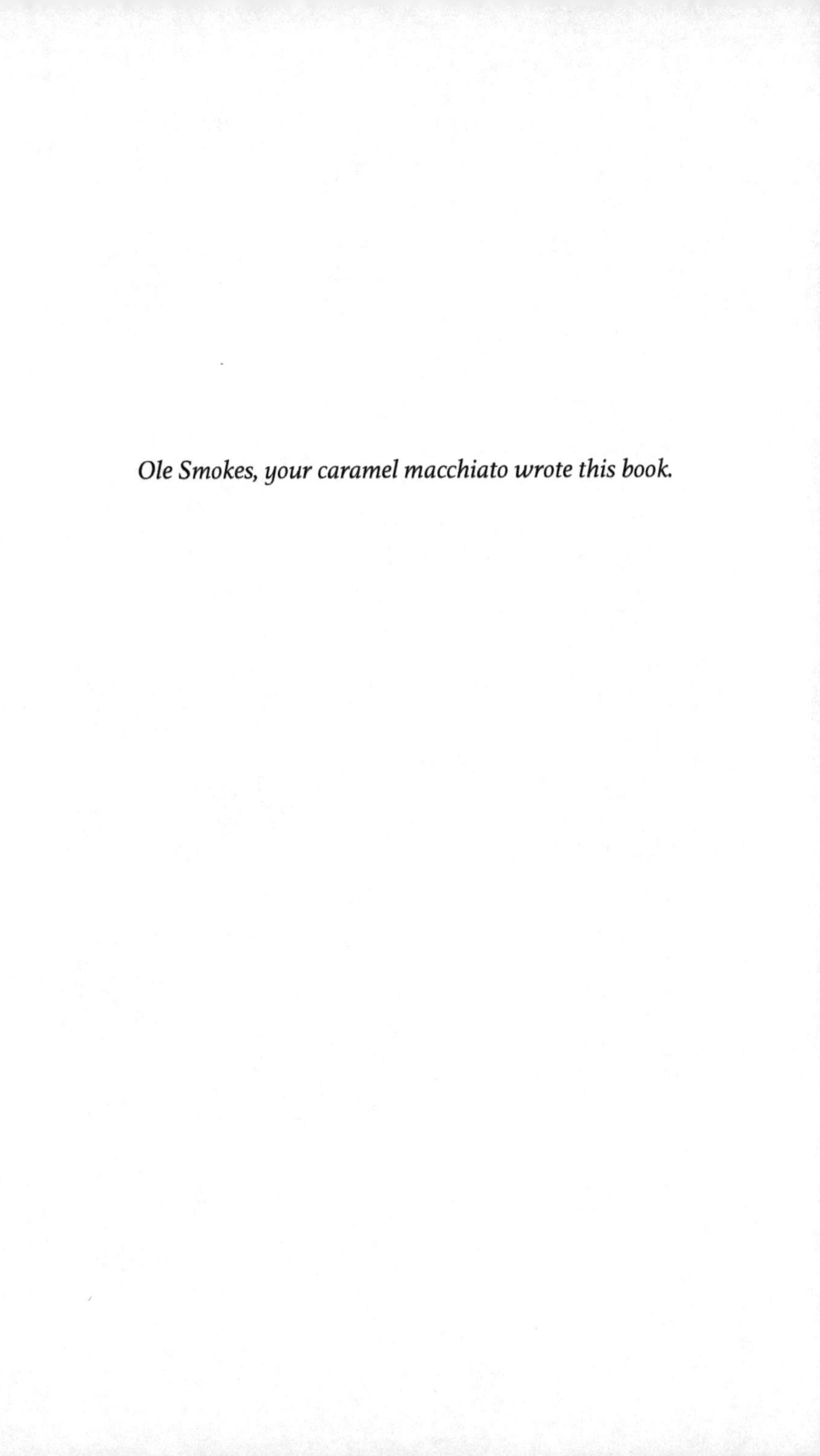

Ole Smokes, your caramel macchiato wrote this book.

ACKNOWLEDGMENTS

It's the end a series, and my first series at that. It's a bittersweet moment for me. I'm sad to let them go, but so happy and proud of myself for all the hard work I've put in and for enjoying almost every moment that goes into a book. There has been so much support for each and every book in this series and I could never thank them enough. First off, thank you. Yes, you. My readers. For continuing to pick up the next book and falling in love with these characters. Thank you to my beta readers, Ellie and Cassia. You two are them best and help me out like no other can. Thank you to my cover designer who has designed all the covers in the Wounded Winds series, and more. I love her work and she's so great to work with. And as always, the biggest thank you to my family and friends for the love, encouragement, and support they give each day. I also need to give a special thanks to my sister for the last minute with this book and the next one coming soon.

I hope you all enjoy Garrett and Nixie's story as we say goodbye to Wounded Winds.

PROLOGUE

Garrett Daly didn't want to move to a new school. He didn't want to make new friends. His little sister bounced with excitement over every little thing, like the word *new* meant shiny and perfect. Well, it turned out that way for her. Not for Garrett.

His new school had bullies. Big ones. They'd left him alone so far, but he caught them staring. It was only a matter of time before Garrett caught their attention. They seemed to pick on almost everyone. Not just mean words, but physically. Only they'd twist it enough to look like an accident. Garrett had enough of seeing kids crying beside their broken bike or bruises growing on someone's head from a ball or the swing set.

"How was school today?" His mom asked as he tossed his backpack in his room and returned to the kitchen.

"Same."

"Same as what?" She turned to him while drying her hands on a towel.

"The bullies are bad there, mom."

"You've mentioned that before, but I talked to your principal several times. She's adamant there isn't a bullying problem. Only a lot of misunderstandings."

Garrett attempted the same *what-do-you-think* look his parents had used on him when he asked for candy before supper.

His mom sighed. "This isn't the best advice a mother should give her nine-year-old son, but if the adults won't believe anyone about the bullies, maybe it isn't the adults who need to handle the bullies."

Garrett frowned. His mom hadn't said someone should hit them back, did she? She tossed him an apple through the air and he caught it. Even if that was what she'd meant, that wasn't what Garrett would do.

The next day at school, he mulled over his mom's words while watching a couple kids time their push down the slide to slam their foot into the back of another kid's knee, sending him face first to the ground. The kid was at least a year younger than Garrett, maybe two. He pushed himself up from the ground, blood pouring from a swollen lip. In that moment, Garrett knew what he was going to do.

Running inside, he went to the main office and searched behind the desk.

"Excuse me, young man. What do you think you're doing?"

"If you guys won't help all the kids being bullied, I will." He found the first aid kit and dashed back outside. He didn't know a lot, but his mom had shown him the basics any time he'd been hurt.

The bully at the end of the slide wouldn't let the kid get up off his knees. Well, Garrett was going to be a target, eventually. Might as well be for a good reason. Garrett shoved the bully's feet, leaving him stunned enough to pause. With a hand under the kid's arm, he pulled him to his feet.

"Come sit over here." He sat the kid down on the swing.

"You know how to use what's in that?" The kid slurred over his swollen lip.

"Some of it." Garrett shrugged and opened the kit.

"I should go in to the school nurse." Yet, the kid gripped the chains and stayed put.

"She doesn't do much, does she?"

"No."

"And neither do the teachers." Garrett pulled out some gauze and the bottle of stuff his mom said cleans cuts. "I think this is going to sting." He poured a little on the gauze, as he'd seen his mom do by pressing the gauze to the top of the bottle before tipping. The kid's eyes welled when Garrett dabbed the cut on his lip. "Sorry." But the best thing was to get it over with.

Once Garrett had cleaned the kid's lip, he found the teeny tiny bandages. He didn't think they were the right thing to use, but it was better than him continuing to bleed. He put a couple over the cut.

"Now, go take an ice-pack from the nurse's freezer."

"Thanks." The kid swallowed hard, then left. Garrett packed up the first-aid kit, but paused as the hairs on the back of his neck stood up. It was his turn now.

"What makes you think you were allowed to do that?" The bully from the slide stood with his fists on his hips.

"Could ask you the same thing." He shrugged.

The bully grabbed the back collar of Garrett's shirt and pulled him up from the ground, the first-aid kit spilling as the handle caught on his hand.

"Put me down." Garrett tried to sound firm, lowering his voice. He knew it didn't work when the bully laughed.

"It's your turn." He tossed him so his shoulder hit the metal pole on the swing set. No choice was a good one. But he didn't deserve to get beaten up for helping another kid. Garrett pulled himself up and set his feet into the ground, running as fast as he could. He ran straight for the woods and off school property. He'd deal with those consequences later.

The bully ran after him, calling him a coward, amongst other names. He hit the tree line and started veering left and right to keep from hitting a trunk with his face. The bully gained ground, the sound of his feet getting closer.

A flash of gold moved around a tree. Garrett frowned, but kept running. The gold appeared again, spinning around a different tree and shooting out behind it like an arrow. Whatever it was seemed to show him which way to go. Garrett followed it when it appeared a third time, flowing out from the back of a tree.

The gold changed his direction enough that Garrett put more distance between him and the bully, but the bully had the tenacity to keep chasing him.

A clearing opened, only small enough for a sunny grass patch. He stopped to catch his breath and listen.

"Where are you, new kid? You can't run forever." Garrett didn't have much time.

A high squawk called out. Garrett looked up but saw nothing. The same squawk sounded out in three quick successions. Garrett turned and on the lowest branch of one tree sat a baby bird. He didn't know what kind, and he didn't have the time to wonder.

The bird looked toward the bully, then pushed off the tree and swooped straight toward Garrett. A golden breeze rushed in behind the bird. A scream stuck in his throat, and he held it in. If he didn't, he'd draw the bully right to him. For now, he'd take his chances with a wild bird and something strange and gold. He put his arms up to fend them off, but created a perch for the bird instead. The breeze hit his face, warm to the touch.

The wind grew in size, billowing around him as the footsteps of the bully drew closer.

Pain surged through his body, but the warmth of the wind followed it all. Something was happening to him and Garrett didn't know what he should focus on—the pain or the bully. The bully won and Garrett kept himself quiet.

The wind encased him before dropping him to the ground.

What was that? He hadn't meant to say that out loud, but yet his voice echoed from somewhere. Everything looked so big.

Come on. We have to get out of here. He's getting close.

Whipping his head around, he saw the baby bird sitting beside him who didn't look much like a baby anymore.

Flap now, questions later. The bird nudged his head at Garrett's side. He looked down and saw his arm covered in feathers. But that wasn't his arm. It was a wing. *Like this.* The bird tried to show him.

"Get back here, now." The bully wasn't far.

Garrett shook from the thought of what the bully would do to a couple of baby birds, so he copied the bird next to him. He fell, hitting his chest and face on the ground twice before he made it into the air. He followed the other bird halfway up the tree. Garrett put his feet out to land, but didn't have the balance. The bird caught his forward motion and righted him on the branch. Just in time for the bully to stop in the clearing, where Garrett's clothes sat in a pile on the ground.

Please don't take them. Please don't take them. Not that Garrett knew if he'd ever be able to wear them again. He was supposed to be a boy, not a bird. He tried not to panic while the bully kicked his clothes and circled the clearing.

"Come out! I can't wait to see how much detention you get for leaving the school grounds. Then coming back without your clothes." He bent to pick up Garrett's clothes, but a loud screech stopped him. An adult version of the bird sitting next to him dived straight for the bully's head. The bully screamed and swatted at the air. The bird came at him again, but this time grabbed Garrett's clothes from the ground. When the bird screeched a third time, the bully turned and ran back toward the school.

Thanks for saving me. Garrett shuffled his feet, feeling odd balancing on a tree branch without his hands gripping onto something.

What was he going to do? The bird snapped his beak after the bully.

Not sure. But it would have hurt. Probably more than whatever that golden wind had done to him. *Are you an eagle?*

No. The bird's voice sounded like he chuckled. *But you can call me an eagle if you want.*

What happened to me?

The bird puffed out his chest. *Welcome to the wild, my friend.*

1

———

He'd only have one shot at this. Get in and get her out with no one noticing, at least long enough for them to get away. His plan assumed his sister was still alive despite his hope for that had died along with the man who took her. Garrett circled the building, taking in each guard he spotted. Their features, body structure, gait—all things to ensure he'd recognize them at first glance. A running tally in his head counted ten cameras around the perimeter, not including any at the front of the mansion or dispersed throughout the trees. The sides and back watched both the ground and the sky from different angles.

Garrett perched on a branch. White spruces blocked in the landscaped mansion that sat on the side of a foothill.

The last several years had been one big *if*. He never expected his sister to survive when taken as collateral. Garrett needed to confirm his sister's death to find closure.

But he'd found a different story, one that meant his sister might not have died, at least not when he'd thought. Bringing him to Fort Vale to stake out Keith Jeffreys' haven.

A money man mogul, a loan shark with fingers in too many honey pots.

Every bedroom on the upper level of the white building had a balcony, and every room on the main level opened up to a wrap-around terrace. In a day he'd already seen ten times the security of the underground fighting ring.

But while Garrett had learned a lot about Jeffreys, he didn't know how he ran his isolated home.

Shaking the chill out of his feathers, Garrett settled on the branch and watched from afar. This would take time. Being a hawk shifter came in handy for surveillance. But he couldn't get too close, not yet. The guards were geared to the nines with knives attached to most of their bodies. They weren't just muscle.

Before arriving in the mountains, Garrett had acquired equipment of his own—binoculars, bugs, and camping gear. Shifters came in many kinds—wolves, bears—but Garrett preferred the inconspicuous bird of prey he was. When debilitating fear for his sister didn't trap him, or someone forced him to doctor captive women, freedom rode through his heart. Taking to the sky, like he'd take to another world. He craved to feel that freedom again. As soon as he either found his sister or gained the closure from her death, that freedom would take over his life. He didn't need to work. Besides, being a doctor had lost its appeal a long time ago.

Guilt squelched every breath he took. He should have done more. But Anya was innocent, just as every other captive woman. Garrett refused to take that risk on her behalf. He did his best to care for the fighters. They hadn't trusted him or realized he'd cared for each one of them.

Being part of that, even forced to be part of that, took away his right to be a doctor. The moment Zachary and his rag-tag group of shifters barged in and destroyed the fighting ring, Garrett quit his job at the hospital. Only his sister mattered now.

Spreading his wings, he pushed off the branch. He first flew away from the mansion before circling back to go around the property. A couple of high cameras turned, sensing his motion. He needed to fly close to the windows. A risk too great at the moment. Even if it killed him, he needed to take his time. One chance, one shot, at getting his sister and getting out.

For the past hour Bugattis, Mercedes Benzes, and Aston Martins had dropped off well appointed guests at the tall, black metal gate. Guards escorted each of them up the drive and inside. It seemed Jeffreys liked to host. Heels clicked on the long paved driveway to the front door, framed with security. Light filled the windows of the main level and soft instrumental music used the breeze to pounce through the air. The crowd wasn't large and, based on the interactions between the guards and guests, they only allowed select attendees.

He tilted in the air to return to the white spruce in which he'd first perched. All rooms on the upper level sat in darkness. Garrett was curious about who stayed in each of the darkened rooms on the upper level.

A yellow glow softened one room. Garrett's attention snapped to the balcony door. A feminine figure stood behind sheer curtains. His flight faltered. The twitch in his wings made him drop in altitude. Firming his muscles, he brought himself back up and spun in the air to veer his trajectory back to the tree. He arrived in time to see the shadow of fabric shimmering to the floor. The figure stepped back.

It was enough hope for Garrett to keep from only going through the motions. There was at least one woman in that mansion. Whether it was Anya Daly or a woman that stood by Keith Jeffreys' side, she was the key to finding out what happened to his sister.

THE DISGUST REMAINED low in her chest as she peeled the skin tight dress off her shoulders. Letting it show only made her more miserable. She let those feelings stew, building strength for when she needed them.

The red fabric had little give. She risked his ire leaving the party early, but she wasn't in danger yet. Nixie Hutton had been here too long, and she'd only done it to herself. Being the only woman living at the estate gave her a modicum of safety, but it wouldn't last. Soon, he'd have another woman to use. It saddened Nixie how gullible young women were. She hated herself for it. The promise of fancy things and luxury lured her and so many others in. But when they said 'Thanks for a great time,' and tried to leave, they learned how trapped they were. It didn't take long to resent luxury.

Pushing the dress past her hips, she watched it drop to the ground. The bright red silk had been the first dress she'd worn here. The first time he'd used her as his arm candy, she'd felt like a million dollars. If Nixie never saw a scrap of silk, sparkling heels, expensive makeup, or a curling iron ever again, she'd die happy.

Reaching her arms behind her, she pinched the spine of her bustier to release the hooks. Nixie had made it through the small party with getting nothing on her dress. She wouldn't give herself more work to do when she could hang the garment back in the closet and wear it another time before setting it aside to wash.

The curtains provided an illusion of what lay outside. Oranges of the sunset shone through the sheer fabric hiding her wooden prison. She took a moment to be grateful that she was still here. Her determination to escape beat against her heart, the drum of an inner warrior fueling her soul. The day that drum died would be the day fear controlled Nixie.

One last deep breath in the sunset hues and Nixie bent to pick up the garments from the floor. She kicked her heels into the closet and sighed as her toes wove into the plush carpet.

Her door burst open, and she sighed for another reason. Dropping the dress, she grabbed the robe hanging on the door. She wrapped it around her bare back and covered her chest before turning on the intruder.

"What?" Nixie threw her head to the side, speaking with more power than she held.

"He wants you downstairs." Brent, one of the few security guards Keith ever sent for her, stood with his hands braced in his belt.

"I've done my job for tonight." She leaned against the wall outside her closet.

"He says otherwise. Put your dress back on."

"No." Nixie didn't move, not an inch. No flinch or twitch of her lips. No lift of her brow or flick of her eye. Once again, projecting more power than she had.

"You'll be punished." An anticipatory sneer lifted his scarred face. Keith liked to punish in front of a crowd.

"Do I look like I care?" The ugliness in his black eyes made it difficult to keep her steady stance against the wall. She didn't release the air building in her lungs until he turned away.

"Fucking brat." He slammed the door on his way out.

She didn't have a reason to leave the party early. It would be smart to save herself the bruises and embarrassment and just go back downstairs. But part of her wanted to hold on to some personality of her own. She'd need it when she escaped. Escaped and lived the most humble life possible.

Remaining against the wall, Nixie waited. Her punishment could stomp back up the stairs to throw her down them or he'd let her wait, thinking the anticipation of what was to come would make it worse. She'd rather not be naked and in the shower if he came for her tonight.

Wonder and an uptight smugness had filled her first days here at the ripe age of nineteen. Nixie had believed she'd struck gold. Offered everything someone could ever want. Gourmet food, safety under guard, jewels and gifts, lavish parties, and the beautiful suite that was her room, her home. But every single one of those came with a catch. She could never leave. Something forced isn't a gift.

Escape was turning into an idea rather than a possibility. Opportunity had thrown itself at her so many times over the years, but she'd always stayed back to protect the others. Not every woman that came here was strong enough to handle Keith. Nixie had always turned his attention toward her, sparing the others the worst. Keith had an odd obsession with her. An amused anger controlled him whenever she impeded his plans or challenged him. Being the only woman left put more attention on her, making escape ten times more difficult. It would have been difficult before, but at least there had been a fleeting chance of outrunning his security with their attention divided between other women. She didn't regret staying for the others, shouldering the burden of their lives.

As the party carried on below and no thumping sounded on the rounding staircase leading to her room,

Nixie dropped the robe. Cool tile shocked her feet as she stepped into her bathroom. A large vanity ran half the room on one side, while the other had a Jacuzzi tub in one corner and a tiled shower in the other. Both pieces over the top. Starting the shower, she stepped under the overhead spray. Her hands came away black from her running mascara as she swiped her cheeks and pushed back her hair.

Keith chose everything for her—clothes, products, hiring stylists to come in and change her to his whim. She was an image. An image to portray his wealth. His wealth was his business, after all.

Nixie washed away the night. For the few moments that she emerged from a shower or bath, she felt like herself, that young woman emerging into the world. It only lasted as long as it took her to crawl into the plush bedding with floral vomit. Bedding and decorations she'd picked out herself as a fanciful young girl. Part of the gifts Keith offered.

The mansion had six other rooms identical to hers, but stripped of their decor while they remained unoccupied. Gifts and luxury, her own palace room, would be what Keith used to lure the next ignorant woman in. Looking back, she should have seen the signs.

Punching the pillow, she pulled it forward to lay her arm across it. Nixie closed her eyes and called for sleep. Keith's punishments no longer held the weight he thought they did —not for Nixie. She'd put on the show, put it behind her and focus on the next day, the next performance. Sleep and her health were more important to hold on to if escape was her goal.

GARRETT HAD MAPPED the guard rotations, recognizing specific guards. But their system lacked strict consistency from the more experienced guards—meaning they'd be harder to predict. He needed to be cautious during their shifts. Several birds of prey flew around this territory. Garrett didn't need to worry about the cameras spotting him. But he didn't want the guards to recognize him if he hung around too much. The cameras aimed at each of the balconies posed the biggest problem for now. He'd worry about the perimeter ones when it came time to flee. But with eyes directed toward the bedrooms, getting inside would be difficult.

When scouting the perimeter, the guards either stayed silent, or they didn't speak of any information regarding the mansion, the security, or Jeffreys. The damn men were too well trained.

Guards worked on either four hour or six-hour rotations —intervals chosen at random with different start times. Guards changed somewhere on the property every hour. Garrett had watched for patterns and holes in their grid over the past week.

Only one bedroom on the upper level had any activity. One woman that often stood in front of the balcony, but had yet to step outside. Her figure and height didn't match his sister's, but he didn't know what the woman wore on her feet to increase her height and years of distress changed a person physically. Captivity altered habits, affecting a person's metabolism, hormone release, stress. Garrett believed the woman who'd undressed behind the curtain wasn't Anya. But he wouldn't feel certain until he saw her face.

When he wasn't flying around the property monitoring

the guards, he perched in the closest tree he dared and stared at the balcony, hoping for a glimpse.

He'd planted listening devices through the nights along the guards' routes on the outside of the perimeter. He'd plant them closer to the mansion with each opportunity.

Jeffreys placed strict measures for each person attending the two events Garrett had witnessed. The guards at the door knew them all by sight. They frisked each one before allowing them up the lane to the house. Getting his own personal inside look wasn't possible and getting an invitation inside would take more time than Garrett wanted. For now, he had an advantage as a hawk and he'd use it. He'd participated in enough illegal organizations. Going undercover into another one didn't sit right with him.

He'd set up a camp for himself outside of their search territory, as close as he dared and still within range of the bugs. His equipment recorded every word, saving the conversations and backing them up for him to listen to when resting. But the moments he allowed his focus to rest away from the guards and security, his glowing eyes narrowed on the single lit bedroom.

She drifted across the room and back. Her head tilted, cascading long waves of hair over her shoulder. Holding her hands in front of her, she twisted them. A slender shadow showed her every curve. Not his sister.

Her head snapped up. A man walked toward her. She twisted away from his grasp, but not quick enough. Grabbing her arm, he yanked her from the room. Garrett's talons seized the branch under his feet. He pulled whatever disgusting power he had left from working in the fighting ring to keep himself still and wait it out. Flying in there to help her would only get himself killed. And her. Captive or sidekick, it didn't matter.

An agonizing hour passed. His feet ached from his fierce grip. The flight muscles in his body and wings remained ready to let loose their energy. She was his target for information.

A quick shadow lurched forward, hitting the floor and disappearing from sight. A few moments passed until she pushed herself up and limped away. Jeffreys hurt her.

Garrett's wings spread wide. He could help her. A ghost from the past had helped him combine traditional and modern medicine. He'd used that to help the fighters when Tyrone had blackmailed him. Those women may not have realized it, but he'd cared for them. Garrett's guilt had almost killed him, believing he'd never done enough.

Eyes hot, he waited for her to reappear. She did. And finally, the balcony door opened. She pushed through the curtain and stepped under the moonlight, still limping as she moved. With a blanket wrapped around her shoulders, she leaned heavily against the rail. As he'd expected, she wasn't Anya. But beautiful chestnut hair with a soft sheen reached the centre of her back. A heart-shaped face with narrow eyes stared at the stars.

Garrett resettled in the tree, giving his talons some rest. She was okay, for now.

Her lips moved as if speaking to herself. Garrett spied the balcony camera. It swung from side to side, searching for the movement that triggered the sensor when she'd stepped outside. She stood in the outside corner. The camera reached the entire door, but never turned far enough to catch the outer corners. Interesting. It was a blind spot Garrett could use.

Wishing he could hear her, he focused on her lips, trying to read them. She spoke too softly to make out the shape of the words. Her eyes closed, and she reached a hand out of the blanket. Tears trailed down her cheeks as she rubbed her injured leg. What had the bastard done to her?

Wiping her tears, she winced with pain as she stepped back inside. Garrett cursed. Fucking cameras. He needed to map their blind spots. Evidence pointed to only one woman in that mansion. And Garrett needed to get her out. She'd come willingly, or he'd force her out. Garrett needed all the information she had.

And he needed to help her.

${{\Large 2}}$

2

Keith was getting careless with his punishments. Never had he waited almost a full week to enact his ire for her disobedience. But he'd let her stew until he cracked, doing his best to crack the bone in her leg. He only got five swings in with the pipe when one guard reminded him how much he liked the heels he forced her to wear. Walking in high spikes such as those was an art. If he permanently damaged her leg, she'd never be able to wear them. Keith's tastes were odd and sick, but in this case, they saved her from disfigurement. But not before causing some damage. The guards had looked her leg over before tossing her into her room, ensuring Keith had only badly bruised her and she needed to rest. It felt like more than a bruise, but Nixie pushed herself up and walked about her room and into the night air, trying to prove to herself she was okay.

The pain had spread faster than a wildfire while she stood on the balcony. But she pushed through long enough to draw a bath. They didn't provide her with pain medication, so her only remedy was a hot bath. Pouring Epsom salt into the water, she dropped her blanket and nightdress. Stepping in, Nixie gripped the side to lower herself while keeping her injured leg straight. She watched the edge of the water creep up her body as the tub filled. The outside of her right thigh bloomed with purples and blues. They'd fade. She'd be fine. But knowing that didn't stop the tears pricking her eyes while watching the colours distort beneath the water's surface.

Once the water covered her breasts, she reached over and turned the gold plated taps. Heat seeped through her skin, warming her muscles and joints, calming the pain in her leg.

Keith had talked of acquiring more girls again. Nixie's emotions swung like a pendulum. His focus would alter and she'd see opportunities to escape. But one look at her bruised leg, and she knew she'd leave the women to more of that if she didn't stay. Whether or not she was here, he'd get more women, but she wanted to help them in whatever small way she could. Even when it meant facilitating their escape rather than her own. Not all got away, the results devastating, but each one knew the risks before their attempt. And the chance at freedom was worth the risk.

Nixie wanted that chance to be higher for her to attempt. She'd survived here this long. She'd continue to do so until the risk of staying outweighed the risk of escape.

Pulling in a slow breath, she held it while sinking deeper. Heat encased her shoulders, neck, face, tingling over her scalp as her hair absorbed the water. Bubbles blew her nose seconds before she emerged, the water line resting at her chin. Not caring, Nixie reached for the bar of soap sitting on the edge of the tub. Being clean and resting had to be her only concern. The sweet smelling shampoos, soaps, and lotions didn't hold any interest. She ran the bar over her scalp and body, letting the water take it away as she scrubbed. Sinking down once more, she ran her fingers through her hair.

Getting out of the tub was more difficult than getting in. While the heat helped, as soon as she put weight on her leg, pain exploded anew. She left the water without draining it and wrapped herself in a towel. The edge of the bed sank under her weight, tilting her forward. Pushing herself back, she freed the towel and squeezed her hair dry.

She eyed the balcony. Air sure to nourish only stifled her as much as being in this mansion. Cameras watched her every move outside. If she thought they wouldn't spot her climbing, she'd tie together every piece of fabric and escape in the most cliched way imaginable. But the cameras recorded everything that walked in and out of that door and everything along the side of the house. There was no way to lower a maiden-made rope or to let down her hair for the handsome prince to climb without them knowing and catching her before her feet hit the ground.

But those two outer corners, she'd learned a long time ago they were blind spots. The only brief moments of outside privacy she had. The first time she discovered it, she stayed there until someone barged into the room looking for her. Her door had banged against the wall and guards yelled up at her from the ground. It hadn't been long enough to escape. Since then, she only spent short moments in the blind spot, not giving them a reason to cover it. Nixie cherished those two corners.

Tossing the towel to the floor, she pulled her still damp body up the bed. She hissed when the weight of the duvet landed on her thigh. Adjusting to alleviate the pain, Nixie allowed her head to sink into the pillow. The moonlight was the last thing she saw as she closed her eyes, imagining tying the end of a long golden braid to the balcony, swinging herself over the edge, then slicing off her hair before making a run for it into the trees. She didn't want a damn prince coming to her rescue. Even a prince was a man with expectations.

THE WOMAN HADN'T LEFT her room in days. Her limp lessened as that short time passed. Garrett had memorized her features each time she stepped outside. Soft freckles dotted her rounded cheeks. Soon he'd learned her moving lips when on the balcony corner was her way of counting. She timed those moments in the blind spots. The woman was a prisoner. And with or without his sister, Garrett would do what he could to help her. The first step to that was getting close to her without alerting security.

Very few windows presented themselves to get to her balcony. And once there, he had to wait for the next window to leave.

The guards passed below, the cameras rotated, and Garrett took flight. Sensors caught the movement, their low frequency humming in his ear. He rotated in the air to stay ahead, pulling himself up the moment he reached the balcony. His talons wrapped around the wood. He stilled, letting silence descend. The cameras resumed their normal movement and no footsteps, even light practiced ones, sounded on the ground below. Mentally timing the patrols for this side of the mansion, Garrett waited, hoping the woman would step outside in the short time he had.

An imaginary clock ticked by in his mind. Leveling his breath, he focused on the door, on her light footsteps on the carpet. Time narrowed down. Guards were about to appear around each corner. He didn't hear them, but his senses struck his spine.

She walked past the door, pausing before facing him through the curtain.

His head twitched at the faint rustle of fabric. Damn it. Time was up.

She stepped toward the door, her hand reaching out. Garrett's lungs seized. He needed to fly now, but not when she was about to come outside. He couldn't leave her. Frozen until the last moment, Garrett stayed.

The door opened, and he lifted his wings to glide down the inside of the railing, staying in direct contact with the wood to ensure he didn't trigger the camera. She paused in the door, but turned her head the same moment the guards' movements rustled beneath them. So faint, but audible to him. They reached their opposite corners, and she stepped onto the balcony, taking residence in the opposite corner, the other blind spot.

Garrett hopped back up the railing, putting himself at eye level. The momentary risk of the passing guards dissipated, and he took in a deep breath for balance. But that breath almost knocked him three stories below to the ground. His talons gripped fiercely to stay where he was, and his golden wind brushed his back before circling her. Chocolate and an earthy tone filled his senses. Dizziness swamped his body, his blood turning light, flowing through his body faster than normal.

My mate.

She was his mate. There was only one course of action, independent of finding his sister. Rescue his mate.

"I always thought birds were smarter than people gave them credit for." Her soft croon calmed him. His next breath came a little easier. "Smart enough to hide from people like them." She tilted her head to the side, over the railing. Her soft curls blew in the breeze as she held her head there. "You're a handsome thing. And the first visitor I've had in a very long time. Well, the only visitor. I'm going to pretend you landed here just to see me. True or not, that's how I'll retell the tale to myself when I'm lonely." She straightened her head and pitched her tone up. "It's not all bad, Nixie. A handsome hawk liked the sight of you enough to land on your balcony."

Ice-blue eyes lifted at the corners as she smiled at him. Faint freckles dotted her smooth skin. Nixie. What a name. And he loved it. A fierce soul and an impish gaze. If Garrett was meant to have any happiness in his life, it was meant to come from her.

His time was running out. Nixie eyed the corners. She knew their schedules as much as he did, maybe more.

"Promise me something, handsome. Come back and visit me."

Garrett would be there every night. And soon would get her out of there.

"Better get going. Even I don't like to be seen by the guards below." Nixie pushed off the railing and went inside, pausing before closing the door. It was almost impossible to fly away from her with her eyes on him. But the guards were close. He had to fly.

Closing his eyes, he blocked out his mate. Taking to the sky, he swooped and spun to avoid the moving cameras. But he didn't go far. Only to the closest white spruce. Perching on the familiar branch, he looked back at the mansion. Nixie still stood just beyond the glass door and the guards passed each other below.

Not that he hadn't planned to help Nixie escape, but

now that he knew she was his mate, fear filled him that he'd lose her before he ever had her.

◆

NOT ONLY HER MUSCLES ACHED, but pain throbbed deep in her right femur. Even without the three-inch heels, Nixie's leg still pained her. But it lessened with each day. Today, Keith wouldn't let her sit.

"Pour Mr. Smith and myself something to drink, Nicole." Nixie blinked to hide her eye roll. Keith didn't believe her given name was Nixie and insisted on calling her Nicole. Many school teachers assumed Nixie was a nickname and had done the same thing. She hated it—the sweet sound that stretched around the 'o' didn't suit her.

Nixie lengthened her stride to slow her legs as she walked to the liquor cart at the side of the room.

"You understand the terms on our contract, don't you, Mr. Smith?" Keith lifted an ankle onto his knee.

"Yes, sir. I do." Mr. Smith squared his shoulders. Nixie winced. He didn't understand. But Keith was about to explain it to him in not-so-clear terms. She'd witnessed this conversation a million times.

"And you don't have any concerns about the interest payments?"

"They are steep, but that's okay." Few ever had the hope of paying in full, but they pushed forward, believing that money from the evil loan shark was their only option. But it was never worth the risk.

"And you understand what happens if you are late on any payments or don't make the interest payments in full?"

The men silenced themselves when she turned back with their drinks, her heels clicking on the floor. The slow staccato adding to the atmosphere. Keith smirked as the intimidation thickened and Mr. Smith's eyes flickered. Damn. Nixie hadn't meant to do that.

She passed Keith his drink first, then turned around to pass over the other. She tried offering a sympathetic smile and a glance to the door, saying *Get the hell out of here, dumb ass*, but Mr. Smith didn't look up.

"Well?" Keith prompted.

"I believe so." The poor man stuttered.

"I don't give extensions, Mr. Smith. If you miss a payment, I will come after you and take the payment. If your payments are less than the agreed-upon amount, I will come to take the outstanding amount and more. If the loan and the interest are not paid off by the date declared in our contract, your business will remain in my name and I will remove you from all dealings. If you're lucky, that is all that will happen to you." Keith had his security in his contracts. Any business he supplied with a loan, he'd transfer that business to him. If they paid the loan off under the circumstances of the contract, he returned the business to the original owner. If not, then he kept it. He did something similar for personal loans, forcing them to transfer land, mortgages, and assets to him until they paid off the loan.

He'd collected enough to make himself an enormous fortune. Paying off one of Keith's loans was near impossible. Just possible enough that suckers kept seeking him out.

"I understand. I hope you'll be understanding if circumstances are out of my control arise."

"That's your problem, not mine. I suggest, Mr. Smith, you remain firmly in control of everything and everyone around you that affects your," Keith gave a quick shake to his head before pulling up a side smile, "our business."

"Wise advice. Thank you." They always thanked him.

They handed everything they owned over to him for the small chance at a Hail Mary, and they thanked him.

"How's your drink?" Keith emptied his glass.

"Great. Thank you." He hadn't had a single sip. Mr. Smith didn't know it yet, but he'd just signed away his life and any future for his loved ones.

Nixie stood on the imaginary X on which Keith had placed her before Mr. Smith had arrived. Agony pushed through her system with her fight not to shuffle her feet. Keith engaged the other man in meaningless conversation, ensuring fear at what he could do while laughing at others' misfortunes. Nixie zoned out, knowing she couldn't help the idiot willing to risk his livelihood and having heard Keith's stories many times before.

Her thoughts drifted to her balcony visitor. It was foolish to believe he'd come there to see her. He was just a hawk looking for a place to land, but those golden eyes were like a deep mirror protecting her soul within it. If nothing else, it made her feel better to imagine someone looked for her, even if it was just a hawk.

"What do you think, Nicole?" Shit. Keith had noticed her lack of attention. He didn't like that. Her leg throbbed, anticipating another blow.

"You always know what I think." She smiled to show off her dimple and widened her narrow eyes, attempting playfulness that sometimes got her out of trouble. Her attitude walked a fine line between cute and insolent. It was always a gamble, but it intrigued him enough he kept her.

"Indeed." Keith nodded to one guard, then turned his gaze back to Mr. Smith. "It's a pleasure doing business with you. I look forward to seeing you again when you personally deliver your first payment."

Mr. Smith stood and nodded his goodbye. He stopped

short when he turned and bumped into the guard that waited to escort him out. Keith waited until the closing of the door echoed against the tile in the foyer.

"Nicole."

Nixie bit her tongue.

"I require your attention at all times. The other night should have reminded you of your responsibilities and the precarious position you find yourself in."

"I'll happily give you my resignation and be on my way if you're no longer satisfied with my performance."

Keith lunged from the chair. His dark presence overpowered her before she stepped out of his reach. Blunt fingers gripped her jaw, pulling her to her toes. His hot breath carried the scent of mint and alcohol. Tanned skin circled almost black eyes. A single strand came loose from his gelled hair with his temper. "I've given you a better life than you could imagine."

"Have you?"

"Ungrateful brat." He spat, the small ball running down her cheek.

"A beautifully decorated prison is still a prison." Her whisper sounded loud between them.

"You are not an idiot, Nicole. Acting like one won't help you." He released her, and she stumbled to hold her weight after the sudden drop. "Return her to her room. Missing a few meals should remind her what she should be grateful for."

Boy, did he have that backwards. Nixie's hatred and determination only grew with every word from his full lips. Nixie would free herself from him.

3
_____

G arrett spent the day at his camp, scouring through his notes, maps, and recordings. He'd already committed it all to memory, but he wouldn't take any chances that he'd missed something. What he'd needed from this time at camp was space. If he didn't get a handle on the dizziness from her presence, he'd get caught, or worse, get them both caught. Visiting her each night was the best way. But that dizziness had lasted most of the night, forcing him back to camp to rest.

The hair on his arms stood on end, his senses detecting another presence. Garrett looked up, and sitting on the opposite side of his campfire was a familiar face. A wise woman that had helped him look after the fighters for years. A ghost, a spirit, another being. He wasn't sure.

"She's my mate, huh?"

"Yes, she is." The translucent woman sat on a log, bracing herself on the heels of her hands.

"Why?" The pain scratching his voice surprised him. He didn't understand why Fate would grant him a mate.

"Did you believe there wouldn't be a mate out there for

you?" She tilted her face with a motherly sadness, her long braid dropping over her shoulder.

"No, I didn't." He'd accepted that fact a long time ago. Not after what he'd done, forced or not, did he deserved a mate and the happiness he'd witnessed in others.

"It's time I told you where shifters come from."

You think? His lips pinched. He didn't dare voice any disrespect toward her. Her tilted lip and quirked brow still scolded him for thoughts unspoken.

"I've never even told you my name. My name is Margaret. I was a witch a long time ago. The end of magic came at a time that put many in danger for a cause that wasn't theirs."

"The witch trials?"

She nodded. "So many innocent women died. Very few were true witches. Very few had any knowledge of the magical beings out there. But those stories spread. It wouldn't have been long before they accused others over people's imaginings and burned them as well. We saved who we could, but all magic stopped and those with any abilities went into hiding. Witches, shifters, and more. We wouldn't risk innocent lives."

"I'm so sorry."

"Shifters were protectors. They were the guards, the soldiers. But as they completed their job, protecting and hiding all who needed it from the fearful public, their species ended. So as not to risk another witch trial or something worse, Fate stopped granting the gift, and no longer allowed it to pass down through bloodlines. Until recently."

"Are you saying all the shifters now are descendants of an original line?"

"Some of you are. Not everyone. You're protectors. Fate saw a need in the world once again. When your species died off, the essence of that magic was preserved in the wind, souls that search for the protectors the world needs. That's your source. And protecting anyone who needs it is your purpose. So yes, dear hawk, you deserve a mate."

"How do I deserve a mate after I did nothing to help free so many?" Some days the guilt simmered low, a slow-moving brook in his soul. But there were times it rushed through him with the strength of a hurricane.

"Why do you think I stood beside you through that?" Margaret's eyes saddened, looking glassy despite being translucent. "You helped them, and I gave you everything I could to help you. If it hadn't been you, it would have been another and more of them would have lost their lives. I don't need to tell you that."

"And Fate expects her to trust me?" Garrett pointed behind him in the direction of the mansion. Why would Nixie trust someone with his resume after living the life of a captive herself?

"You both want the same thing. Peace," she whispered. "Get through these trials and you'll both have peace."

After finding his sister, Garrett planned to live quiet and alone. Maybe to some, that sounded like peace.

"Please, don't doubt yourself." Margaret pleaded, her hands clasped in her lap.

"I have more questions." He'd give no promises. But he needed to know more.

"I'll answer everything I can."

"Is my sister alive?"

"I'm unsure. Fate doesn't always tell me everything— only what She thinks I need to help any of you. I've asked. But she gave me no answer. I'm sorry."

"How do I get Nixie out?"

Margaret winced and Garrett knew she didn't have the

answer to that either. "But when you do, I'll help you in any way I can to ensure you get away."

"Thank you. Are there any records of past shifters? Or at least family trees?"

"Family trees, yes. They destroyed the few physical records that existed to keep people safe. But I have so many stories."

"I'd love to hear them. There are a few other shifters who would like the same."

Margaret smiled. "I will tell you all every story I know. When this is over and you've found the peace you want so bad."

The sun had set and Garrett's blood ran quicker. Looking over his shoulder, he imagined the mansion in the distance, and the balcony that called to him.

"Go to her."

When Garrett looked back to thank her, she'd disappeared. The log sat empty and the space around him chilled.

Garrett put out the fire and tucked his camp away so they wouldn't easily find it. Stripping his clothes, he called on the magic, the wind, and shifted while taking to the air. Fate had a plan and gave him a mate.

A GUARD in front of her and a guard behind her, Nixie walked barefoot to her room, her shoes dangling from her fingers. Missing meals wasn't anything new, but he didn't restrict her access to food often. Nixie had learned to stash little things away in her room to eat for those days. And she made a habit of nibbling on anything she could during the day. Keith always hoped for a better outcome, and Nixie gave it to him for the first few days. Not because she was starving and grateful for his generosity, but because it made life easier for just a short while.

Nixie shut the door in the faces of the guards. They had no sympathy for her. Were they just as evil as Keith, or did Keith have their undying loyalty despite any morality they may have? The result was the same, as was their treatment of her. So if she had the chance to slam a door in their face, she did.

Returning to her room became a monotonous event, but it served as a small comfort for her. A slice of peace and perceived privacy. In her closet, Nixie tossed her shoes at the wall, then reached behind her to unclasp her bra, pulling it out from under her dress. Silks and fancy dresses hung in front of her and each shine and elegant drape only made her sick to look at. What she wouldn't give for a pair of sweatpants.

Grabbing a throw, she wrapped her shoulders before heading out to the balcony. She'd tried to squash the eagerness at seeing the hawk again. It was silly to think he'd come back. But the night air pulled her out. Keith didn't concern himself with her entertainment, meaning she had nothing for herself in her room. She could have a friend. As sad as it was that her friend came in the form of a wild animal, at least she had something to look forward to—a reason for her genuine smile to escape.

Sliding the door closed behind her, she walked to the blind spot in the left corner. She watched the thick trees on the other side of the wide empty lawn. When the guards passed below, Nixie leaned back rather than over the railing. It was also a chance to adjust her stance, kicking her foot to the side to trigger the camera, so no one came to her room looking for her.

Her leg still ached, but she wasn't ready to go inside yet. Not until she was sure those golden eyes didn't at least lurk in the trees.

Shifting her weight once again, Nixie sighed. She needed rest.

A short screech echoed in the distance and a slight flash of gold headed toward her. Nixie held her breath as the golden dots stopped moving. He landed on a tree.

"Come on, handsome." Nixie's whisper wouldn't stretch across the night, but she released the plea, anyway. The guards turned the corner on their next round, going out of sight. The hawk spread his wings, leaping off the branch. He soared high, spun tight, and spiked down. The camera at the front of her balcony moved to track him. Nixie moved to trigger the sensor toward her.

The hawk landed with grace in the same corner as the night before.

"You aren't only avoiding the guards, but the cameras, too. You aren't an ordinary hawk." She'd called him smart the night before, but hadn't realized how true that statement was. "Do you belong to someone?" Maybe someone had trained him. Falconry was still a thing. That would be some serious training for him to avoid being seen by the security here. Now she understood why he'd stopped at the tree first. He'd timed his arrival.

Nixie tilted her head. Neither of his feet had a band of any sort. Didn't falconers put something on their birds—the equivalent of a collar for dogs or cats? With no evidence to support the theory, Nixie let go of the hope of a messenger.

"I'm thrilled you came back."

His eyes glowed. Nixie smiled when he cocked his head.

"I needed the company tonight. I'll need your company for a few days, so I hope you keep coming back."

He shuffled his feet and moved to the adjacent side of the corner, turning himself so he faced her.

"There won't be many chances for me to leave my room for the next few days, and I'm about to get very hungry."

Sharp talons sliced into the wood. Nixie frowned.

"You don't need to worry about me, handsome. I won't starve. I have a few things stashed away." She'd lost it if she believed this animal understood her and had been angry on her behalf. But it was nice to think someone cared.

Nixie leaned against the railing, relieving her leg of some of her weight. The hawk lifted one foot, turning it over. One talon curled back and forth as if beckoning her forward. The bird was just being weird. He wasn't smart enough to give her a come hither. But he paused and repeated the motion.

"Really? I'm not making that out to be something it's not?" She pointed at his beckoning talon.

He made the motion one more time, settled his foot, then tilted his head down, golden eyes striking her from across the balcony.

"Okay." Turning her gaze toward the trees, she made her gait casual as she crossed in front of the camera. The last thing she wanted was for the guards to come investigate something she saw. She settled once again in the corner in the blind spot—only inches away from the hawk.

From a distance, she claimed him as handsome and smart. Up close, the traits that made him a deadly predatory animal flashed like red flares. His beak and large, sharp talons could do some real damage.

He moved, adjusting his wings. Nixie jumped, then froze, afraid her uncontrollable moment of weakness startled him, giving him a reason to lash out. Her eyes had closed, and when a sharp talon or beak didn't strike, she opened them. His body relaxed, pulling in a breath before making a show of releasing it.

"Definitely smarter than the average bird," she muttered.

The hawk inched closer, leaning his head forward. Nixie stayed as still as possible, only moving her eyes and not her head to follow his movement. Soft feathers brushed the exposed skin of her arm holding the blanket. Two strokes and he stilled. His head tilted toward the end of the mansion, then a talon pointed toward her glass door. After a moment, he launched from the railing.

"Goodnight," Nixie called softly after him. She walked back toward her room, getting out of sight before the guards came.

Nixie was beginning to believe the visits from the hawk weren't only a wondrous sighting of wildlife.

GARRETT HAD AS MUCH of the escape plan complete as he could without knowing more about what happened inside that house. Once he got Nixie to the trees, he knew what to do and had several contingencies ready. But the problem lay between the house and the trees. He needed inside information.

He had hoped to visit his mate a few more times before showing her his true self, but time wasn't their friend. If Anya wasn't in that mansion and still alive somewhere, Garrett needed to find her. Let alone the raging need to get his mate to safety. Garrett always had patience, even under the most urgent situations, but having a mate in danger changed that for him. Having a mate that wasn't getting any food at the moment enraged him.

After hiding his camp, he shifted. Wrapping his talons

around the small pack, Garrett took flight toward the mansion.

Landing on the railing of Nixie's balcony, he waited. The light shone in her room, but he didn't hear any movement. He'd rather not make a sound to call her, so when the guards turned the corner again, he swung down on the inside of the railing.

The door behind him slid open. Turning his head, he pinned her in place with his gaze until the guards passed. Silk pajamas hung from her body, long pants and a tank top that dipped dangerously low. His blood burned, and magic thrummed within him. His body wanted to shift, to feel her skin against his.

Damn it.

Garrett tore his eyes from his mate and peeked through the bars to see the guards disappearing. He climbed back up to the top and held up the bag so Nixie would come toward him rather than the other corner.

"You brought me something?" A few of her freckles jumped off her pale cheeks. Dark circles lined her eyes, fueling his anger. She stepped closer. Her scent overwhelmed his rage and infused sweet chocolate into his system.

Garrett lifted one foot and shaped it like a bent arm in front of him, then pointed to her arm with his beak. Nixie would find out who and what he was tonight.

"You want me to do something." She frowned at his foot. He repeated the motion. "You're one strange animal." But she lifted her right forearm and held it parallel across her body.

Garrett pulled a small cloth from the side of the pack he'd carried with his beak. He threw it over her arm and attempted to straighten it.

"Like this?" Nixie spread out the cloth. It would protect her arm from his talons. He might be fast enough to outmaneuver the cameras to get to the balcony, but he couldn't beat them to get through the door.

Holding up the pack, a small bag the size of a lunch kit, he took it in his beak. With slow movements so as not to scare his mate, Garrett hopped from the railing to her arm.

Her narrow-set eyes widened, resembling a majestic doe. She gasped, cutting off an audible yelp. A yelp she could have made an excuse with the guards who heard her, but stepping back into the camera for them to see him would have ruined his entire plan. Garrett took a deep breath and watched his mate mimic him.

"Okay, handsome. Now what?" Her voice quaked, and her arm trembled beneath his weight.

Garrett nodded to the open glass door, then ducked against her body, indicating she hide him. When he looked up to see if she understood, her eyes returned to their normal shape.

"Are you sure I've not gone crazy? What animal can communicate like this?"

He waited for her to answer her own question—to decide to trust him.

Pulling her head up high, Nixie tucked her arm close to her body and wrapped her other around him to make it look like a natural stance from behind. She stepped back and turned at the same time, walking toward the door. Once they crossed the threshold, Garrett hopped off her arm and glided to rest on the back of a chair, taking the cloth from her arm with him.

Nixie reached back and closed the door.

"I've brought a wild animal into my room. One who can communicate better than some humans."

Garrett held out the pack, his talons wrapped around a loop at the top.

"That's for me?" The silk pajamas moved like slow waves over her hips as she walked toward him. She grasped the side of the pack and Garrett let go. Her blue eyes watched him as she pulled the drawstring loose.

Backing away, she sat on the edge of the bed before pulling out the contents.

"Food? You brought me food." He'd packed her a sandwich and a thermos of soup to give her sustenance tonight and a handful of protein bars and dried fruit snacks. He hoped to have her out of here before he needed to bring her much more.

Her hand fluttered over her stomach and a tear played connect-the-dots with the freckles on her cheek. Reverently, she unwrapped the sandwich. She ate slowly at first, closing her eyes over each bite. But soon she had it gone and was drinking the soup, infusing colour back into her skin. Just as he'd intended, the soup warmed her from the inside. Not only physically, but he hoped it provided an essence of comfort.

Packing away the remains, she blushed. "Thank you. Whoever, whatever you are, whoever sent you, thank you."

Garrett inclined his head, then glided down to the floor. He hoped she still thanked him after what he was about to do.

Nixie tensed on the bed. Garrett closed his eyes and pulled on the magic within him. The wind gathered around him, warming the skin beneath his feathers.

"What's happening?" Her panic was alarming. He snapped open his eyes that now glowed bright. Nixie had planted both feet on the floor and her hands braced herself against the mattress. He held her gaze, freezing her panic as the pain swept through his change. The magic fiercely moved the bones in his body, elongating to excruciating lengths.

Nixie didn't look away until the golden wind dissipated in the air and he stood in front of his mate as a naked male.

4

N ixie lunged from the bed and scrambled around the side, further away from the man standing in her room. Not a hawk. A man.

"Please don't scream."

"Why would I scream?" It wasn't as if she'd just witnessed some unimaginable, impossible, inconceivable act of magic. Was it magic? Or was it a hallucination?

She felt her way along the bed to the nightstand, situating herself within reach of the ceramic lamp. Not that a lamp would hold back a man the size of him. Nude as he was, she saw not only his height and breadth, but each indent from each muscle. And so much *more*. A hardened and erect *more*. Silk pajamas had been enough cover for her when standing in front of a hawk, not in front of someone like him. But Nixie wasn't yet ready to abandon her position next to her only weapon.

"I won't hurt you. My name is Garrett." Brown hair flowed to the tops of his ears. A frown sat over eyes that had dimmed from the bright gold to an odd hazel. Despite his statement that he wouldn't hurt her, he looked like he might. But his voice, while low, carried a soothing cadence.

"What are you?" Nixie rested her hand on the nightstand. His eyes followed her movement.

"I'm a shifter."

"You can shift from animal to man. Very original."

His lips lifted. A pure smile gave way to a dimple in his left cheek. She'd lived around men with nothing but evil intentions for so long that the light from this man almost blinded her. No reason or logic accompanied her decision to step away from the silliest of defenses and reach for the two throw blankets on her bed. Nixie tossed the balled up fleece through the air and Garrett caught it. She wrapped the other around her shoulders while he covered himself, tucking the blanket into itself low on his hips.

"You aren't the trained bird of a falconer, then."

"I'm not." He still hadn't moved. One hand rested on the blanket.

"Thank you. For bringing me something to eat." She looked away, embarrassment flooding her. Why, she didn't understand. But she'd taken every bite and sip of what he'd brought her.

"You're welcome. How long will Jeffreys deprive you?" His dimple vanished and fierceness of an angry man shadowed his eyes.

"You know who he is?" This wasn't a random happenstance as she'd thought.

Garrett nodded. "How long?"

"Not long." She didn't want to tell him that Keith had made her go hungry for up to a week when she really pissed him off.

"How often?"

"Not." Although the frequency had increased.

"I came here looking for someone."

Nixie tried so damn hard not to react. "Who?" She clamped her teeth onto her tongue to keep her expression neutral. But her eyes, they wouldn't stay still. It had been too much to hope that someone came looking for her. That the kind hawk had been there for her, even as a friend. The hurt of knowing she wasn't missed or wanted was old and stale, but pungent nonetheless.

"Anya Daly. My sister."

She saw it now. The same hair colour and shape down his nose. A miniature and feminine version of Garrett had stayed here for a short time. "I'm the only one here."

"Is she..." When Nixie thought he wouldn't ever look away from her, he did. His pain slashed across the room, making her problems seem so small.

"I'm not sure. Keith didn't kill her."

A statement that might have given someone hope only increased the wave coming from Garrett.

"The women that are forced here don't last long. They don't provide the image Keith looks for. He sells them, including them in part of a business deal."

He took a breath, and the air calmed. His focus turned back to her. "Are you saying he doesn't force everyone to be here?"

"No." Shame blasted up her core, and she lifted her chin to fight against it. She may have been stupid enough to fall for it, but she didn't deserve it. Staring at the balcony door, she waited for his censure. But it didn't come.

"Nixie." A soothing rumble carried her name and his bare feet padded over the carpet. When she thought he'd come closer, he paused at the end of the bed. "I'm here for you, too."

She allowed herself to enjoy the pull from his eyes.

Shaking her head, she shattered the moment. He didn't know who she was until he showed up. He might be in here now for her, but he hadn't come here for Nixie Hutton.

Garrett stepped away from her.

"I know who he sold her to. Only his name. Not how to find him." She'd tried to retain names and information over the years. She might not know how to use any of it to free herself, but at least something would come in handy now to help Garrett. And maybe help Anya.

"It will be enough." It wasn't. Anya had been sweet to every other woman here, but she lit into Keith and every guard she could. Some blows she'd endured should have killed her. Nixie remembered watching her head swivel back, pain evident in every one of her features except her eyes. The fire burning there reduced it all to ashes. Nixie admired her so much and wished she could have gotten to know her for longer than two weeks.

"Alexander Merk." Seeing that man only once had been enough to make Nixie hide. Anya would have been better off at the hands of Keith Jeffreys.

"Thank you. How's your leg?" Garrett tilted his head and his eyes dropped.

"How do you know about my leg?" Her hand dropped below the end of the blanket, settling against her thigh. She didn't remember saying anything to him about it.

"I've been watching you limp." He glanced up then back down to inspect her silk clad leg, as if he couldn't read how nervous she was.

"Oh. It's fine. Just bruised."

"What did he do?" His smooth resonance caught. She studied him, looking for an outward reaction to match what she heard.

"It's okay."

"I'm a doctor. I'd feel better if you'd tell me what he did."

Before she could stop herself, she popped her shoulders and adopted a mocking tone. "Trust me, I'm a doctor." Nixie closed her eyes and shook her head. "I am so sorry." Sometimes, she had such little control over herself. The one trait that always got her in trouble and the one that saved her ass more than once.

Peeking with one eye, Garrett smiled wide, his glowing eyes crinkling at the corners. "Don't apologize. That's exactly how it came out." He sat on the side of the bed and waited.

"He," she started, but had to wet her lips. Admitting to someone what she went through wasn't something she was ready for. She wasn't even free yet. This was information that should take months of distraught therapy to pour into the lap of a trained professional. But right now, she had him. And she wasn't about to push away someone who cared for her enough to bring her food. Someone whose golden eyes were her only promise of freedom.

What Nixie didn't want to think about was the other ways those golden eyes affected her.

"He hit me with a pipe." Horrid words dropped from her honeyed voice. Garrett had witnessed the abuse of others and the familiar rush of rage returned. But a vivid image of someone hitting his mate burned his body with bright flames.

"A pipe?" The scratch in his throat hurt and his question dropped off.

"A PVC pipe." So specific. Nixie's heart rate thumped in his ears, doubling its pace.

Garrett cleared his throat. "You've been walking well. Any pain in either your hip or knee joints?"

"Not since the first couple of days." She brushed her hand over her thigh as if to brush away the bruise.

"The colour of the bruise now?" Without seeing her leg for himself, he needed as much information as she'd give him.

"Blue and green. It's been about a week."

"That's good." He wanted to ask her more.

The blanket she held slid down, exposing one shoulder. Shifting her weight, she cocked her hip. "What's your plan? Naked and in my room isn't an advantage."

He laughed. She had a point. Standing, he towered over her by a foot, and Nixie was a hair taller than the average woman. He inhaled her scent, making it harder to keep his hands relaxed and at his sides. He sobered and took a step closer. "I'm going to get you out of here. But I need your help. I know everything that goes on out there." He pointed toward the balcony. "I don't know what happens in here and how the two connect."

"You didn't come here for me." Nixie walked away from him, her head down. But when she reached the other side of the room, she turned with her chin up and a smile that didn't reach her eyes. "You should go find your sister."

Garrett didn't respond right away. He studied her, wanting to understand. She blinked rapidly before going into her closet.

"She's important right now. I'll be fine on my own." The walls muffled her voice. When she emerged, she held the folded blanket in her arms and had pulled a long sleeve shirt over her pajamas.

He hadn't been wrong. She didn't want to be here, so why wouldn't she accept help from him to escape?

"Garrett?"

"I'm not leaving you here, Nixie."

"I'm not who you came for. It's okay." She shook her head and set the blanket on the bed.

Garrett couldn't stand it. He was guilty of enough in his life. He wouldn't add to it by leaving any woman in the hands of Jeffreys. But leaving his mate, whether he deserved a mate, Garrett would rip out his own heart before leaving her behind.

He moved around the bed, pleased to capture her eyes when she stopped busying herself with the blanket and the bed. Touch her, he had to. He ran his thumb along her jaw, applying pressure when she tried to look away from him. If she'd tried to step back, he would have let her, but her accepting his touch told him how much she needed it.

"You don't have anyone looking for you, do you? No one to miss you?"

Her gasp was slow, as was the time it took her to swallow. The smallest shake of her head broke his heart.

"I'm here. For you. Help me get you free."

Nixie shuddered, and tears glistened over her eyes, but didn't fall. He wanted to do more than run his fingers over her jaw, but it wasn't the time.

"Everything will be okay." He let his hand drop. "In the pack I gave you, there are a couple of listening devices. They are small and discrete. Do you think you could plant them or at least wear them?"

"I'll try. They have a large security office. I've never been inside. Guards are in and out of there on rotation, just like everywhere else. It's just another station to them, so eyes are always on it."

"Do they get alerts to other devices when something triggers a motion detector or camera?" Garrett moved across the room and settled himself on a chair. He'd given her enough to process in one night.

"Only if triggered by the guard in the office. Too much wildlife and the guards are always on the move."

"That's good."

"I don't see how that matters." She walked to the balcony door, but stayed out of sight. "They're everywhere all the time. And if we slip past them, they'll find us."

"Listen first." He hoped they'd give him a weakness. A way to cut their feed and keep their attention elsewhere while he escaped with Nixie.

"Okay." She clasped her palms over her elbows. "Is this all a dream?"

"No, Nixie. It isn't. I'm sorry. This is a lot to take in. I hope you'll trust me, though." His gaze locked on hers and he couldn't stop the heated flash. Her lips parted. With sharpened vision, Garrett knew his eyes glowed. His mate. Why the hell would Fate give her to him?

"What have I got to lose?"

Garrett didn't want to answer that. It wasn't only what she'd lose, but what he'd lose, too. Pushing back against the glow in his eyes, he nodded toward the balcony. "I need you to block my path out of here."

"Cause walking backwards onto the balcony won't look weird." Her hands dropped to her sides, and she shrugged a single shoulder. Garrett held back his laugh.

"Put the blanket back over your shoulders. I'll sit on your arm behind your back while you hold the blanket in front of you with the other."

Nixie frowned, but retrieved the folded blanket from the bed.

"I'll bring you more food tomorrow night. Do you have enough until then?"

"I do. Thank you." She wrapped the blanket around her shoulders and waited. Garrett pulled the one from his hips and set it on the end of the bed. Heat filled his body, and the magic flowed through him. Nixie's eyes widened as she watched him shift. She froze in place and Garrett feared he'd scared her. But as the golden wind disappeared, Nixie turned around, her chin resting on her shoulder. He held her gaze while he flew from the ground to land on her arm she held beneath the blanket at her back.

Nixie slid the door open and walked to the corner. Garrett climbed onto the railing. With a sigh, he said a silent goodbye to his mate.

HER BEDROOM DOOR banged against the wall. Brent stood there chuckling as Nixie sat up from a dead sleep with an almost scream.

"He wants you downstairs today. You have fifteen minutes." He slammed the door with the same force he'd used to throw it open.

Keith never gave her long, believing the image he wanted was instantaneous. That with enough practice, she could snap her fingers and make it happen. Nixie had made him wait on more than one occasion. He'd learned not to have his guards haul her out of there before she was ready. He'd punished her for the scene and horrible display of herself, but he never moved her before she was ready again. They seemed to come to a truce. She would be prompt and he wouldn't have her dragged around in unkempt states by his guards.

She had a five-minute shower and pulled on a simple dress and blow dried her hair. After checking her time, she pulled the pack Garrett had left her from its hiding spot in her closet. She found the bugs in the front pouch. Taking two of them, she closed them in her palm while she hid the pack. The door burst open again.

"Time's up," he bellowed.

"Too bad." Nixie called from the closet. Listening for his footsteps, she relaxed when he didn't move.

She didn't know how these things worked or how much clearance they needed for Garrett to hear clearly, but the only place on her she felt safe putting it was inside the bra of her dress. The other, she stuck to the bottom of her shoe, high in the centre above the heel. It would be the first she dropped off.

Nixie threw on her attitude like she would a jacket and stepped out of her closet. "What does he want me for?"

"He has a breakfast meeting." Amusement dripped from the corners of the guard's sneer. It would be like Keith to use her during meal meetings while he starved her.

She followed the guard down the hall and the two flights of stairs. Gold trimmed white tile wasn't high-heel friendly and had become a sport over the years. Paranoia forced her eyes back on the stairs, retracing her footsteps. What if the bug fell off her shoe? How stupid could she be? She should have considered that, or at least tested it out in her room. Let alone, all he'd hear would be the clicking of her shoe against the tile. She should slap herself across the head. *Way to go, Nixie. You're so smart.*

Just a brat who thinks she is.

Only Keith sat at the dining table, but the staff had laid out food, all covered and keeping warm.

"Good morning, Nicole. I hope you're feeling better than the last time we spoke."

"Oh, you know me. I don't stay down for long."

"Indeed. Sit." He pointed to the empty chair beside him, the one devoid of a waiting plate and cutlery.

She sat, knowing that if Garrett hadn't given her food the night before, this meal would be as tortuous as Keith intended—not that Nixie would have given him any hint of her hunger.

"My guest will be here soon."

Many of Keith's meetings took place over a meal or at least nearby with a drink. While she hadn't thought of planting a bug at the table, now that she was here, she realized it would be one of the best locations aside from the security office. She wanted to get rid of the one on her shoe before she lost it somewhere in the house. But as usual, the guards were ever alert and watching her closely. When Keith's guest arrived would be her best chance.

A guard preceded a man dressed in a black suit that didn't quite fit right and another guard trailed behind him. Keith stood, raising a brow at her to do the same. She rolled her eyes, ensuring he saw them, and stood. Instead of greeting his guest, she made a show of ignoring him, knowing it would cause trouble for herself, but it gave her the opportunity to see where all the guards had their attention. There were too many for all of them to divert their attention away from her. Keith employed an excess number of staff. They missed nothing.

Nixie sat before allowed, while Keith still talked to his guest. She reached down to scratch her leg, extending it to her ankle and just inside her shoe. The heel slipped off when she pushed her fingers to the bottom. She kept her bored look at the table, on the covered dishes. Let them all think she was dreaming of food.

Reaching for the bottom of her shoe, she tucked it back over her heel, bringing the bug back up with her fingers.

She considered placing it under her chair while tucking herself in at the table, but if someone ever tipped the chair over, they might find the small microphone. Moving her body, she shielded her hand as she stuck the bug under the lip of the table.

A sigh of relief filled her lungs, but letting it loose would alert anyone watching her. Nixie had to carry on with the attitude until given a reason not to. Which would mean another punishment. But if it meant she'd soon be free, she'd take whatever he wanted to dish out, as long as it didn't kill her.

A server arrived to uncover all the dishes.

"Please, help yourself." Keith waved a hand over the table. Mr. Baggy Suit scooped large spoonfuls of eggs and hash browns on his plate. He paused when he reached for the bacon.

"Your lady not eating?"

"No. A lesson to reinforce her place." Keith reached for the dish nearest him.

"I've tamed all of my girls. You won't have any need for lessons with them." The man was trying hard to mirror Keith's mannerisms and speech to put him on the same level. Keith's reach and abilities swung too far for anyone to be on the same level. It was pathetic to watch them try.

But his words registered. Nixie hadn't been paying attention, concerned with acting a part. His girls. He wasn't here for the usual business deal. Keith was bringing in more women.

"A minor correction is always needed, but I appreciate your confidence."

"How many are you looking for?" He shoveled a forkful of eggs into his mouth, enough to push out his cheek.

"One. If she works out, I'll consider getting more from you."

"It won't work out." Nixie couldn't keep her mouth shut. Maybe it would be a better life for her here, a solid roof, good food, and a warm bed. The man sitting across from her didn't look like he concerned himself with the comfort of the women. But another prison wasn't freedom, and this prison had better security.

"Nicole?" To his guest, Keith sounded like he was curious in her opinion, but Nixie heard *choose your next words wisely*.

"Women you force into this house have never lasted long, tamed or not."

"Sounds like your lady is jealous." Crumbs of food fell from Baggy Suit's mouth as he grinned.

"You're not aging so much that you no longer have the energy to lure them in yourself, are you, Keith?" It was beyond the wrong thing to say. She'd recently been beaten and starved over less, yet the blades glinting in Keith's grey eyes cut through to satisfaction over hitting him where it hurt. And Nixie would do it again at every opportunity.

5

———

Garrett jumped from his seat, his fingers pulling at his hair. His mate was going to get herself killed. Did she always act this way with Jeffreys, or had Garrett's arrival fed her boldness? He knew the answer, and it gave him no end of worry.

He'd had to lower the volume from the moment Nixie took the bugs from the pack, but as soon as she settled, he'd listened, strengthening his patience with every word from her mouth.

Garrett wasn't sure if he could stop Jeffreys from getting more women, or shut down whatever business his guest had. He wanted to, but if he did, he'd find another like him to shut down as well, and then another, and another. The trail would never end.

Nixie and Anya were his priorities.

His body stilled with coldness, frosty shards spreading as Jeffreys spoke again.

"I don't want to punish you again so soon, Nicole."

"Too lazy for that, too?" Her quick retort came out husky.

She didn't think twice before speaking, as she'd done with him the night before, an utter stranger.

Damn it, Nixie.

"Too much of a good thing erodes quality. I once found your bratty nature amusing, because you behaved otherwise." Careful precision sharpened his words. A prelude to a controlled temper. "That seems to have changed. It's time for you to shut your fucking mouth or I guarantee you will miss me and everything given to you here when I hand you off to someone else."

Garrett held his breath, praying she wouldn't say anything. An eerie silence reigned through the speaker, the tension with it.

"One woman. I'll contact you for more if I'm satisfied." Jeffreys clipped as his conversation turned back to his guest.

Garrett listened to the two men broker their deal. The conversation wasn't anything new to him, but never did the tides of bile in his core lessen the more he heard it.

An instinct that Nixie's life in that mansion was coming to an end shook through him, despite her attitude. He had to consider the possibility of an easier rescue from someone other than Jeffreys. But what his mate would endure in that short time wasn't worth it. And that depend on if Jeffreys intended to get rid of her. He'd kept her for so long.

Getting captured or killed while making a run for it in the woods, or the damage she'd endure from the next person.

"Tell me, how do you tame the women you have?" Gleeful curiosity simmered through Jeffreys' voice.

"Pain and starvation are effective."

"I haven't had the same experience."

"You aren't using enough of it." He mock whispered as if divulging the secrets of the world.

"I'd rather not scar them. The image they provide is the only purpose I have for them. I hope you remember that when choosing which one to sell me."

"Of course. You can cause a lot of pain without scarring or permanent damage." Garrett had more than enough knowledge to know the truth to that statement. And the damage that kind of torture created. The kind that would steal her spirit. Jeffreys called her a brat, but Garrett saw she was full of life.

"Interesting."

"I'd be willing to give a demonstration." Jeffreys' guest's voice pitched, excitement evident.

Silence stretched and Garrett's heart stopped. He didn't know if he'd be able to listen while they beat his mate.

"When you deliver next week. I'd like to see a demonstration then. On Nicole." That was Garrett's time line.

"And the life here looks rather cushy. You might consider relocating her." Garrett's research suggested Jeffreys didn't welcome others' opinions, but his guest spoke freely, seeming to think himself special.

"I'll take that under advisement." A chair scraped. "Where are you going?"

"I prefer surprises, and you two are dropping all sorts of spoilers." The woman sounded so calmly flippant.

"Sit. Back. Down. Nicole."

"The little girls' room, Keith. It's right over there." Her heels faded away from one speaker and kept up with the other. A door clicked shut and his mate's whisper sounded. He turned down the conversation between Jeffreys and his guest.

"Garrett? Oh God, I hope you're listening. I wish there was some way for you to give me a sign that I'm doing this right. I think I'm in trouble. I planted one bug at the dining room table. I'll try to plant the other as close to the security office as I can. I might not get another chance." Deep breaths rushed over the microphone.

His mate did well with the first bug, but getting as much information from that security office had the best chance at success.

NIXIE BOUNCED off a hard chest when she exited the bathroom.

"He wants you back at the table."

"That isn't news to me." She shook her head and tried to move around the guard, but he wouldn't let her pass.

"I don't understand why you do this to yourself. Why do you give him attitude?" It might be a question from someone who cared, but these guards didn't give a shit.

"This life would be so boring if I didn't." She rolled her head to look up at him with her best mischievous smirk.

"There's the catch. Keep it up and there won't be a life to have. But it's your funeral. At least the rest of us find it amusing how much you can piss him off. Now get moving." And there was the true nature of the guards. They only had mere curiosity and amusement at her expense. They were good little soldiers who did what they were told. But they were damn good at their job.

The guard followed her back to the table, retaking his position only a few feet away. Nixie paused before taking her seat. A full plate of the breakfast food sat in front of her chair. Both Keith and his guest looked at her. She sensed the trap. Keith never went back on his word.

"Are you not going to eat, Nicole?"

"You made it clear that I'm not allowed." This would be much harder if Garrett hadn't given her food the night before and if she didn't have the snacks stashed away in her room.

"Offering you food would imply your punishment is over."

"Imply being the operative word."

His guest stroked his chin, watching the exchange carefully.

Nixie met Keith's gaze, hoping he'd either spring his trap or just make his point.

"Take her back to her room. I'll visit her later." Keith didn't direct his statement to any particular guard or look away from her until she stood. Turning her back on him, she used the clicking of her heels as a breathing measure. She didn't have time to worry about what Keith had planned for her now. They had to pass the security office to get back to the stairs leading up to her room.

Where could she plant the bug?

The guard stepped close to her heels.

She saw the door on her left. Put it anywhere on the trim and they'd spot it within a day. If the guards didn't, then the cleaners would. There, the bottom of the door. She only hoped there was enough room to slip her fingers beneath it to place the bug. Scratching her chest, Nixie took the bug from inside her dress. Holding it in her left hand, she inwardly winced, knowing this would hurt.

Her left foot stepped in front of the door. She tilted her foot, so she came down on the side of the long heel. Her ankle rolled. Nixie couldn't fake fall to save her life, but making herself roll her ankle in heels? That she could do.

She cried out, her shoulder slamming against the door as she slid to the floor. Sucking in the pain, she focused on the bug tucked in her fingers. Her ankle would be fine, but it would hurt later and needed ice.

The guard mumbled under his breath and stepped forward to reach for her. Nixie braced her hand against the door so she'd be able to slide her fingers beneath it while getting up. But the door opened, releasing her weight. She flopped to the floor just inside the security office. Her fingers stretched out, dropping the bug.

Panic flared, and she kept her eyes on the floor to search for it. It hadn't gone far. Nixie slapped her hand over it and pushed up at the same time. One guard sat in a wheeling office chair right in front of her, holding the door open above her. One other stared at her from a long desk of screens, while another never took his eyes away from them. The guard escorting her back stared at her from the doorway, his feet straddling her legs still laying in the hall. Darkness shadowed each pair of eyes.

Oh god, they'd seen it. They saw the bug she tried to hide.

"Quite the show." The guard in the door drawled.

"Show?" Nixie felt the quiver in her throat, but kept it out of her voice.

"All that just to see inside the one room you can't go. It doesn't help you." He moved back.

"Off the floor, brat. I have work to do." The guard in the chair nudged her with his foot. She let the motion stumble her lower to the floor again. The star-shaped feet holding the wheels on his chair were right in front of her. So much better than just under the door.

Nixie braced her hand, holding the bug on one of the feet, her fingers sliding beneath it. She stuck the bug inside and pushed herself off the floor and out of the office. The guard slammed the door.

She did it. Adrenaline coursed harder through her body, giving her a little thrill. They hadn't seen the bug.

Carrying her heels, she limped in front of the guard back to her room. He closed the door and locked her in. She rushed to her bed and flopped back on it. Air felt like a rare commodity as she sucked it in with all her might. She didn't want to know what would have happened if they'd seen the bug. That thought alone made her wonder if it had been worth the risk. But it was done now, and she'd been successful.

Her lungs calmed and her stomach reminded her to eat. The snacks Garrett left her beckoned, but she didn't know when Keith would show up or what he had planned. It was best to wait until she'd be alone for the rest of the day.

She didn't have ice in her room and she hadn't asked the guard for any because they wouldn't bring it to her. But what she did have was running water and a cloth.

In the bathroom, she turned on the tap and left it to run until frigid. Nixie limped into her closet and pulled out the pack from Garrett. Two more bugs sat in the front pouch. She didn't know him or trust him enough to allow him to listen in on her, but with Keith as mad as he was and coming to her room, she wanted him to hear anything that might help. Tucking the pack back in its hiding place, Nixie took the bug out to her room. She worried little over where to put it. They didn't search her room. Why would they when they had eyes on her at every other moment? She stuck the bug on the back of her empty nightstand and returned to the bathroom.

The water was a poor substitute for ice, but it was better than nothing. Wetting a cloth, she rang it out and went back to bed. Propping her foot up on a pillow, she laid the cold cloth over her ankle. The swelling wasn't much—only a day or so, and she'd be fine.

Her eyes drifted, wondering how long Keith would take before his temper got the better of him. The moment her lashes touched her cheeks, a key unlocked her door. It didn't burst open with a bang like earlier, but swung open with the slowness of nails on a chalkboard. The silent sight gave her cringe-like chills.

She sat up as Keith stepped into the room, letting the door shut behind him.

"You are a smart girl, Nicole." A raw calmness leveled his tone, like that of a disappointed authority figure. "I heard of your show in the hall."

Nixie tilted her head to hide the gasp through her parted lips. Maybe she hadn't been so successful, and they'd only allowed her to believe she'd been.

"What did you think you'd gain?"

A chance at peace. She raised her brow rather than voicing her deepest wish.

"No smartass comments anymore?" Keith stalked toward the bed, his hands behind his back. He may only deal with money mostly, but Nixie understood the predator still had claws. "If only I believed that meant you've learned your lesson."

"Looks like you're pretty smart, too."

"There she is." He lowered his chin with a growling sneer. He dropped his hands, a new pair of shoes dangling from one. Glittery, bedazzled, tacky, and extremely high. She wished she had the strength to stab that spike through his eye.

He tossed them onto the bed and stood beside her feet.

"The inside of that office is off limits. And tricking the guards to open the door is beneath you. Nothing in there will help you." They hadn't found the bug. He believed she'd only wanted to see inside. "And of course, there is the matter of your disrespect over breakfast." His eyes dropped to her foot, elevated by the pillow.

Nixie didn't have time to prepare herself for what she saw coming. Keith grabbed her swelling ankle and wrenched it to the side. She tried to roll with him, but he placed his knee over her hips to keep her in place. Metallic liquid coated her tongue. She bit harder to keep herself from crying out.

Keith's lips curled, and he wrenched harder. Nixie screamed, unable to hold it back. If she didn't give him what he wanted, he'd break it. He'd never gone that far before. Did nothing to infringe on the image he wanted by his side. But an angry blackness glowed from his eyes. She'd pushed him too far, or had the path he'd been on led to this no matter what she did or said?

He let go of her foot, but she didn't stop screaming. The wailing lowered to painful sobs. The pain in her ankle heated as it swelled.

"You can eat when you can walk in those."

The door shut, but Nixie hadn't reopened her eyes. She let the pain loose through her sobs. Only one thread of silver ran through this day. The guards or Keith wouldn't bother her for at least a week. With nothing to help her ankle now, Nixie cried herself to sleep.

GARRETT ROARED INTO THE AIR, covering the sound of his mate's screams. Heat filled his body, magic rising, attempting to take over.

"Calm down." Margaret's voice, faint like the wind, came

from behind. Garrett whirled on her.

"How the hell am I supposed to calm down?" He gritted his teeth to keep from roaring at her. A woman he respected, and the only help he had to save his mate and find his sister.

"Your mate needs you to stay calm."

"I've witnessed abuse and pain. I've stayed silent and patient, ready to treat them. This is different. I've lost all control."

"Gain it back. She needs you to do what you do best. Go to her, treat her, help her."

The rage wouldn't calm. Bringing it down was like trying to fly through a hurricane. The winds bashed his control back and forth against concrete walls. He packed another bag, this time with first aid supplies.

"Don't go yet. Listen, Garrett. Listen." Margaret pleaded before fading away.

He'd do what he wanted for once. He didn't need to listen to her, not when his mate needed him. But then voices caught his attention. He growled, realizing Margaret hadn't meant to listen to her.

Dropping the pack, he turned up the volume on the bug from the security office. Jeffreys voice rang clear, fueling his anger, but he forced himself to listen.

"Select guests for next Friday. We'll welcome the new girl, make a point to a client or two and if Nicole can't walk by then, we'll get a demonstration of how others might handle her. The party will begin early. I have business to discuss with them before the new girl arrives."

An idea formed in Garrett's mind. Creating chaos while guests were present would give more distractions to the guards for an escape. He had nine days.

Garrett went back to the bag, loading another thermos of soup and a sandwich. He'd bring her something more nutrient based next time. He'd heard enough to know she had at least one injured foot or ankle. Taking everything he'd need to treat a sprain, he shifted. He'd wait in the trees.

The woods were quiet under the afternoon sun as he flew through the treetops. Perching on his favourite white spruce, Garrett eyed her balcony. He couldn't get into her room without her help.

Her screams and sobs had faded and no other movement sounded over the speaker before he'd left his camp. She'd most likely fallen asleep from the pain.

Hours ticked by. Shadows moved like a motion picture over the ground, but Garrett didn't budge. Sunset turned the sky and the trees into a picturesque haven, but still Garrett waited.

The curtain moved and Nixie peered through the glass. Garrett let his eyes glow, so she'd see he waited for her. The door slid open, and she hopped onto the balcony, meeting him in the corner.

"I'm not sure if I can carry you in."

Not with the way she hopped.

Garrett passed her the bag and held up a single talon to tell her to wait. She had her usual blanket around her shoulders, holding it with one hand, the same hand that now held the bag.

Reaching one foot out, he clasped the blanket and tugged, hoping she understood.

"Okay. Get on."

Clutching the blanket with both feet and his beak, he nodded for her to move. Angling her back to the camera. She kept her free hand on the railing and half hopped and half shuffled her way to the door. Her hand reached out to grab the frame, and she pulled herself the rest of the way in.

Garrett pushed off her while she slid the door shut. He

began the shift before landing so that the change put him on his feet. Rushing the change hurt, but not as much as his mate did.

Nixie let out a squeak when he scooped her up to set her on the bed. Leaning in, he whispered in her ear, "Where did you put the bug in your room?"

She pointed to the back of her nightstand. Reaching around, he felt it and pulled it off the fake wood. He took it to her closet where she'd hidden the pack the night before. He tucked it back in, muffling any noise it picked up.

"Why?"

"In case any guards find my camp. I don't want anyone to overhear our conversations."

"Do you think they'll find your camp?"

"No. But I won't take any chances." Garrett sat beside her on the bed and took the bag he brought with him. Pulling out a medication bottle, he shook out two pills and passed them to her. Then he pulled out a bottle of water and the food. "Take those and eat while I look at your ankle."

"Bossy."

He hoped the look he sent her didn't scare her, but his emotions were still raw from hearing her cries. "Do you have any allergies?"

"No." She popped the pills in her mouth and tilted the bottle of water to her lips. "You heard it, didn't you?"

"Everything, and more." Garrett paused from looking at her swollen and bruised foot and lifted his gaze to hers. Her cheeks bloomed red, making most of her freckles fade with the colour change. "What have you been doing with your foot since?" He'd address her embarrassment later.

"I fell asleep after he left, but when I woke up I used cold cloths and kept it up on pillows."

"That's good. It's helped. But it's still very swollen. Those pills will help, and so will this." He pulled out a jar with a homemade poultice in it. One of the many remedies Margaret taught him through the years. He often found better results in the long run.

"What is that?" Nixie wrinkled her nose and turned her head. Either the look or the smell of the poultice would cause that reaction.

"Good for you."

"What kind of doctor are you?" Supreme doubt coloured each word.

This time, he smiled. "I worked in the emergency room." That didn't explain his use of a poultice now.

"Work or worked?" She unwrapped the sandwich.

"Worked." Garrett rubbed the poultice over her ankle. Nixie ate while she watched, but asked no more questions. It wasn't a story he wished to share right now, anyway. He'd tell her everything in time. For now, Garrett's focus was on her.

In the bathroom, he dampened a cloth with cold water. Nixie had finished the sandwich when he returned.

"You're still naked." She bit her lip and busied herself with the soup. His cock hardened as she tried to hide her darting eyes.

Garrett sat back down and placed the cloth over the poultice. "Does that bother you?" It didn't bother him, but that was part of life for a shifter.

"No." She squeaked, frowned, and shrugged in a drawn out awkward moment.

Garrett trapped her gaze, seeing the pink rise under her skin as she stilled. "I can't shift with clothes on and they won't fit in that bag. My priority was you, not covering up."

"It's okay," she whispered.

"Now that I'm done," he placed his hand on her other

ankle to keep the contact, "can you tell me why you antagonize him so much?" He wanted to shake her.

"Didn't you hear my answer when the guard asked me?" He imagined she gave him the same expression she sent him now. Nixie spooned up some of the soup, taking her time to blow on it before sipping.

"Yes. And I want the real one."

Nixie huffed and stuck her tongue in her cheek. "Why do you get the real one?"

"That's for you to decide." He couldn't tell her to trust him, but he hoped she did. "Nixie."

Her face blanched, and she held the soup in her lap. Her struggle to speak hurt to watch. Garrett wanted to hold her, comfort her, but it was too soon. As least he thought so. Nixie licked her lips and leaned her head back against the mountain of pillows. "As soon as I realized I was trapped here, I let my opinion fly free. It's the only part of me that still is. If I stop, if I bend to his will, every piece of me will be gone."

"That's both sad and beautiful." He was so damn proud, even when he wanted to shake it out of her to keep her safe. "It must take a lot of strength to hold on like that."

She shrugged.

"It does. I'll tell you how I know that someday."

"You could tell me now." She lifted the soup to balance against her chest while she ate.

"Your story is more important. We have nine days until we can get you out of here."

"Nine days?" Her frown snuffed out the second of hope Garrett saw flash in her eyes.

"Jeffreys has a business meeting and will host an event to welcome the new girl. That's when I'm getting you out of here."

6

Nine days until Nixie was free. If she didn't believe it, didn't allow herself to hope, then she wouldn't be true to herself. All her efforts to hold on with bratty comebacks and all the attitude she could dish out would be for nothing if she didn't let herself believe in Garrett's ability to get her out of here.

The medication settled into her system and coolness breathed into her ankle, easing the throbbing pain. Garrett sat next to her feet, his large hand resting on her good ankle. The heated contact sent tingling threads up her leg, like silk from a spider floating in the wind. Why did she trust him, enough to admit something so personal? Both his eyes and voice were warm, comforting in a way her heart recognized.

"Can you tell me how long you've been here? How you got here?" Garrett's thumb drew circles as he moved his hand up and down her shin. She was all too aware of her bare legs beneath the dress she still hadn't changed out of, and it was all another stark reminder that the man touching her was naked.

"Eight years."

Garrett waited. His eyes carried a low glow. Muscles tensed and shifted under tanned skin as he adjusted himself on the blankets. Nixie closed her eyes when they trailed to places they shouldn't.

Shame, red-hot and sharp, poked the inside of her ribs. "You don't need to know the answer to your other question."

"Maybe not. But maybe it will give a bit of insight that could help."

She hoped that was true, because she was about to lay herself out, raw and vulnerable to his judgment. "Keith is all about money and business, and about looking the part." Nixie circled her finger in the air to encompass the mansion. "A money man and loan shark that believes if clients don't see certain things, they won't fear him. He might be right. I don't know and I don't care. But part of that image is women. Arm candy. Spoiled girls fawning at his side. He used to put in a lot of legwork to get those women."

Garrett's eyes softened. It was enough sympathy to make her sick. A yawn overtook her, cutting off her ready remark to tell him to take his pity and shove it. By the time she looked back at him, his features had hardened, and he reached for a blanket. He shook it out and draped it over her legs.

"I grew up with foster parents. I can't complain. There were many who had it bad. They treated me well and provided necessities, but caring enough to become an actual family never quite happened. I barely scraped by enough to graduate high school and move out. They helped me move, said their goodbyes, and drove away. So when someone came along promising things that were too good to be true, I jumped at the chance. I'd been struggling to make ends meet, and I was just naïve enough to fall for it. He promised me everything I wanted. He was kind and attentive. Until the day I said I was ready to leave. Then this place didn't appear so marvelous anymore, and he wasn't kind or attentive. The catch—once a woman walks through that front door, she never walks back out with her own free will."

Garrett packed up the remnants from the bag he'd brought that she'd strewn across her lap. Her own disdain for herself soured the silence. Nixie fought another yawn while watching him move around. Intelligent, tall, lean, and defined—a magical being that decided to rescue her out of pity. Right now, it didn't matter why he was helping her. She'd take the freedom, thank him, and run with it.

He tucked the bag under the bed and sat beside her. Long fingers swiped her hair off her face and tucked it behind her ear. A sweet gesture that Nixie realized she'd never experienced.

"Being alone is scary, Nixie. Don't hate yourself for your decisions."

"I have to blame someone."

"But that someone isn't you." His touch and voice changed, hardened, scolded. He rose to her defense without knowing her. That's all she'd ever wanted—someone in her corner.

"I'm getting sleepy. I'm not sure if I can get you back outside."

"Why would I get you settled and then expect you to walk me back outside?" Garrett tilted his head and braced his hand on the bed on her other side. He bracketed her between large arms, immobile, vulnerable, yet she knew this man wouldn't harm her.

"You're staying?" The hope of a little girl tightened her throat. The drugs didn't allow her to apply her filter to her tone.

"I'm staying." He leaned down and pressed his lips to

her forehead. A simple touch that charged her nerves. She didn't understand.

"Why would you do that?"

"Do what? Stay?"

"No." Her lips moved up and down, but she couldn't bring sound to the word kiss. Lifting her hand, she placed two fingers over the spot he'd kissed.

"Oh, that. The same reason I'd do this."

He wouldn't.

He would. Garret leaned down, holding her gaze until his lips touched hers. They moved gently, supping, capturing her top lip between his, then moving down to capture the bottom. He tasted her and shock filled Nixie at the taste of him. The cold air in the changing seasons, like the fresh air that whipped at her face when she'd gone skating or sledding. Or the sweetness that came with the first flowers after the thaw. Fresh and wild. The very things she wished for.

One large hand cupped her bare shoulder as he tilted his head further to lick along her lips. Just as she parted them, ready to open to him, he lifted his head.

Heat rushed through her. Her eyes travelled down his body, little shame at her perusal until she reached his erection.

"Large and in charge," she muttered. "Oh, God." Nixie turned her head away to peer across the room. The heat that had rushed in her blood turned to deep embarrassment.

Garrett's laugh, deep and low, shaking the bed. "Nixie, it's okay to look." He turned her face back with a knuckle at her chin.

"Look? Sure. Speak? I should be banned." Her cheeks must be a dark burgundy by now.

"No." His thumb brushed her lips. "At least not around me."

Nixie yawned, using both hands to cover her face.

"Get some sleep, little one. I'll be here when you wake up."

Warmth invaded her body as he tucked her in and walked around the bed to settle on the other side. With his feet stretched out and crossed at the ankles, he leaned his head back against the headboard. She'd watched his entire progress.

"Close your eyes, Nixie."

She sighed, letting the medication finish seeping into her system. She relived the kiss in her mind while sleep pulled her under just as she realized he didn't tell her why he'd kissed her forehead.

HE SHOULDN'T HAVE DONE that. It had been inappropriate, ill timed, and irresistible. Why was he not surprised that she tasted spicy? Garrett threw another blanket over his lap, intertwined his fingers on his chest, and closed his eyes while he listened to Nixie settle beside him. The medication he'd given her would also help her sleep while the swelling went down in her ankle.

He'd wanted to bellow into the night again at the sight of her ankle. Large and a deep purple. The cold cloths she'd used would have helped some, but not enough for a sprain that bad. Jeffreys' expectations for her to heal in a week and walk in ridiculous shoes were unrealistic. It was bad enough Garrett needed her to run in nine days. He'd carry her as much as he could, but he needed her to move that initial sprint on her own.

Nixie's breathing became deeper, and Garrett allowed himself to open his eyes. She looked fragile sleeping in the bed. Already too thin to be skipping meals. He'd help her sustain herself until the time came to escape. That escape plan was still forming.

But it wasn't the only one he needed to work on. Once they got away from here, Garrett still needed to find his sister. He wouldn't put his mate in danger again by bringing her with him. Taking her to Alder Ridge would be safest. But he'd vowed not to include the other shifters and put them in danger as well.

Garrett shook his head. One rescue at a time.

Getting up from the bed, he added his blanket to Nixie's for another layer of warmth. Pulling on the magic, he shifted. If a guard were to come in, it was a lot easier for a hawk to hide than a man. He perched himself on a chair near equidistance from the bed, the closet, and the balcony, giving himself as many options as possible.

Exhaustion and adrenaline worked like a teeter totter in his body. Closing his eyes, he tuned into the sounds in the rest of the house. The voices on the other levels, and the movement of the guards on duty, their steady, faint pace. No one approached Nixie's room.

Sleep thinly enveloped him. Muscles stayed tense while his body and mind rested. Nixie should sleep for several hours, but Garrett would catch any hitch in her breathing or the light snoring that escaped her throat.

Hours later, Garrett stirred with a change in the air. The guards were switching shifts. Their footstep patterns changed and their conversations rumbled through the house. Not that Garrett heard enough to make them out. But it wasn't the only disturbance that woke him.

Nixie moaned with pain and the blankets had balled up

over her waist. Turning his head, he peered out the glass door. The moon was bright and shone at an angle that said it was the very early hours of the morning. The medication he'd given her should have lasted longer than this. But it wasn't too soon to give her more.

He listened for movement outside her door, and when he didn't hear any, he shifted and retrieved more medication from the pack. Once on her side of the bed, Garrett grasped Nixie's shoulder and squeezed.

"Nixie."

Her face scrunched up, and she turned her head away. Garrett slid his hand up her neck and to her cheek. He should have kept his hand on her shoulder. When he turned her head, her eyes cracked open above her flushed cheeks.

"Hi, little one." He pulled his hand back.

"Garrett?" Her sweet vulnerability shot straight to his cock. He gritted his teeth and cleared his throat. If kissing her earlier had been inappropriate, then kissing her now would be worse.

"Your ankle is hurting. Take these." He'd tried to lighten his tone to keep from demanding her, but he couldn't concentrate on that when all his blood had rushed elsewhere.

"How did you know?" Pushing herself up, she held out her hand to take the pills from him.

"You moaned in your sleep." Garrett kept his voice hushed in the shadowed room.

"Oh."

Garrett handed her the bottle of water from her nightstand and watched her down the medicine.

"What time is it?" She set the bottle on the nightstand

and laid back down, sleep trying to pull her under despite her pain.

"Don't know, but it's very early. I'm going to redress your ankle and you need more sleep."

She nodded, her eyes already weakening.

He used the cloth to wipe the poultice from her skin and took it to the bathroom to rinse. Returning with it chilled once again, he sat next to her ankle. The swelling had gone down, inserting relief into his chest. Garrett applied fresh poultice and replaced the cold cloth. When he looked up at Nixie, she'd closed her eyes and had a small smile tilting her lips.

"Thank you." Soft and muffled, she sighed.

Garrett wasn't sure how he was going to manage the next nine days. Telling her she was his mate, bound to him by Fate, wasn't fair under her circumstances. Even after he got her free, it wasn't right. Garrett looked at his mate, awed by the strength she had to put herself forth the way she did.

He hadn't seen Fate wrong yet, but that didn't stop Garrett's doubts that maybe she got this wrong.

NIXIE WOKE, knowing she wasn't alone. She kept herself still in bed while she turned her head, expecting Garrett to be asleep beside her. But a hawk sat on a chair on the other side of the bed. Warmth moved down her body with his golden eyes. Stretching, she tested her ankle, moving it up and down.

"Good morning." Nixie sat up in bed, gripping the blankets that fell to her lap.

Garrett tilted his head and hopped off the chair. Nixie winced from the painful sounds as he shifted. A gold breeze flowed in and around him, clouding the image as he changed into a man.

"Good morning." Gloriously naked, he walked around to her side of the bed.

"Why did you shift back to a hawk?"

"Easier to hide or escape if someone had come into your room in the night." He sat down next to her foot and lifted the cloth after using it to wipe off whatever paste he'd smeared on her. It looked and smelled awful, but Nixie had to admit it had helped.

"I doubt anyone will be in here for at least a few days. And then it may only be to make sure I'm alive."

"You're probably right. But I'll be no good at getting you out if they catch me beforehand." He lifted her ankle, leaning over it to examine it from all sides. With the swelling gone, his hand could wrap around her entire ankle, yet he only balanced her heel in his palm.

Her belly fluttered. Had anyone ever cared for her like this? She didn't think so. He'd said he was a doctor—this was his job and a normal interaction. Nixie didn't remember a single childhood doctor visit that carried the same warmth and genuine concern that Garrett gave. There was something more to his touch. She couldn't put her finger on it, but Nixie wondered if he was like this with all his patients or was it something about her?

She didn't know which answer she wanted to that question. The world needed someone like him, someone that cared too much. But for once, she wanted to be special. That would only confirm how foolish she was if she let her attraction to him grow, because he made her feel special by doing his job.

That attraction was there, front and centre. It didn't help

that the man wouldn't cover up. And the kiss. Why would he kiss her?

Garrett set her ankle down. "I want you to keep taking the medicine. Once this afternoon and then again when I return tonight. You need to stay off your feet as much as possible and keep it elevated."

"You're leaving?" Nixie wanted him to stay. The company was nice.

"I am. There are things I need to do. I have to plan a way to distract the guards and take out their surveillance at the same time. And I need more information on Alexander Merk."

"Okay." Her face trembled as she let her lips lift into a tight smile.

Garrett moved closer, sitting next to her hips. "I'm coming back." His voice wasn't all business. A low current wove through the sound.

"I know."

"I'm also helping you with whatever you need to get settled before I leave."

"Oh." There went those flutters. He had to go that extra step, making her feel special again. Stupid. Nixie needed to let the idea go. That wasn't why he was here. And she didn't want anyone. Did she?

"Let's get you up and to the bathroom." Garrett tucked his arms beneath her knees and back and stood, lifting her from the bed with an ease that scared her. It was a smooth glide into the air and across the room. He set her down.

"I can take it from here."

"Holler if you need help." He wiped away the frown that started on his brow.

"I will." She wouldn't. That would shatter her *I'm special* flutters. Garrett left, the door shutting behind him. Nixie let out a long breath, letting her mind blank for the moment. No thoughts of Keith and his plans for her. No thoughts of escape. And no thoughts of handsome, naked, shifter hawk doctors.

Washing her hands, she eyed the shower reflecting in the mirror. If she had to sit in bed all day and after yesterday, she needed the refreshment. Just a quick one was all she needed, or could manage. She hopped across the tile to keep the weight off her foot. Her arms were straight out to her sides to keep her balance.

The bathroom door opened, and she spun, startled from her concentration. Wobbling, she lost her balance. But before she could either put her foot to the floor or fall on her ass, Garret wrapped an arm around her waist and pulled her up. She landed hard against his chest, her toes no longer touching the floor.

"What are you doing?" His breath was warm against her cheek.

"I was going to take a shower."

His eyes dropped low, the gold darkening. Why did she feel like she got caught stealing a cookie?

"Before I settled back in bed for the day." The longer he stayed quiet, the more she felt she needed to explain.

"A shower is fine, but not without help." His eyes gentled, and his arm held tight.

"Help? For a shower? From you?" This wasn't just an extra step, but an extra mile. And maybe a little too much for a sprained ankle.

"I don't see anyone else here." His lips twitched and a dimple in his left cheek flashed for a moment.

"I can shower myself. I've been doing it for years. I'm an expert."

"I'm sure you are. But I'm not leaving, in case you slip."

Nixie tilted her head back to really look at him. He wouldn't budge on this. She saw that much in him. The determination to care. He had a heart of gold to match his eyes. She shook from the vulnerable position she'd be in. But if he had come here to hurt her, he wouldn't have helped her with her injury.

"I'll turn around, but I'm waiting right here." He still hadn't let her go, holding firm while she thought it over. She realized, despite his determined demand, if she ordered him from the room, he'd leave. He had a comforting presence that called to her to trust him.

Nixie nodded. Garrett set her down next to the shower and reached in to turn the water on. His eyes raked down her body before he cleared his throat and turned around.

"You don't have to stand so close." He hadn't moved. She only had a few feet between the shower and his back to undress.

Garrett took half a step forward.

She didn't know there were that many muscles in someone's back. As the steam filled the room, her eyes traced down each line. Not good. Heat pooled in her belly with a slow trickle to her core.

"Nixie." He whipped her name through the steam. She gasped and looked up, catching his eyes in the mirror. They glowed bright, cutting through the reflection. "Get in the shower." His voice garbled, he closed his eyes and looked away.

Nixie shimmied out of her clothes and stepped in. There was no hiding her reaction to him now. He'd caught her, eyes round and peeking into the proverbial cookie jar.

7

———

It took all of Garrett's strength not to turn around and grab Nixie again. Her eyes had heated with dilated pupils and a sheen of desire that sparkled in the misty room.

Gritting his teeth, he kept his eyes averted while he listened to the whisper of her clothes from her body to the floor. He conjured the perfect images to match the movements he heard. Her skin bare and smooth.

No. This wasn't right. He had to push the thoughts away. She was hurt and needed help. That was all. He was only here in case she fell.

The glass door slid open, and he imagined her holding the handle for leverage to hop in. The water running down her body.

Garrett shook his head. Guards nearby. Jeffreys downstairs.

Her hair, long and wet, covering places like a game of peek-a-boo.

He growled. His sister. He still had to find his sister.

"Garrett?" Her voice made his cock jump. He winced as it throbbed.

"Something wrong?"

"I was going to ask you that."

Fuck. He needed to get a hold of himself. "Nothing's wrong." So many things were wrong, but he wouldn't tell her he couldn't control his reaction to her.

He forced the sound of the water to the back of his mind and tried to focus on his surroundings, listening for anything outside her room. Getting her out of here needed to be his only focus. Not the idea of claiming a mate. He didn't deserve the reward of having a mate, and she didn't deserve the ties that came with being one. He'd deal with the repercussions of not mating later.

Take out security, distract the guards, get her to safety, then go after his sister. If only it was that simple.

The water shut off. "Pass me a towel, please?"

Garrett took a towel from the shelf on the other side of the room. When he got back, a small hand poked out of a two-inch opening in the door. She had her wrist pinned while she waited. He put the towel in her hand and she opened the door enough to pull it through. Turning back around, he waited until the door slid open.

Nixie had towel dried her hair enough that it didn't drip and wrapped the towel around her body. She hopped on the wet shower floor.

"Stop." That would make her slip, if nothing else. He reached in and wrapped an arm around her waist, pulling her out. Once she was free of the door, he hooked his other arm under her knees.

"You don't have to carry me everywhere."

"You already have to walk on it to get me out of here. Carrying you keeps you off it the rest of the time."

"And I have a deadline to heal."

"Yes." He set her on the bed and walked to her closet. "What do you want to wear?"

"Nothing I have in there. But I guess pajamas would be best."

He looked at the clothes in her closet and didn't see a single suitable thing. Dresses and silks filled the closet with more than enough for five women. But none of it comfortable or reasonable. The set that would provide her the most cover was a silk t-shirt and pants set. Pulling it from the hanger, he went back to kneel on the floor on her side of the bed. Holding the pants out, he waited.

"Why are you doing this?" She swung her legs off the side, but didn't put her feet into the bottoms.

"Doing what?"

"Everything? Why did you come back when you found out your sister wasn't here? Why have you given me food, tended my ankle? Why are you helping me with things you don't need to?" She licked her lips. "Why did you kiss me?"

Garret let the pants sit on the floor and straightened his body so he was eye level with her. He wouldn't tell her about being his mate, not yet, but he could give her the basic truth of it. "Because I won't leave someone behind when there's a chance of saving them. Because he's depriving you of food and because that's what I do. And I kissed you for the same reason you took your time to look at me before your shower with enough desire in your eyes to swirl the steam around the room."

She gasped, soft and short. Her eyes dropped to his lips, and he did the same. His hands fisted the bedding on either side of her hips. Closing his eyes, Garrett sat back on his haunches, pulling away before taking things too far, too soon. He held the pants out for her again. This time, she slipped her feet inside. Pulling them up past her feet so she didn't trip, he helped her stand, balancing her with a grip on her shoulders while she dressed beneath the towel.

She straightened and placed her hands on his forearms. Those narrow eyes had a powerful call. He cleared his throat.

"Is there anything else I can bring you tonight? If I can carry it, I will."

She moved her head back and forth in slow motion, her eyes not leaving his. She was struggling with the moment as much as he. But that still didn't give him the right to kiss her again, no matter how much that flame between them grew.

"Okay." He stepped back and left her to get things he thought she'd need while he was gone. Her hair brush, extra blankets, protein bars, water, the poultice, and a cold cloth. When he returned, she had the shirt on and the towel sprawled on the floor. "As soon as you get back to bed, put the poultice and cloth on your ankle and keep it elevated. Change it again this afternoon. I'll be back once it's dark."

Garrett itched to touch her, to at least get close to her, but he couldn't control the temptation. He rushed to pull on the magic and begin the shift. Flying to the door, he waited for her to wrap the blanket around her shoulders and hop to the balcony. She paused for him to hop on her back and grip the blanket. Once out of the camera range, Garrett perched on the railing.

The air was crisp and the morning beautiful. He'd learned to appreciate the insignificant moments like this. And when he knew he needed some distance from his mate to control himself, he instead leaned around her as they looked at the different shades of the morning light shining through the trees. If only he could have this peace every morning, with his mate by his side.

Nixie was used to boredom, but now it felt like torture. It was one thing to not move because she didn't have a reason. It was another to not move because she couldn't. Throw in her thoughts on Garrett and agony settled hard in her belly.

Slamming her head back against the pillow mountain at her back, she groaned, loud and annoying with a long suffering eye roll. There was something wrong with her if she had the hots for the paranormal creature that visited her in the night.

"Get a hold of yourself, Nixie. He's just a kind man and you're not so special. He'll get you out of here and you, not-so-young lady anymore, are going to live happy and alone." She stabbed her finger at her imaginary self sitting in front of her. "Get some goats! Goats are cute!" After throwing her hands into the air, she fell back onto the bed. It was a good thing Garrett hadn't replaced the bug in her room and she hadn't bothered getting it either. He didn't need to hear her monologue. "Whoa, you're crazy, woman." She dropped her voice, mimicking a man that sounded nothing like Garrett. "I'll drop you off at the next bus stop and see you around. Not."

But she hadn't imagined it. She hadn't imagined the change in his voice when he said her name or the way he'd admitted simple attraction. His touch burned and ignited thoughts and feelings long gone. The first few years here, she'd held on to dreams and a fanciful future. But as time passed, she knew she didn't want any of that. She wanted to live alone and in peace. Be self-sufficient, someone to be proud of. She couldn't be proud of herself if she latched onto a man, the one to rescue her, no less.

Nixie needed to remember that. Remember her goats.

She wouldn't abandon her future kids, John Boy, Mary Ellen, Jason, Erin, Ben, Jim Bob, and Elizabeth, give or take a few Waltons.

Only once that day had someone walked past her bedroom door. They'd banged three times against the wood asking, "Still alive, brat?" If Keith hadn't ordered them not to open her door, her "fuck you" response would have snapped their temper. They wouldn't have laid a hand on her, not without Keith's permission first, but sometimes she got to them enough they liked to scare her. It didn't work like it used to. She knew the rules of this place.

But if the last few days had taught her anything, it was that the rules changed. The air fizzled with it. Her time spent here was ending. She only hoped it was far away from here and not in the ground or on the other end of a pain stick.

The least she could do was help Garrett with a plan to get out of here.

"Those damn guards are too meticulous. I can't imagine anything pulling them all away." She spoke aloud to stave off loneliness. Had to talk to someone to stay sane, might as well be herself. "There are too many cameras and sensors to take out all at once, but what if we took out their ability to see what they saw? The security office. But that would only make the guards more alert at each of their stations. Why not just blow the house up and run?"

Nixie kind of liked the idea of blowing up the place, with Keith and his rottweilers inside. Except she was still inside, too.

She sighed and watched the light change through the balcony doors. As soon as dark hit, she moved from the bed. Using a chair to help herself hop across the room, she sat and waited for Garrett to show.

Golden eyes flashed in the trees and Nixie opened the door to make her way to the blind spot. He carried another pack in his talons, but didn't hop onto the blanket. Nixie eyed the stars, silently pointing out the constellations she remembered. They needed to stay out there long enough the guards wouldn't suspect her short hops in and out.

The guards would make their next turn around the corner soon. Garrett nudged her arm, and she turned to face him. He clutched at the blanket with one foot and balanced with his other against her arm beneath it. Keeping her back to the camera, she hopped inside. Nixie made her way back to the bed while he shifted.

"How are you?" Garrett stood on the other side of the bed, glancing between her face and her ankle.

"Good. No new swelling or pain. I've done nothing other than the best impersonations of a bump on a log all day." She kissed the tips of her fingers and threw it in the air.

Holy shit cracker. His smile. Goats, think of the goats. Don't think of what those heated eyes and that devastating dimple were doing to her body. Arousal zigged and zagged and zipped and popped like a ping-pong machine until it hit the goal between her legs. All from a fucking smile. Nixie looked away, heat filling her cheeks.

Garret moved, graceful strength carrying him around the bed. He sat next to her ankle and repeated the same examination as he had that morning. "It looks good. What time did you take the medication?"

Oops. She'd forgot. She twisted her lips as if she were thinking. "I was just so busy. I just didn't have the time to stop and take them."

"Uh huh." There was that look again. The prominent brow that said "caught you." He took out the pills and passed them to her. "Too busy plotting to blow up the mansion?"

She froze with the pills on her tongue. Wincing, she swallowed them down with water before she gagged on the chalky texture. He'd heard. "I'll blow you up." She slapped her face. "Shit. Nope."

THE LAUGH that bellowed from him felt good. Garrett should have told her he'd replaced the bug before he left. But then he wouldn't have heard her fears regarding him, or her blurting about goats. And he wouldn't have heard the premise for a good plan.

"The idea has merit," he said once settling from his laughter.

Her skin flushed to the shade of a rose, and her delicate lips parted.

"Not that one. However, I'm happy to discuss that later. But your idea to blow up the house."

Nixie straightened her shoulders and brushed her hands over her cheeks while pushing her hair away from her face. "Except that I'm stuck inside said house."

"We wouldn't blow up the entire house. How would the guards react in the event of a fire?" A big enough fire that needed most of them to manage, and that also took out the security office, might give them enough of a head start out her balcony window and into the woods. He'd already planned his escape routes and contingency plans.

"I think that would depend on a few things." Her freckles danced as she thought.

"Maybe during a meeting where they need to evacuate several people and tend the blaze." He'd already decided what night to get her out. The one with the most distractions.

"And also come for me." She hesitated. "Although we'd have a few minutes before they did."

"A few minutes is the biggest window we'll ever get." No matter what distraction Garrett could cook up, he needed to get them off that balcony and far into the trees in only a few minutes.

"As long as there are people more important than me in the house."

She was right, but he hated it. Every other man in this house needed to burn in hell. "Not a single one of them are worth more than you." He wouldn't embarrass her by raising her comments about not being anyone special. She didn't need reminding of everything she'd said to herself that day or her terrible impression of him.

"I know that." Her hoarse whisper quaked.

"Do you?" He moved closer.

"It's all about perspective, right?" One slender shoulder lifted.

"No." Garrett tapped his own chest when he'd rather touch her heart to strengthen his point. "It's here. I've seen a lot of evil like Jeffreys and I've met many people. Perspective has nothing to do with it."

"How did someone like you end up with people like Keith?"

Luck of the draw. "Someone took my sister to blackmail me into working for them. I was his on-site doctor for his underground women's fighting ring." Garrett hadn't done enough for those women.

"I take it the women weren't volunteers, either." Disdain dripped as her features tightened.

"No. I never knew what he did with Anya. If he had her,

killed her, or sold her. I've thought she was dead for a long time. I tracked her to Jeffreys and came here to find closure. But now I need to find out if she's alive or not." Garrett didn't want to feed the hope that she might still be alive after all this time. But how could he not want his little sister to be safe?

"I'm sorry. Rescuing me is delaying that." She watched her hands twist in circles on her lap.

"Don't be sorry." He used his knuckle to lift her chin. Blue eyes shimmered with vulnerability. Every emotion she had was on display. How could someone still give so much after she'd lived the way she had?

Her lips parted above his touch. The atmosphere changed quick enough to give him whiplash. Garrett pulled his hand back. As much as he wanted to explore, it wasn't right. Not here. Not now.

"I brought you more to eat." Reaching for the pack, he pulled out the containers. "I'll take all the packs and containers back with me tonight."

"What? Do I snore?" She unscrewed the cap and picked up the spoon. He wondered if he could throw her off as easily as she did him.

"Like a trucker." The spoon dropped, and so did her jaw. Those slim eyes shot darts into the centre of his head. Worth it.

"I was joking."

"So was I, little one."

"Damn right you were." Nixie threw one more I'm-watching-you look and picked up the spoon. "Tell me more about shifters."

"What do you want to know?" Garrett stood and pulled a chair to her side of the bed. The bed was too tempting.

"Everything. Where or what do you come from?" Nixie

pulled herself up further against the pillows and eyed him over her food.

"You saw what looks like wind when I shift. It is a wind in a way. Those winds preserved the magic for the current generation of shifters." He leaned forward with his elbows on his knees, clasping his hands in front of him. He still hadn't bothered to cover up, but he didn't need to spread himself wide.

"Current generation?"

"I've recently learned the original shifter species died off, or the abilities remained dormant a long time ago, over three hundred years ago. Fate saw a need to bring them back, so here we are." Here he was trying to get through all this and be done with it, and it turns out this was why he was here.

"Fate, huh?" Skepticism lifted one side of her face.

"Yes, Fate. She's real, and nosy." He needed to ask Margaret why Fate chose mates.

Nixie giggled. "Keep talking," she drawled, spinning her spoon in circles.

"We have increased strength and speed and the senses to match our animal counterparts. When we first shifted, the wind paired us with an animal in the wild, our pair. Many shifters grew up with their pair, building a bond stronger than siblings. Others only see their pair once in a while."

"Why?" She looked put out with her indignant frown over sad eyes. The blue paled as she waited for his answer.

"They may have lived and grown up in a city and shifted with their pair while on vacation. But pairs have increased abilities and a lifespan to match their shifter."

"What about your pair?"

"Eagle. He's nearby." He'd been helping to scout the areas around the mansion and all the escape routes.

"Eagle? But you're a hawk." Her light pink lips disappeared. She pulled them in to stop the snicker in her throat.

"Nine-year-old me didn't know the difference." Besides, Eagle had liked the name. Still did.

"That's cute." Her grin burst free. "What else?"

Garrett hesitated. Did he tell her about mates? Was it fair to tell her without revealing she was his? The longer he stayed silent, the more she'd wonder.

"Garrett?" That moment of silence had given her enough reason to feel cautious. Her voice was only a whisper.

"Just thinking. Only one more thing." He didn't trust himself not to claim her. "We're a secret." He winked.

"But I know."

"Yes, you do." Because she was his mate. Only some family members and mates knew.

"Lucky me." She wiggled her shoulders. Garrett smiled, but wondered just how lucky she was. She'd be bound to him when what she deserved was her freedom. Margaret had said Nixie wanted peace. Garrett vowed he'd make sure she had it.

8

Nixie had become superb at single-footed life. She always thought she had good balance until she stopped wobbling around her room. Two feet on the ground, even in ridiculous heels, was better than one foot and hopping.

Garrett hadn't spent the night again, but he came every night with food and always examined her foot. As long as she continued to stay off it, he said the muscle would heal enough she could make a run for it when the time came. A short run, at least. And she kept most of her strength from the food he brought. By night time, she was hungry, but she sustained herself throughout the day with the protein bars and snacks he brought her.

She'd bugged him for stories while he visited. Hearing about his friends that lived in a town called Alder Ridge while she ate whatever he brought her that night. He'd told her more about the fighting ring he'd worked for. Hell, Nixie had it easy. Those women had to fight to keep their life. Until one wolf shifter came in to rescue one of them and Garrett helped him rescue them all.

His eyes dimmed to a dull yellow whenever he spoke of that time. Garrett hated himself for the role he played. Nixie might not have a lot of experience with other people and how to read them, but the guilt rolled over him like dark smoke. The man didn't realize how good he was.

But for four nights, he hadn't touched her unless examining her ankle. She pretended she didn't see him pull his hand back every time he stretched it out. He heard her talking to herself that second night. Yet, no touch or kiss since. Nixie considered that a good thing, at first. The attachment wasn't right for her. How did she discover her true feelings toward the person getting her out of here?

These past few days carried their own sense of peace and normalcy without interruptions from Keith or the guards. Their knocking decreased since they always saw her from the balcony camera. This time gave her the opportunity to examine the attraction she felt toward Garrett. Her conclusion? It wasn't going away, and it wasn't fanciful.

Darkness fell into the room and she made her way outside to wait for Garrett. Worry crept in when she had to wait longer than usual. They had no way of contacting each other when apart. Something Nixie would ask him for. It would be important as they got closer to the big day. The possibility the guards had discovered him or his camp scratched at her.

The familiar gold glow weaving through the trees calmed her, for now. Discovery was a genuine threat. And Nixie was useless until she got out of here.

Garrett landed on the railing, a new pack in his beak. Since she'd already been outside long enough, she motioned for him to get on.

No longer needing to worry about swelling as much in her foot, Nixie sat on the end of the bed while she watched

Garrett shift. Pain and magic mixed, but she held in her wince. The sight turned beautiful as the wind came forth and covered him.

"Sorry, I'm late." The wind finished dissipating, and Garrett sat down on the chair, taking his usual position with his elbows on his knees and hands clasped, blocking her view of his come-and-go erection. "I was late getting back to camp after looking for information on Alexander Merk."

"That's okay. But it got me thinking." Nixie swung her foot back and forth to keep from setting it on the floor. "Is there any way you can leave me a phone or something to contact you or for you to contact me?"

"The closer we get to day nine, the more I think of that as well. Something could always go wrong, and I want to make sure you're safe." His eyes and voice changed simultaneously—a fierce shade and tone before clearing. "I'll get you something."

"Thank you." Was he affected by her as much as she was of him? He was always so calm, even when his eyes changed, that she couldn't be sure she hadn't imagined it. "What did you find out about Alexander?"

"That he's dead." His clasped hands turned into fists.

"What? What about..." She trailed off, not knowing how to ask about his sister.

"They killed or severely maimed anyone who worked for him." Muscles ticked along Garrett's arms and legs. It wasn't the right time to notice those. But she did. Nixie wanted to run her fingers over each one to soothe his frustration.

"They killed them?" Murdered? Not just killed in a skirmish?

Garrett nodded, his jaw tight.

Nixie waited. If he wanted to tell her what he'd found out about his sister, he would.

"No one knows what happened to any women or others he had captive. But there are rumours. Some say set free, some say taken."

"Who?" The shock of it all reduced Nixie to simple questions.

"Again, no one knows, but there are rumours. Those are the only trails to follow." Dejected eyes left her face and landed on the floor. Her entire centre clutched with the need to go to him, to hold him. She imagined those square shoulders hid his pain and fear well, to the rest of the world. But Nixie saw more.

"Are you okay?" she whispered.

"I never had much hope that I would find her alive. And I'm trying to keep it that way." Garrett's voice didn't waver, but he didn't look back up at her.

"I'm so sorry you have to push all that away. But I understand why you do." She'd lived with that fine thread tethered to her freedom for a long time.

"You've held onto your hope of getting out of here." He tilted his head enough he looked at her with an upward glance.

"Yes, but that doesn't mean I don't give myself one hell of a reality check every once in a while." She let her lips twitch into a sad smirk. "I know the chances of escape. They're better with you here, but that doesn't mean we won't get caught." She couldn't be the reason he never found Anya. "Can you promise me something?"

"Anything." As quick as the word left his lips, so did his frustrations. Sharp attention landed on her, waiting for her to speak. Nixie had to clear her throat and take a breath. His attention was heady, setting her nerves on fire, an instant blaze. Focus. She needed him to make a promise.

"Promise me that if things go bad during the escape and

capture is inevitable, that you will shift and get away for good. Don't let yourself get caught. I've been here for years and I can handle it. You need to go after Anya."

"I can't promise you that." A hoarse rasp muffled his voice. "Nixie, I can't leave you behind."

"Well, you can't very well come back and save me again if they catch you too." Casting her seriousness aside, she shrugged her shoulders and gave him her best *well, duh* expression.

He grinned, letting his dimple out in full force. Oh, that deadly dimple.

Nixie didn't expect to live if the guards caught her trying to escape, but she needed to give Garrett a reason to stay free. And if she was going to die soon, Nixie didn't want to spend her last minutes wondering if she should have done something about her attraction to Garrett. Maybe this wasn't her chance at freedom, but a little slice of life before it all ended.

Pushing off the end of the bed, she stood, catching her balance before hopping toward Garrett. He jumped from his seat and met her before she made it two hops. Large palms slipped beneath the blanket and cupped her elbows.

"What are you doing?" His fingers flexed.

The smell of him invaded her senses, as did his body heat. Placing her hands on his arms, she let the blanket she always had covering her shoulders drop to the floor.

"This." Leaning up on the toes of her one good foot, Nixie pressed her lips to his. His head jerked back.

Stupid. She'd imagined it all from him. Not that it made sense, but it wasn't as if she had experience reading a man's reactions. A few, many years ago. But she hadn't thought about men in this way for a long time. Heat flooded her, climbing up her neck. Retreat.

His grip tightened and the frown over his eyes tightened. Garrett pulled her closer and bent his head to claim her lips in a way she'd been too afraid to do herself.

It was a bad idea. But his blood rushed, his skin heated, and his control vanished. Garrett tasted her, nipping, licking, claiming her mouth as his while he grappled with himself in his mind to regain the reigns of his control. He couldn't lose that. If he did, he'd have her on the bed and buried inside her in minutes. And they'd both enjoy it, he'd make sure of it. But he wouldn't mate her and he wouldn't take her here. Not under this roof.

He drank her sweet spiciness like he would an aged whiskey, enjoying every sip. He kept his hands on her elbows, holding her close, for fear they would wander to places she wasn't ready for. Places he wasn't ready for.

Running his tongue along hers, she matched his motions. And when she moaned, he growled. Damn, the temptation was too strong. Each moment he thought he had his control back in his hands, it slipped through his fingers.

Her body softened and her balance wavered, forcing him to band an arm around her waist, leaving the other without purpose at her elbow. The things he could do to her with one free hand.

Garrett tore his lips from hers, forcing his head up and back. "You need to stop me, Nixie."

"Why?" She panted, pushing her breasts against his chest, the silk hiding nothing from him.

"This isn't right." He nodded to the bed and the room, hoping she understood he meant the setting, not the kiss.

"My opinion flaps better than your wings. If I didn't want

you to kiss me, I wouldn't have done it first. And if I don't want something, you'll be the first to know. I promise."

Damn, this woman. His woman. "And what is it you want right now, little one?" He was about to cave, but he mentally set limits for himself. This wouldn't go too far.

Her gasp melted her snap attitude. "I want you to kiss me, and I want you to touch me."

Garrett wanted that and more. His hand left her elbow and rested on her hip. Pulling her against him, he pressed his erection to her belly so he could capture her gasp. He held nothing back, didn't try to. He let his control hover out of reach.

Small hands moved over his chest and up to his shoulders. Signals fired through his system, telling him he needed to move that hand. Gliding under the silk shirt, his palm reached her ribs. Her soft body stilled with each inch he moved. Anticipation dragged on, for her and him. He stretched it out as he tasted her lips and tongue. Small strokes with his thumb left a zig-zag trail until he reached the underside of her breast.

The moment his thumb moved over her nipple, Nixie pulled her mouth from his to take a deep breath.

"Is that the touch you want?" Garrett didn't manage more than a harsh whisper. He bent his head to nip at her jaw and down her neck. Her pulse throbbed and called to him. If the time ever came, he knew where he'd leave his mark.

"It's not enough." How did she make a whine sound so demanding?

"It's not." Garrett pinched her nipple between two fingers, then settled the nub in the centre of his palm to soothe the ache.

The bed behind her beckoned him. He didn't need to lay

her down to do the things he wanted, but he should get her off her feet. Now was the time to gain a tight grip on his control.

Lifting her off the floor, he backed her to the bed. He laid her down and braced himself on his knee while he pulled them up toward the pillows. Claiming her mouth again, he teased her breasts, pinching, kneading, circling, until she writhed beneath him. Her moans carried urgency, and Garrett held back his grin.

The next time he thrust his tongue into her mouth, she nipped it. Lifting his head, he caught her gaze. Her eyes rolled back the more he played.

"Is this touch good?" Her beauty captured him. Not only her physical beauty. There was so much to this woman, it would take him years to discover every facet of her.

"Yes," she hissed. Swollen lips parting, he held himself back from claiming them again. As frustrated as he was making her, she was sure to bite him again as he carried out his next move.

He moved his hand lower, over her belly, slow and light. Her skin pebbled and hitched with her breathing. "And this?"

"Yes, Garrett."

He couldn't stop himself, not without giving her something. When he slid his fingers below the waist of her silk bottoms, he asked again. "And this touch, little one?" He approached the limit he set for himself.

Her eyes snapped to his, and her head lifted off the pillow. He had to lean back to keep her from smashing into his nose. "You really don't need to keep asking."

His chuckle held a seductive promise that filled his core —one he needed her to hear. "I'm not asking because I want your permission. I'm asking because I want to hear you to beg."

➤

Beg? Sure, Nixie could do that. Anything for him to move his hand lower and give her a release unlike any other. Something about the way her body responded to him, the pleasure he gave her would never compare.

"Garrett, please. I... It's been..." She didn't have the right word to give any confession. "Please."

"Shh, little one. That's all I needed." He kissed her again, at the same time his fingers moved over her clit. Her knees had a mind of their own and moved further apart, inviting him in.

Sparks spread from his fingers. She thrust her hips up, searching for more too soon, but Garrett moved with her, not changing the pressure or his motions. The slow downward pet and circles were too much and not enough. Nixie lifted her hands above her head to fist under the pillow.

Nixie had no end goal, only a desire to experience something in case the escape went to hell. And Garrett more than provided.

His pressure increased, taking her another step closer to a peak she craved. That ultimate pleasure, ultimate release, ultimate freedom. When his lips nipped along her jaw and down her neck again, she realized she'd stopped kissing him back, too focused on the small fires racking her body.

Tilting her hips, Nixie silently begged him for more. He obeyed.

One thick finger circled her entrance and thrust in once. Then two fingers circled and filled her. His other hand cut the sound that escaped her short.

"As much as I want to hear how loud I can make you cry out, this isn't the place." He was right. The guards may not check on her often, but they did patrol outside her door once in a while. Especially if her cries echo down the stairs. But his pumping fingers were too much. She continued to whimper behind his hand. "Do I need to keep this here?"

She nodded, his hand moving with her. He didn't seal his grip, but only muffled the sounds she made.

Garrett kissed her nose. "Very well." He moved his fingers in a way that made the sensations almost unbearable.

Her blood rushed through her body and she bucked with his hand, but there was still something missing.

"But, if I can't kiss you here," he touched his nose to the back of his hand, "I'll have to kiss you elsewhere." As his meaning sunk in, her pleasure focused and her walls tightened around his fingers. That grin with his deadly dimple sharpened the edge she lay on.

Nixie whimpered again as he kissed down her body, pulling her nipples between his teeth as he passed each one. Her hands clutched his around her mouth when his tongue circled her naval.

With the change of angle to his arm, he pulled at the waist of her pajama bottoms, exposing the top of her mound. Cool air washed over her clit. He blew on her twice more before his tongue lashed out to expose her clit from under its hood and latch on with his mouth.

That was it. That was what she'd needed. His fingers worked harder as he sucked. Sharp spears helped her climb, each lash a new step toward her climax. The closer she got, the more his hand wouldn't be enough, but she had no power to stop him—to stop herself.

Tearing the pillow out from under her head, she held it

over his hand and her mouth in time for her little world to explode. Garrett followed her movements as her hips bucked, but he changed nothing. His tongue and thrusting fingers forced her into a million other mini explosions. When she couldn't take anymore, her knees tried to close, and he released her.

Lifting his hand, he pulled the pillow away. When Nixie opened her eyes, his fierce ones glared down at her. His hand stroked her centre as she continued to shudder.

"I'm at a loss for words, little one." He swiped her hair off her forehead.

"I'd have enough for both of us, but that portion of my brain has gone into a coma."

There it was, that show stopping, body melting grin.

"That's sexy."

His look intensified.

"That was meant to only be a thought, but you heard it, didn't you?"

"Yeah." Garrett kissed each cheek. She assumed where she blushed, and kissed her lips again. Gentle motions that soothed and ignited at the same time. He pulled away before her body reheated. "I hate to ask you to move, but I need to leave."

Her heart sank. "Why? You could stay." He'd given her the most amazing moment of her life and he didn't want to stay with her? He pulled his hand free from the silk.

"If I stay, things are going to go farther than either of us are ready for." The warning growl must have been an over dramatic reaction. Nixie wasn't expecting the stars and the moon, only something she could hold on to and not regret if she faced her final days.

Pushing on his shoulders, she put space between them. "How do you know what I'm ready for?"

"Trust me." He growled, and his cock twitched against her hip.

She lifted her brow, still expecting an answer, despite her body's reaction to his.

"It wouldn't be just sex." As nice as that sounded, Nixie didn't understand.

"That's exactly what it would be. Just sex." Sex hadn't been her plan. She'd only wanted him to stay, but now she argued out of spite.

"Not with you." The change in his voice made his meaning clear, but to top it off, he fisted her hair and held her in place while he devoured her mouth, giving Nixie a taste of what it would be with him. Not just sex. While the feeling was inexplicable, she got a glimpse. She wasn't ready.

Releasing her, Garrett closed his eyes while he backed off the bed. She sat up to watch him shift.

Saying goodnight to the hawk wasn't any easier than saying goodnight to the man.

9

Garrett paced his camp, already fighting with temptation before he left the ground. He'd spent the day chasing down rumours of Alexander Merk's killers and gathering supplies for the escape, hoping to drown out his thoughts of Nixie. He had to go back to her, but with each step across his camp, he tried to imagine a reason not to. But it always came back to if he didn't, she wouldn't get a meal for the day.

True to his word, Jeffreys hadn't sent any food or help for her. His recordings had caught her name in a few conversations from Jeffreys and the guards. Jeffreys lamented the brat in her, wondering why she had ever appealed to him. And the guards had musings over what would come of her when the week was up. None of them would get the answer they expected. His plan only put them a few minutes ahead of the guards at best, but Garrett would get his mate out of there.

He looked up at the dimming sky. If he didn't get moving soon, he'd be late, leaving Nixie to wonder again. She may not have said she'd been worried, but Garrett had felt the concern from her, the reason for her asking for a way to contact him.

Cleaning up and hiding all evidence that pointed to Jeffreys' mansion, he snatched the small pack and stepped outside. He pulled in the magic as he hiked those first few steps, shifting as he walked. Taking flight, he followed the familiar path, veering to watch for new patrols. Reaching the end of the tree line, he saw Nixie waiting for him on the balcony. Despite how well her foot was healing, Garrett had demanded she stay off it as long as possible, knowing she needed it to run. Within the next day or two, he'd let her walk on it to build some of her strength back.

Avoiding the camera and guards became second nature. As did their maneuver inside her bedroom from the balcony.

Nixie took the pack to the bed while he shifted. He sat, leaning forward with his hands in front. He wanted to touch her. Leaving his camp, he knew keeping his distance from her would be torture, but he hadn't anticipated how much. Now that he'd tasted her, he needed to taste her again only so he could breathe.

"How is your ankle today?" Keep the conversation where it needed to be and leave before he tumbled her back to the bed.

"It's getting better every day." Her eyes brightened. "I've been flexing it to work the muscle. Still no weight on it, I promise."

"That's good. I've put a burner phone in the pack. Keep it hidden, but where you can get to it and only use if you have to. I've attached my number. It's another burner phone. I won't call you either. Not until it's time."

Nixie reached into the bottom of the pack and pulled out the phone. She clutched it to her chest. "Thank you."

"Eat up, little one." The meals were a hearty substance and the protein bars staved off her hunger through the day. She didn't look ill, pale, or lost any weight.

"Tell me what you did today." She opened the thermos and ate while her eyes latched onto him, eager for whatever he had to say.

"I gathered supplies for the escape. And I chased some rumours."

"Okay, first. What supplies?"

"It's a good thing your room isn't on the side of the mansion as the security office or where Jeffreys holds his meetings."

"You're really going with fire, aren't you?"

"Low grade bombs shot from out of camera range with an arrow. First one will hit the security office and the rest will line that entire side of the house and out the front lane."

"Keep the guards all going in one direction."

He nodded. "We won't have long before he sends someone to get you or before they position themselves back on this side of the house."

"If any time at all."

She wasn't wrong, but it was his only chance. He needed to get them ahead enough to stay out of sight until they reached one of the getaway vehicles. Three stashed in different directions. Which one they chose would depend on the position of the guards.

"So you bought bombs today." Excessive cheer broke her smile.

"Yes, I did." Things he'd rather not own.

"And where does one go to acquire such unsavory material?" With pinched lips and a quirked brow, Nixie took on the persona of a head mistress while enunciating her syllables.

"To unsavory people." People he hoped to never cross paths with again. Never with his mate by his side.

"What else?" She relaxed and continued to eat.

"Have you ever gone zip-lining?"

"No." Her spoon froze in the air and she frowned.

"You will. Our escape is out the balcony."

"I had hoped for a ladder."

"Too big to carry."

"Zip-line it is." She finished the thermos and tucked it back in the pack. "What about the rumours?"

"They led to more rumours. But I don't think that's all they are. It's a group of people. They exist. How to find them, though, I'm not sure. Maybe if I keep questioning people about them, they'll find me."

"That doesn't sound like a good tactic."

"It's one I'd rather avoid." From what he'd learned, them finding him would result in questions followed by death. Garrett hoped that some of what he'd heard was an exaggeration. He'd put his search for them on hold until Nixie was out of here and safe, in case he triggered their attention prematurely.

Silence settled as Nixie finished eating. Garrett captured every glance she tossed up. Memory of her taste exploded on his tongue and heated his blood. She was perched on the end of the bed, one leg stretched straight and the other bent to make a four shape. The blanket lay discarded beside her since they'd first come inside. That was a first since he'd been coming here. That blanket had been her shield. Now he needed it to be his.

He didn't stop himself from browsing her body through the silk. His cock swelled, making him wonder if he had enough control to stop himself as he did the night before.

"Garrett?" Nixie packed everything back in the pack and

stood. One long look up her body and he swallowed his tongue.

Standing, he reached behind her and snagged the blanket off the bed to wrap around his hips. "Is there anything you need help with before I leave?"

"Really?" Her eyes narrowed. Looking down her nose, she gestured to the blanket. "Now you cover up? After last ni..." Her playful smile receded like the tide. Garrett watched what little confidence she'd had in facing him without her shield change to utter humiliation. Crossing her arms over her chest, she looked away. "No, I don't need anything."

He couldn't do that to her. Garrett couldn't let her believe he didn't want her or that he regretted anything. "Fuck." His hoarse growl erupted, startling her. She caught herself on the bed at the same time Garrett dropped the blanket. He wrapped an arm around her waist and toppled them onto the soft mattress.

RELIEF CRASHED at the same time they crashed onto the bed. He wanted her as much as she wanted him, but that didn't help her confusion. Why had he covered up and tried to leave so soon?

Leave a girl alone to think all day and she's going to come up with a well-choreographed plan of her own. But would he accept it?

Heat bloomed—the centre of it was the kiss. It was more than a kiss. There was no one word or even a decent description of the way he claimed her mouth and controlled her body with only his lips. Every time he tilted his head, he changed the intensity of the flames within her.

The hand at her back slid up to brace her nape and his other roamed free up and down her side, but never touched her bare skin. His erection pulsed at her hip as the rest of his body stayed as rigid as steel. This wasn't anything like she'd planned. Pushing his shoulders, she broke the kiss.

"I don't understand."

"What don't you understand, little one?"

That, she wanted to scream. How his mouth and his voice were saying one thing, but his body and hands said another. "There is something wrong with this that you don't want, yet you still kissed me and laid us on the bed. Why are you holding back?"

"I explained that last night." He braced his hand on her hip and put more distance between them. "I don't want to take this too far, but I couldn't let you believe for even a second that I don't want you or that I regretted last night."

"I don't want just another kiss." She took a chance to make it clear what she wanted from him.

"Nixie, I can't give you more." His eyes closed and his fingers flexed. "I won't take you here."

"Take me?"

Garrett rolled on top of her and pressed his erection to her centre, the length grinding against her clit. "Yes, take you. Fuck you and so much more."

Nixie's doubts vanished. That one motion, those few words, told her everything she needed to know. But he wasn't getting free of her with just a kiss again. "Stand up."

Garrett stiffened, and his jaw clenched hard enough she heard his teeth grind. He stood. She followed him up, but stayed sitting on the bed.

He stepped back, creating empty space between them. She reached out and grabbed his hand to pull him back.

"Nixie?"

"I dare you stop me."

His eyes flashed molten gold. Nixie ran her hands up his bunched thighs. The man wouldn't relax.

The second her fingers touched the velvet skin over his length, he twitched. Moving her fingers around, she wrapped her hand around the base.

"Stop." His demand had just as much power in his whisper as it did in his full voice. But he didn't move. And he didn't repeat himself as she stroked up to the tip and back down.

Angling him toward her mouth, she waited for him to say it again. He didn't, but his hand shot into her hair.

"Do it, little one."

She swirled her tongue over the head and his eyes closed. His hand tensed, but he didn't force her motions. That was her goal. She wanted to crack that rigid control—not break it. Only a crack to allow them both a little more to hold. As much as her core craved him inside her, she thought there was something sweet about waiting for her freedom.

Sucking him in to the back of her throat, Nixie hummed and stroked her tongue on the thick underside. She moved back and forth, enjoying the taste of him. Nixie dragged on the slow torture until his hips moved. Small thrusts and nothing more. Not enough to hinder her movements or to take over.

That was when she struck, upped the ante, doubled her bet. Gripping both his hips, she pulled him closer to take as much of him as she could. Grinding teeth echoed through his growl, and he thrust once with her. He froze in place, everything tense, as if he waited for her to deny him. Nixie continued like nothing happened.

And he broke.

Pricking pain covered her scalp as Garrett tightened his hold in her hair. He pulled to tilt her head back, and he reared up. With shallow, quick thrusts, he moved in and out of her mouth. Nixie relaxed and took everything he gave her.

His eyes bore into hers and in them she saw that crack she'd hoped for. She couldn't look away, couldn't blink. And it seemed neither could he. That moment filled her with something she didn't want explained. Nixie only wanted to hold on to it forever.

His cock swelled in her mouth and his other hand cupped her chin—the gentle touch at odds with the fierce hold in her hair. She knew what was coming, tasted the beginnings of it. His lips moved, but instead of the words he tried to form, a low roar, trapped in his throat, erupted. The sound rumbled through his body rather than through the room.

Nixie swallowed around him, his release jetting down her throat. Garrett tried to pull out of her, but she sucked harder. His knee bent, but he caught himself. He'd almost buckled to the floor. Satisfaction turned up her lips around him, pausing her ministrations. Garrett used the chance to pull her off him.

"Payback, little one. I think you've earned it." His voice had changed. Rough and almost slurred. His grip in her hair didn't lessen. He used it to guide her back up the bed, laying her down before he released her.

Ridding her of her bottoms, Garrett stood beside the bed, his erection rising once again. Nixie stared in awe at the stamina he had. When her eyes roamed to his face, she gasped from the savage grin.

Nixie realized in that moment she was in way over her head.

BEST FUCKING ORGASM of his life. Was it all Nixie? Or was it because she was his mate? Did it even matter? Not right now, it didn't.

Garrett dropped the silk shorts to the floor. He wanted her naked, but it would be too much for him to handle. The only reason he trusted himself this much was because she'd already sucked him dry. But that satiation wouldn't last long. Not while he forced her to come apart beneath his tongue and touch.

He pulled one leg off the bed to hang toward the floor. Reaching down, he rubbed his thumb over the hood covering her clit with upward strokes, all while watching her face. Her lips parted, her breath rushed, and her eyes fluttered to escape his gaze.

"You don't know what you've tempted."

"Oh, I'm learning." She pulled in a breath as her words whooshed out.

Garrett chuckled. "Yeah, little one, you are." He'd tried so damn hard to hold back with her mouth wrapped around him. But she wouldn't let him. He should feel bad for how hard he took her, but he didn't, not with the salacious look she sent him when she'd finished with him. It had been her plan to shatter his control.

He increased the pressure of his thumb and switched to circles. She tilted her hips up, and he gave her what she asked her. Turning his hand, he dipped his fingers down, sliding them into her heat. But when she moaned, he pulled away.

Her head lifted off the pillow, and she froze in panic.

"Not a sound, Nixie." Low and guttural, his command flowed.

She relaxed and pinched her lips together. Garrett returned his hand. Clenching his fingers, her hips followed his movements. He wanted to sink himself into her body. An urgency to get her out of there, jump from the balcony and be damned, crawled over his skin.

No, he wouldn't put his mate in that kind of danger. He had to settle with giving her what he could for now, what the minx asked for.

Curling his fingers, he paused. His ears hummed, his blood rushing through, but something around them was changing.

"Garrett?" Nixie breathed.

"Shh." He focused, his hearing cleared. Footsteps, light and practiced, approached. "Someone's coming." He pulled his hand from her, hating the wince pinching Nixie's face. He picked up the pajama bottoms and passed them to her.

"What do we do?" She whispered and slipped the silk up her legs.

"You handle them like you would any other time. I'll hide." Garrett groaned thinking about her antagonizing the guards. He grabbed the pack from the bed and dashed into her closet while shifting. Shoving the pack in her hiding spot, he pushed himself deep into the closet. His dark feathers blended in the night and he shielded his body with the things she had on the floor.

The bedroom door opened. Garrett listened to the foot-steps and movements. Two guards entered her room.

"What do you two want?" Nixie's voice was steady and sure. He didn't sense any apprehension.

"The boss sent us up to check on you." The bored male voice filled the room.

"Odd. He made it clear I wouldn't see another face until the time was up. Yet here are two ugly mugs to gaze upon."

Garrett imagined the smile playing on Nixie's lips. Damn it. As much as he wanted to laugh and feel pride, he wanted to shield her and shut her up.

"You're looking well for someone who hasn't eaten in almost a week." Garrett didn't miss the suspicion that clung to the guard's boredom.

"So kind of you to notice. It takes effort. Now, why don't you tell me why you're here?" They didn't fool his mate.

"The boss wants to know why you're always going outside." The second voice echoed, deeper than the first.

"How many years here and he asks that now? I've gone outside daily since he first brought me here."

"He wants us to search your room."

Garrett tensed. Any thorough job and they'd find everything from the food to the burner phone, including him. Panic sloshed in his gut. His choices were few and not one of them guaranteed his and his mate's safety.

"Is it just me, or has Keith started to go a little crazy?" Nixie's Harley Quinn-like-lilt stilled the room. Footsteps that were lazily roaming paused. "Search a room that is locked and has no way in or out. Does he think I twitch my nose to make my furniture sing and lavish me with magical gifts? Why would he think you'd find anything more than what he's provided?"

No answer or movement came from the guards for several moments. Garrett readied himself to either fly or shift. Fly and trust Nixie to hold on a few more days, hoping that Jeffreys wouldn't strike at her until the end of the nine days, or shift and fight the guards, getting Nixie out of there tonight.

"Make it quick," mumbled the first guard. Footsteps moved from one side of the room, over the tile in the bathroom, then around to the other side and pausing just inside the closet. Black boots stood two feet apart. The guy was big. Garrett looked up to see him dressed in the same black clothes as all the others. Short, dark hair and narrowed eyes moved over everything in the closet. When he cast his inspection to the floor, Garrett closed his eyes to hide the glow and stopped breathing. Jeffreys didn't hire idiots.

10

———

Shaking started in Nixie's fingers. She controlled it for now. But panic spread and created deep roots. If she tried to stop them, they'd only search harder. As it was, they weren't being thorough. Her words got to them. Their hesitation proved that.

Brent stood inside her closet, while Macon stared at her. She had to keep a tight control over her reaction. When she wanted to leap across the bed and pull him out of there, she had to maintain her bored and irritated expression toward Macon. They'd butted heads a few times over the years. He was a no-nonsense guy. Even he knew searching her room was a waste of time. Well, it would be if one didn't know about shifters, specifically a man that shifted into a hawk. Wings made it simple to get inside her room without being seen.

Hangers scraped and clanged with one quick swoosh before Brent stepped out, shaking his head.

"Your days are numbered. What they're counting down to is anyone's guess." Curiosity lined Macon's eyes.

"The boss has been a little unpredictable lately." Brent shrugged.

"Interesting times ahead." Macon whistled and shut the door behind them.

No sound came from the closet, but Nixie didn't dare move. Not yet. She doubted the guards had left the hall, expecting her to check on anything she had hidden now that they'd left.

Controlling her breathing, she counted each one. Never had they or Keith infected her with such fear and panic. But never had the stakes been so high.

Garrett stepped from the closet, the sight of him blowing her away. The moment caught up with her. How close they'd come to getting caught rushed through her body. She shook uncontrollably. Garrett moved over the bed. Settling beside her, he pulled her over his lap.

"Easy, little one." His warm whisper brushed the shell of her ear. Large hands rubbed up and down her arms. "You did a great job, Nixie. I'm so proud of you."

He had no idea how those words affected her. They settled like dead weights dropped onto a beanbag chair.

Her shaking slowed as he moved his hand over her arms and shoulders. His steady strength filled her.

"That was so close."

Garrett's lips pinched and his silence froze her in place before she settled herself against his chest.

"What is it?" Nixie turned on his lap.

"He found the packs." Garrett kept his voice low.

"What? No, he shook his head when he came out. He didn't find anything." She might act like a brat to hold on to her sanity, but she didn't want to consider what Keith would do with this information. But why hadn't the guard said anything? Why didn't he search further?

"He found them."

"What did he do? I don't understand." He hadn't been in there long.

"He peeked inside one of them, but that's it. He left them where they were."

"Did he see you?" No way they would have left if he'd seen Garrett.

"No."

"I don't understand why he wouldn't say anything. What do we do?" All bets were off. Nothing was certain or predicable any longer.

"There is one way in and out of your room and it's the balcony. Those blind spots won't be blind for long." Garret lifted her to straddle his hips.

"Why search my room now?" Nixie tried to ignore the reemerging desire. It was too risky now.

"Your trips to the balcony are consistent. Did you always go out at the same time every day before I arrived?" Strong fingers tucked her hair behind her ear.

Nixie dropped her face. She was an idiot. "No."

"I didn't think of it until now either, little one. But I need to leave. And you need to lie low until I can get you out of here." Heated palms cupped her face and lifted her gaze to his. Fierce eyes pleaded with her. Nixie didn't ask what he pleaded for.

"So, this is it. I won't see you again until then."

"No. If I can drop off food somehow, I will, but I wouldn't count on it. If I were them, I'd place guards just inside the tree line facing your balcony."

Nixie felt the ticking of the clock inside her chest. If things went to hell, this could be her last moment with him. He may not have changed her life, or changed her, but the impact he had on her was physical. She couldn't let him go without him knowing that.

Settling her hands on his bare chest, she moved them up to the sides of his neck. Corded muscle flexed under her palms.

"Thank you for flying in to see me." She leaned forward and kissed him. She moved, waiting for him to respond. His hand gripped her hair and pulled her back.

"This isn't goodbye." Garrett kissed her, harsh and full, claiming her in a way that would never be. It ended with frustration. He lifted her off him and set her on the floor. Nixie balanced herself while he stood and retrieved the packs from the closet. "If you can keep the burner phone hidden, I'll leave it."

"I want to try."

His thumb swiped over her bottom lip. "Be careful, Nixie."

"Garrett. If it comes down to me or your sister, choose your sister." Nixie had tried to get him to make that promise earlier, but he wouldn't. She didn't want to be responsible for him not finding Anya.

"No, Nixie. I won't choose." Garrett shifted and flew to the balcony door, peering through the glass while she hobbled over. Would they have guards in place already? Macon might. He didn't bullshit.

Garrett gave a single nod and clung to Nixie's back, settled on her arm under the usual blanket she'd wrapped around her shoulders. She moved to the corner, sticking her tongue out at the camera on the way. Garrett didn't hop off right away, and she didn't move her arm. Relaxing her hip against the railing, she forced herself to relax while she scanned the trees. She didn't see anyone, but that didn't mean they weren't there. Soon, Garrett hopped off her arm, landing for only a second on the railing before taking off, twisting and weaving to avoid the cameras. He must have felt it was safe to fly.

Nixie stayed against the railing, taking in the air as much as she could. In case they locked her in from the balcony. Three days. She could last three more days. As long as Keith and the guards left her alone. Keith had a plan for her. She had to believe he wouldn't ruin his own plans.

He barely made it in time. As he settled on a branch, Garrett caught sight of the guards hiking through the trees to get into position. Exactly what he'd expected. He stayed until they settled. When they hadn't moved and Nixie had gone back inside her room, Garrett took flight toward his camp. He needed to move it.

Eagle caught up with him in the air.

They've been consistent until now. What just happened? Eagle leveled himself beside Garrett. He'd been scouting every day around the mansion. Sometimes following anyone that left.

A guard found the packs I've been taking to Nixie. But they didn't search further or tell Nixie they'd found it. They've seen the pattern in her movements and are now concentrating on her balcony. I can't go back. Not until it's time to get her out.

Now that they're suspicious of her, they may not leave their post when we set the fire. Eagle descended toward the camp.

Garrett shifted seconds before he landed, setting his feet to the ground. "I need to pack up and move. Keep watch for any guards searching this way."

Eagle nodded and took off.

They knew someone had to give those packs to Nixie, and they'd come looking for him. His camp was as minimal as possible, and he hid everything when he wasn't there, but there would always be a trace. As long as that trace didn't lead them to him or give away his plan, then he still had a chance.

He shook his head as he listened to the recordings from the bugs while he packed away the rest of the equipment. Nixie wanted him to leave her behind to go after his sister. But she didn't understand what she was to him. What it meant to have a mate. He wouldn't leave her behind even if she wasn't the one Fate chose for him, but that wasn't the situation he found himself in.

His plan was still the best shot at getting her out, but Eagle was right. With growing suspicion, those guards wouldn't leave their post so easily. And they'll be searching the woods for the person helping her. For him.

"I want every guard and employee here questioned. Someone has been helping her." Garrett recognized the guard in charge from Nixie's room. "And I want guards posted outside of her balcony, unseen. I'm not waiting to find out if it's from the inside. If you spot anyone, do not engage. Come to me. Only me. This doesn't reach the boss's ears."

That was interesting. They didn't want Jeffreys to know. Not that it affected Garrett's plans. He had no way to use that against them. This was an in and out job. But he might need more help than he wanted.

Garrett listened to the rest of the recordings that talked of plans for the night of the party. Positions and rotation schedules, including the new ones outside of Nixie's bedroom. He had everything else packed by the time it finished. Pulling out his phone, he dialed Zachary while he packed up the last of his things.

"Hello?"

"Hey."

"Hey, Doc." Zachary's voice cleared with recognition.

"I need a favour." Garret was about to ask for more than he'd planned.

"You got it." A deep, sincere rumble cloaked his voice.

"You don't know what I'm about to ask."

"Doesn't matter. What is it?"

"I was only going to ask you to pick someone up for me and take her home with you to keep her safe, but I think things may be more difficult than I thought. I need help, but I don't want to put you and yours in danger. You don't need these guys on your tail."

"Location?" he clipped, his focus sharp.

"Zachary." Garrett didn't want them to blindly jump into the crosshairs of Jeffreys and his guards without knowing what they were up against.

"Location, Doc. This is what we do." They'd all come together and helped each other without question since they'd all met. And they included Garrett, even though he didn't feel he belonged in their clan.

Garrett gave him directions on how to find him and where to meet up. He didn't need to set up much of a camp. Only enough he could continue to listen in on the guards and Jeffreys. Three more days and all his recordings and information would get passed on to someone who could do something about it. Garrett was wiping his hands of this one. That had been his plan all along. His only goal had been getting his sister. And now that goal included his mate.

"How many of us do you need?"

"I'm not sure." He wanted to say just Zachary, limit the damage and contact as much as possible, but Garrett's plan may not draw away enough guards for only the two of them to handle.

"Then all of us."

"No."

"Too late." Zachary snapped, aggression pushing back.

"Fine." Garrett snapped back. "I'll fill you in on the details when you get here." He sighed. "Zachary?"

"Yeah?"

"Thank you."

"I'm going to pretend you didn't say that." The call ended. Silence echoed in his ear.

With that done, Garrett loaded up and got out of there. He checked his three different escape routes he had ready, making sure they hadn't found them. Eagle found him before he left the last one, landing on his shoulder. His talons were sharp, but they'd both learned over the years how to keep them from piercing skin.

"Everything good?"

Eagle nodded, but then pointed back toward the mansion with his wing. He planned to go back to continue to scout.

"I'm staying clear of the woods for the night. Find me if she's in danger."

His pair flew away. Garrett trusted him. But sleep wouldn't happen tonight, not when he needed to stay away from his mate.

For tonight, he'd focus on his sister. Once Nixie was free, he'd send her to Alder Ridge with Zachary to keep her safe while he went after his sister. He had rumours to chase. And rumours almost always had a thread of truth.

TICK TOCK. Nixie had felt every second of the past three days hammer away at her composure. Protein bars kept her from starving, but they didn't satisfy her hunger. Garrett had taken the packs but left the bars hidden in her closet.

Having Garrett around every night had spoiled her. Loneliness crashed hard after he'd left. But Nixie had dealt with it before. The difference now? She missed Garrett. And she worried about him. Worried about tonight.

Late afternoon crept closer with the lowering sun. She needed to be ready for whatever happened. Either she'd need to run with Garrett or she'd have to face Keith and the future he decided for her. With a mildly weak ankle, she walked fine and even managed the ridiculous heels Keith had thrown at her for more than a few minutes.

Stepping from the shower, Nixie dried off in the bathroom. Leaving the towels behind, she padded into her closet. Nothing practical ever appeared, no matter how much she wished for it to be different each and every day. Bright colours of silks, skirts, and lingerie blinded her. Searching through her choices, she tried to find the best possibility to run in. Keith had picked everything in here. If she made it downstairs and he didn't like what she wore, he only had himself to blame.

A bright yellow bustier caught her eye. Not comfortable, but it would keep everything in place. She pulled out a black lace, long, layered skirt. It wasn't a hot summer night outside. The length and layers would be welcome to stay warm. They'd also love to tangle in whatever they could in the woods.

Twisting her lips, she pulled on silk sashes from two of her robes. Tossing it all on the bed, she set about getting herself dressed. Fastening the bustier in place, she adjusted herself. It was tight, but her girls weren't going anywhere. Nixie slipped on the skirt and laced up the thin ties at the back. Damn, she looked good. A feminine badass. Maybe she didn't hate all the clothes Keith gave her and made her wear. But she sure as hell resented them and what they represented.

Now, to make this outfit work on the run. Bunching the skirt up on one side, Nixie slid the pink sash under it and up through the waist. She pulled the other end around the outside of the skirt. Tying the ends together, she tightened the knot until the skirt bunched beside her upper thigh. She could untie the sash and let the skirt down if she needed to. Using the teal sash from her other robe, she repeated it on the other side of her skirt. The result was a puffy, over-sized Tarzan loincloth that left her legs free and kept the skirt in place instead of flowing around her.

She threw her foot into the air in a pretend Karate kick and chuckled. Yeah, sure, a feminine badass. Nixie liked the idea, but all she needed to do tonight was run. She hoped.

Nixie finished getting ready by drying her hair and piling it into a fancy knot on top of her head. The makeup sat on the vanity. That was more effort than she wanted to put in. But if she ended up downstairs with Keith, Nixie didn't want to give him a blatant reason to punish her. Thin eyeliner, a shadow, and barely enough mascara. She'd pass.

On the bed, the shoes Keith wanted her to wear sparkled under the light. The thought of the pain they'd cause after only an hour of wearing the unrealistic things stirred her belly. But she'd still prefer running through the woods in her bare feet.

Nixie sat and allowed an odd calmness to descend. Tonight was the first night of the rest of her life.

She snorted. How much more dramatic could she be? It didn't matter the truth to that. No more worrying. No more dwelling. She'd either be free or she wouldn't. Nixie accepted either fate. But that's as far as she'd allow. If freedom waited for her, then that's what she'd have. Never again would she let anyone call the shots for her.

11

———

His blood electrified, ready to get this over with, ready to make his move, ready to free his mate. Garrett waited for the others to arrive. Eagle continued to scout the mansion, returning every so often to check in.

He'd expected Zachary and Nathan, maybe Asher too. But when he thought the shifters would arrive in a truck, they came barrelling through the woods with their pairs in tow. Zachary with Smoke, Nathan with Bear, and Asher with Kai. A screech rent the sky, tearing Garrett's gaze above. Eagle flew back in, circling two snowy owls descending to land. Holly and her pair, Chloe, landed with the others. Holly on the ground and Chloe on Smoke's back. Of all the shifters here, he'd known Holly the longest. She'd been one of the fighters he'd tended in the fighting ring. It surprised Garrett the others had let her come, that her mate had allowed it. Being a conservation officer, Garrett doubted Anthony would condone the outside of the law antics they were about to play with.

They all shifted, spirals of winds and magic helped them all change, then created a playful pattern in the air before they dissipated. Nathan and Asher pulled clothes from small bags they'd carried and passed them around.

"All of you didn't need to come." He'd meant it for all of them, but his gaze was hard on Holly.

"Bite me, sky rat." Despite her insult, her lips lifted. They hadn't gotten along inside the fighting ring. Garrett never blamed her for her animosity, considering his position pinned him as the enemy, as one of her kind that betrayed her. With time and space, they'd become friends. As he had with the other shifters.

"Do you think we didn't try to stop her?" Zachary stuck his hands in his pockets and leaned his bare back against a tree. "Even Anthony couldn't convince her to stay behind."

"It was hard enough to convince our mates to stay behind. Gwen had a bag packed and waited by the door." Asher stood next to his pair, his hand in Kai's fur.

"The only thing that kept them there was that we didn't know what we're walking into." Nathan's voice didn't carry far. He lowered his chin and crossed his arms.

"So, what have you been up to these past several months?" It was Zachary that stepped forward.

"I've been searching for my sister."

"You've found her?" Holly moved and reached her hand toward his arm. She was a fierce little thing.

"No. I have another trail to follow for her. But I've found someone else that needs rescuing before I can finish my search for her."

"Someone who?" Holly lowered her hand and the others all tilted their heads. The sight could be comical in a different situation.

"Her name is Nixie. She's been captive here for several years."

"Fuck that. Let's get her out." Holly jumped back, ready

to help a kindred spirit. But the others still looked at him with suspicion.

"I need you guys to take her back to Alder Ridge. The guy who's kept her is Keith Jeffreys. She has no ties to Alder Ridge and he won't look for her there, if he goes looking for her at all. But I need her safe while I search for my sister."

None of the men moved and only continued to glare. Holly, realizing she'd been the only one jumping into action, looked between him and the others.

"Fine. She's my mate." Garrett conceded as the others wouldn't budge until he did.

"There it is." Zachary grinned, and the others followed.

"That wouldn't matter. I'd still want to get her out of there." Garrett needed to make that clear. Mate or not, he'd never leave her behind. He wasn't only asking for help because she was his mate.

"Of course." Asher sobered. "But we just wanted to hear you say it."

"Nosy bastards," Garrett muttered.

"Let's get to work." Nathan lumbered forward. Garrett filled them in on Jeffreys, his dealings, security, and the guard rotations, including the recent changes outside Nixie's room. He'd laid out his map and started pointing.

"I have escape vehicles ready, here, here, and here. I was going to do this alone until the other night when I called. With suspicion on Nixie, I can't be sure the guards will leave her unattended at all. Someone needs to incapacitate anyone who's left watching this side of the mansion." Garrett ran his finger along the tree line outside Nixie's balcony. "I only need enough time to get to one of the escape vehicles and get a head start."

"Whatever vehicles you don't take, we will. Could help as decoys if they're found." Asher shrugged.

"Good. I have a few different destinations ready as well. I won't know which one I'll go to until I have Nixie away from here and am sure no one is following."

"How are you getting her out?" Zachary stared at the map. "I don't see a clear option."

"I'm shooting low grade explosives along this side of the house."

"How will we get close enough?" Turning the paper, Zachary tapped the guard positions marked by red dots.

"I won't. I've attached them to arrows. The first room I'll hit is the security office to take out the cameras. Then I'll set enough fires to have the guards running. Jeffreys has a meeting and then a party this evening. I'm timing it for the end of the meeting and the beginning of the party. More people to occupy the guards."

"And Nixie?" asked Asher.

"We're zip-lining from her balcony." Garrett pulled out his crossbow-like contraption from his pile of equipment.

"Where's your hat?" Holly looked up, staring at his head.

"What hat?"

"Indiana Jones always wears a hat." She circled her finger near his head.

"Very funny. I didn't take to conventional sports growing up."

"That's obvious."

Garrett ignored her chuckle and got back to work. "Holly, you and Chloe join Eagle in the air. The more eyes up there, the better. The more ways to communicate from up there, the better. With so many of you here, I could use another shooting the explosives with me."

"I'll do it." While Zachary and Asher looked a little perplexed, Nathan spoke up, his eyes still on the map.

"When did you learn archery?" Asher nudged Nathan's shoulder.

"I'm not your average bear." His lips lifted to the side, but his gaze stayed down, continuing to study the plan. The grump didn't crack a joke often, but of course when he did, it was cheesy. Holly shook her head, trying not to laugh.

"Okay. Zachary, Asher, and the rest of the pairs need to be in these woods." Garrett made two imaginary lines into the trees on the map. "Take out the guards and keep the path clear."

"Blow up half the house, get her out, and run like hell. Pretty straightforward."

"Don't say it, Holly." Zachary's warning was low and quick, warding off silly superstition. They all felt it the moment she said *straightforward*. Fate didn't like anything straight.

"What? It seems pretty simple, and with all of us here, it should be easy."

"Damn it, Holly." Zachary growled. Nathan glared, and Asher hung his head. Garrett had been afraid this was too simple, but there was no other way. He had to take the risk.

"Let's go." Garrett nodded. Zachary and Asher hiked off with the pairs. Holly stripped and shifted. Meeting up with Chloe and Eagle, the three of them flew away. Nathan waited next to Garrett. He showed him the explosives and split them into a second bag. Retrieving his spare bow, he passed it over and watched Nathan look it over, settle it in his hand and test the draw.

"I'll take the front of the house and the lane. You get the back and the security office." Nathan tossed his gear in the back of the truck.

"We need to take the cameras out, but spread out the shots."

"When do the guests arrive?" Nathan hopped into the passenger side.

"Soon."

Garrett had planned to fly into position, but with another shooter, he could hand the keys to Nathan to drive the truck back while he flew in to get Nixie. Garret parked the truck near Nathan's position. Stripping, he tossed his jeans in the back and pulled out his equipment to set on the ground. He nodded to Nathan and shifted, trusting the other man to follow through.

His talons gripped his gear and flew into position. Shifting back, he attached the explosives to the arrows. Eagle screeched once above him, signaling that all was clear and everyone was where they'd expected them to be.

The first car arrived at the gate. Then the next, and the next. Garrett took stock of each person searching guests at the gate, and then again at the door. Thirty minutes. That's how long the meeting lasted before the first car arrived with the first guest of the party. Garrett pulled out his burner phone and sent a text to Nixie.

Get ready.

READY FOR AN HOUR, Nixie tucked the phone in her bustier to wait for anything from Garrett. Should she take anything with her? Nixie considered a change of clothes. But even that didn't hold any appeal for her. None of this was hers. She wanted nothing from her years here. Glancing down at her outfit, she imagined watching it burn while wearing the world's comfiest and baggiest sweats a girl could find.

There was nothing more she needed to do to get ready.

Keith's meeting would start soon. She'd heard the first

car arrive through her open balcony. The cold filled her room, but she kept it open a crack for Garrett. Nixie hadn't stepped foot on the balcony all evening, not wanting the guards she assumed were watching her to think she was waiting for someone, adding to their suspicion.

Her bedroom door swung open, and she jumped, holding her hands over her chest. Brent blocked the entire entrance. His gaze roamed over her bare legs. "Boss won't like that."

"I was bored." Nixie recovered from her surprise. It was way too soon for them to come for her.

"He's ready for you."

"Now? But..."

"Fix that or I'll fix it for you." He pointed to her skirt. "And don't forget the shoes." He said the last with a smirk that conveyed a love of torture. She knew these guards did more than watch the mansion and babysit her.

Nixie sat on the bed and pulled the shoes on, fastening the barely-there, unsupportive straps. The phone dug into the top of her ribs and side of her breast. Brent's black eyes didn't leave her for a second. She had no time to take it out and hide it. She'd been so sure he wouldn't come for her until the party, not during his meeting. It had been stupid to stash the phone on her person and to ready herself to jump off the balcony so soon. Not stupid, but cocky. She preferred to believe she'd been thinking positive.

It wasn't the first time she'd tried on the shoes. Over the past few days, Nixie had walked around her room for a few minutes to a time. For two reasons, to ensure she could walk in them and as an exercise for her injured ankle. The practice had been worth it to learn how to compensate when she stepped the wrong way, threatening to re-injure herself.

Walking toward Brent, she held her chin high and carried herself with years of a practiced sashay.

"I said to fix the skirt."

"But how will he see the shoes?" Nixie stuck one foot out and spun it in circles.

Pain gripped the back of her neck and she planted her toes back to the ground to hold as much of her weight as possible. He pulled her up and held her in place. Brent had moved too fast for Nixie to notice his intention. Picking at the knots of the sashes, he let them fall to the ground as her skirts covered her legs.

Nixie struggled to breathe, struggled to hide her pain. Putting on an act was much harder now that she that freedom was only a breath away.

"I don't have time for your shit." He shook his head, his nose so close to hers. "Sometimes I wonder if you enjoy imagining your funeral."

"Death hasn't been in the cards until now." Nixie rasped. If his hand wasn't big enough to snap her neck with a simple twist, she would have spat in his face.

"Little do you know." He dropped her. The balls of her feet tensed and on the ground. She would have collapsed, hurting herself or breaking a shoe. Still, she rocked while her balance steadied. Unlike the rest of her.

She'd always had this small sense of safety. Safety from the worst. Sure, it was a prison, but Nixie hadn't been at risk of being harmed badly. Or so she thought. Brent's words rang with revelation.

But there was no time to wonder about her years here. He stepped out of her way and reclaimed the grip on the back of her neck to propel her forward. At least the man had enough sense not to shove her while she wore the heels. The fact he was touching her at all told her things had changed for her here. According to him, they never had, only the rules.

Nixie kept her arms at her side, hoping to obscure the phone tucked in her top. It was tight enough the thin bulge showed if anyone looked hard enough. She would have to remind everyone, 'I'm up here.' The fact he was bringing her down earlier than planned said she couldn't just blend in the background like she sometimes did.

She took her time on the stairs. The deep mumbling slowed and stopped with each click of her feet. Anticipation slithered at her like a flying snake, weaving through the air to force its way down her throat like Ursula's magic. Something was very wrong. This wasn't how tonight was supposed to go. If she didn't get back upstairs, she'd get caught in the fire, or caught by the guards when they attempted to rescue everyone.

"Gentlemen." Keith spoke seconds before she rounded the corner at the end of the hall. Five men plus Keith formed a semi-circle beside the long table. "I'd like to introduce you to Nicole. Some of you have met her before."

Nixie recognized most of the faces. The others were new and deadlier than some of Keith's guards. They looked deadlier. She'd still put her non-existent cash on the guards.

"She's the special treat and entertainment at tonight's event. I wanted to give you all a first glimpse as I may be amiable to putting her up for auction. My decision lies in her hands at the moment."

That was pure bullshit. Keith already decided. He wouldn't have even hinted at the offer if he still thought he'd keep her. This really was the end of the line. Although she didn't know how any of those other men would treat her, she knew she could have it much worse than under this roof. Nixie didn't want to find out.

"Where are your manners, Nicole?" Keith lowered his chin and glared. Didn't take much to get off to a rocky start with him.

"My apologies." She thickened her consonants. "These shoes are so distracting." Lifting her skirt, she allowed one foot to peek out and pointed her toe. "Pleasure to meet you all." She didn't need to roll her eyes when her voice did it for her.

"You've had her a long time, Jeffreys, and you still haven't tamed the brat out of her?" Nixie recognized the scratchy voice. The long-haired man had been here several times over the years. His disdain for her had always been obvious, and Nixie enjoyed throwing her attitude around from wall to wall in front of him.

"I'll admit, I used to find her amusing. I've grown tired of it. If tonight doesn't fix her, maybe I'll consider giving you first dibs. Although I do have someone else coming to tonight's event who may be interested. He's offered me an even trade."

The man bringing the new girl. He didn't scare Nixie. But the scratchy voice did.

"Let me have some time with her, and if I'm interested, I'll pay you double." Despite his offer, he didn't seem eager to cart her away.

"I'll consider it." Keith spoke slowly, a sign the offer surprised him. "For now," he turned to Nixie, "Nicole can make our drinks."

"Vodka, lime, and cyanide, right?" Her sweet smile only fanned the embers in each pair of eyes, including Brent and the other guards around the room. Hell, if this was her last night, she'd make it a good one.

The drink tray was in the corner. She glided across the room, taking her time while thinking of a reason for Keith to send her back upstairs. There wasn't one. Staying quiet and demure will keep her by his side and acting out will have her handed over to Scratchy. Eww, what a horrible name. Her back was to the table as she scrunched up her face, but not some guards. Quirked brows and dark glares forced her tongue out between her lips like a five-year-old.

Nixie wondered if she would have held onto her bratty nature if Keith ever let the guards have free rein with her. Or would she still hold on to it if Scratchy took her? Was her strength real or only free because of her circumstances?

Now wasn't the time for *what-ifs*. She focused on getting clear of down here and back upstairs where Garrett could find her.

Setting the drinks on a silver tray, she moved back across the room to the table. She didn't let her struggle show to keep everything, including herself, balanced. As she delivered the drinks, Keith gripped her wrist.

"The next round better be a hell of a lot quicker."

Nixie waited three heartbeats before responding. "Don't you like the new shoes you picked out for me, Keith?"

"Behave yourself, Nicole. For once." His grip tightened until painful and then released her. He turned back to the other men. Nixie went straight to work on the second round, to ensure they were ready and also to keep herself away from them. If it weren't for the guards, she could slip away with what little attention they paid her.

Was his purpose in bringing her down early just to make his offer for her auction known?

She felt eyes on her as she poured the next round of drinks. She didn't want to turn around to see who they belonged to. None of the options in the room appealed to her.

"Nicole, there are some empty glasses on the table."

Nixie picked up the tray and turned around. The eyes staring at her had been Brent's. She passed his spot against the wall and pushed off and followed her. Her pulse pounded, thumping in her ears.

She set the tray down on the table and, before she could pick up the first glass, Brent grabbed her wrist and swung her around.

"What are you doing?" Keith didn't jump with fury, only questioned his employee.

"You have a problem." He held her arm in the air, exposing the bulge of the phone, but no one had noticed it yet. Except Brent.

"Where is Macon?"

"He's busy and put me in charge of the evening."

Oh, no. Garrett. Panic clawed its way through her lungs. Was there a trap set for him?

"Then what is the problem?" Keith pushed his chair away from the table and turned in his seat to look up at Brent and Nixie. Brent ran his fingers along the top of her bustier until he reached the side. Digging two fingers in, he pulled out the burner phone and held it up for Keith.

The chair crashed to the floor as Keith surged to his feet. He snatched her from Brent's hold with a painful grip on her jaw. "What the fuck is that? And where did it come from?"

His grip on her jaw kept her from answering, even if she wanted to. Brent stood behind him, thumbing the screen.

"It's a burner. Only one number in it. No names."

"Do you recognize the number?" Keith asked Brent but spoke in her face.

"No. But she just got a text. It says get ready."

Glass shattered, and the house shook enough to loosen Keith's grip. Another shatter and shake from the other direction toward the front of the house. Smoke billowed out from the hall and from the kitchen. Minor eruptions cascaded along that entire side of the house.

Keith threw her at a guard standing behind her. "Don't let her out of your sight."

Chaos erupted among everyone else, guards rushing toward the fires and others rushing to get the guests out. Just as Garrett had planned.

The guard took a firm grip on her arm to steer her toward the main entrance. She slowed their progress by trying to kick off her shoes. He paused, allowing her to bend down to rid herself of them, but Nixie took a tight grip around the toe and came up swinging.

"Ha, those damn things are useful." Nixie leapt back as blood poured from his cheek. "Holy shit, they're sharp." Leaving the other shoe on the floor, she kept a tight grip on her sparkling weapon. She searched for an escape, for anyone coming after her. They all made their way toward the main entrance, not paying her any attention. Except for Brent. His gaze caught hers over the heads of all the others. Turning, she ignored him and ran toward the smoke and orange glow from the hall.

FIRE BLAZED AND BURNED. The security system went down after the second explosive into the office. Garrett fired off the rest of his arrows in quick succession, hitting right on target every time. Explosions lit up the entire east side of the mansion. Nathan hit his targets, setting fire to the front side of the building and along the lane mind entrance gate.

Taking stock of the guards and the chaos, Garrett knew this was the best he was going to get. The more time they had to accept what was happening, the more organized they'd become.

Setting down his bow, he shifted. The wind swirled the smoke around him, pulling it into his lungs. He coughed and hacked from his throat as he took the shape of a hawk. His talons wrapped around his gear and he sent off a screech to let Nathan know he was in the air and after Nixie. Nathan would soon make his way out with the truck.

Garrett took the most direct route, holding his breath while flying through the smoke over the top of the mansion. He stooped over the roof and surged through the balcony door, pushing it open. Her room was empty. Before he allowed unhelpful panic to settle, he tried to scent her, but all he could smell was smoke.

He set the gear at the balcony door and shifted.

"Nixie?" They'd underestimated Jeffreys and his guards. They must have come for her at the moment of the first explosion. "Fuck." He cursed at the empty room. As he reached to pull his burner from his gear, the bedroom door burst open and Nixie came through. She held her skirt up with one hand, covering her mouth and nose while she coughed into it, and the other hand had a death grip on a bloody shoe. Soot covered her face and bare arms and ash stuck in her hair.

"Garrett?"

"I'm here. Let's go." There wasn't time to ask questions.

Nixie bent to the floor, picking up two silk strips.

Garrett's nose might not be useful due to the smoke, but his ears were exceptional. Someone had followed Nixie. Without a thought, he gripped the waist of her skirt and pulled her behind him. He met the man at the door with a straight punch to the nose before he even knew what he was walking into. But it wasn't enough to knock the big bastard out. He reared back and entered the room with his own well-aimed fist. Garrett's only saving grace was his quicker reflexes, but he still took the hit to the shoulder.

Nixie moved around behind him. He didn't have the time to turn and find out what she was doing. The guard was a fucking tank. And not the only one. Garrett recognized his face. He'd committed most, if not all, of the guards to memory in his early days here.

Garrett tried to get a grip around his neck to get him unconscious, but the guy was too quick, too strong, too well trained. They grappled until they swung each other around. The guard now stood between him and Nixie.

The grin that lifted his lips twisted into a snarl. He reached his arm back to grab at something. Spinning his body, he moved from Garrett's view. Nixie dodged his grip while hacking at him with the heel of her shoe.

"You don't give a fucking hoot about me, Brent. Leave us alone!" She growled through her teeth. Her shoes caused more than enough damage to take his attention from Garrett. With a single direct punch to the temple, Brent tumbled to the floor.

When he looked at Nixie, she had her skirt tied up on either side with the silk. He nodded to her skirt. "Efficient. Now, don't let go of that shoe." Garrett rushed to his gear and pulled out his zip-line. He'd modified a few pieces of different equipment to create his own. It shot anchors in both directions so he could launch himself from almost anywhere within the right range.

Strapping the rest of his gear to his torso, he pulled Nixie out to the balcony. He doubted Brent would stay out for long. With the zip-line on his shoulder, he shot the backwards anchor first, securing it to the building. Then he aimed for the closest tree and shot. The anchors took hold, and Garrett gave them a firm pull. The launcher itself acted as the handles.

Garrett wrapped an arm around his mate. "Hold on." She had a tight grip with her arms over one shoulder, the shoes still tight in one hand, and her legs wrapped around his hips. He stepped up the railing and kept walking, sending them zooming down the line. The scream caught in Nixie's throat rang in his ear.

His feet touched the ground, and he retracted the line as Nixie slid off him, her body shaking.

"We have to keep moving." He nudged her into the trees. Monitoring her ankle, Garrett followed, sensing Zachary and Asher nearby. They slid from their shadows, startling Nixie. She stumbled backward into Garrett's chest.

"Garrett?"

"They're friends."

"Trees are clear now. Incapacitated about ten of them. Take your pick of escape routes." Zachary waved his arm forward, but his eyes continued to dart around the woods.

Garrett paused, his shoulders tensing. "That seems too easy."

"Don't have to tell us that." Asher's eyes still hadn't landed on either him or Nixie.

"Macon was missing earlier. Brent said he was busy." Nixie's hair flopped sideways as she looked up at him.

Zachary and Asher flanked the two of them, urging them to keep moving.

Garrett hoped they were wrong. Eagle, Holly, or Chloe weren't near in the air to sound off any warning. "Too easy."

12

I t would take one hell of a sharp knife to cut through the
tension coming from the men around her. Scratch that,
a fucking sword. Nothing less. The words *too easy* dripped
with dread like a bad omen. Nixie sucked in air through her
teeth as her bare feet pounded against rocks, twigs, leaves
and more. But she wouldn't be the one to slow them down,
being the cause for any harm to Garrett or his friends.

"You're hurting."

Damn it. She'd hoped he hadn't noticed. "Not at all." She
hiked faster, keeping in her yelp from a sharp rock.

"Don't lie." Garret scooped her up from the ground. She
landed against his chest, settling into him, trying not to sigh
with relief. She would not be a burden.

"Boys, behind you!" The feminine voice sounded like an
echo in the trees.

"Margaret?" Garrett called.

"You know her name now?" Mr. Bright Blue Eyes on the
right swung around, searching behind them.

"Yes." Garrett set Nixie down on the ground and held
her behind him while he turned to face whatever threat this

imaginary Margaret warned them of. Nixie hadn't seen any woman, and the voice had come from all around them. None of the three men searched for her, only trusted in her warning, and turned around.

Three growls vibrated from the men. Nixie poked her head to the side and saw Macon emerge from the trees.

"I was certain I was only being paranoid when thinking someone had been getting in and out of your room through your balcony. Thought it was a fool's job to hide in wait under it. I still don't know how you did it, but I'm glad I wasn't wrong. However, that just won't do. I can't have a weakness in my system. You're going to tell me how you did it."

Garrett shook his head while Macon advanced.

"A very elaborate rescue for a brat. Impressive zip-lining equipment."

The growls deepened.

"Interesting. She had no connections when Jeffreys brought her home. How has she formed new ones now?" Macon looked between the three shifters. Nixie assumed they were also shifters since they were all buck-ass naked. A fact Macon didn't seem interested in getting the answer to.

The dark-haired shifter took a step forward, silver flashing from his eyes.

"I wouldn't do that." A handful of guards stepped from the shadows.

"The fucking wind has been blowing in their direction this whole time." Mr. Silver muttered toward Garrett. Macon frowned, but Nixie understood. Garrett had said shifters had increased senses. They should have known they were being followed, unless nature conspired against them. Hence the need for the warning from Mystery Margaret.

She stuck her finger out beside Garrett's arm, air tapping the heads of the guards.

"What are you doing?" Garrett tilted his chin down, but didn't take his eyes off Macon.

"Counting." That should have been obvious.

"Six, Nixie. There are six of them."

"And four of us." Not terrible odds. But she knew what those men were capable of. She was only just learning about Garrett and his friends.

"Three. You keep your ass behind me." Garrett's foot moved back only an inch, ready to launch himself forward.

"Then why the hell did I bring this shoe?" She tapped him on the back with the non-bloody end. "Don't you tell me where to keep my ass."

"Nixie." That threat pooled heat in her belly and more in her palm with the urge to slap him.

"Did you forget who saved your ass back there?"

"You're kidding, right?"

"If you two are finished, we need to move this along." Mr. Silver spoke quick then struck for the nearest guard.

"Let it go, Garrett." Bright Blue surged forward, clashing fists and arms.

"Easy for you to say." Garrett squared off with Macon and the final three.

"Yeah, we left ours at home." A punch to the gut and Mr. Silver barely budged. He moved into the blow and wrapped his arm around the back of the other guy's neck.

"Four against one. Or is it two?" Macon tilted his head to peer around Garrett at Nixie.

"It's two." She stepped out, brandishing her shoe. "Why? Why did you follow us? You don't care about me, none of you do. I was just a babysitting job for you. Why go to this trouble to take me back there when I probably wouldn't even be there past tonight, anyway?"

"I've already said. I want to know how he got past my system to get into your room. Tell me and I'll let you all go."

"Your cameras are easy to fool." Garrett spoke with utter calm, but his body vibrated next to hers.

"No, they aren't." He lifted two fingers and the three guards left moved toward them.

Thankful she'd retied her skirts, Nixie moved one foot back and firmed her grip around the toe of her shoe. She looked forward to adding fresh red to the already dark and dried blotches on that glittering spike. Who was she kidding? She'd be no more than a painful annoyance. But she intended to fight for her freedom and to protect Garrett by being the best damn painful annoyance she could.

✦

HE HAD no way to stop her. His mate stood beside him, fiercely ready to attack with a shoe. The woman was fucking brave, and Garrett's chest constricted. But his focus had to stay with the threat in front of them.

Nixie ducked away from the man coming at her, and the other two charged at Garrett before he could swing in and help her. He dodged one while ramming his shoulder into the second. Tackling him to the ground, Garrett swung hard at his jaw. His eyes rolled back in his head. Rough hands pulled Garrett off the man and tried to shove him to the ground, but he got his feet under him enough to lunge upward. The guy side stepped.

A quick glance showed Zachary and Asher holding their own. Asher still fought the same man, and Zachary had Macon coming at him. Garrett took a hit to the jaw when he took the time to search out his mate. Nixie swung her shoe at every opening she had. A bruise darkened on her shoulder, but she continued to be quicker than the guard.

Garrett blocked the next punch while he smiled with pride at his little mate. Damn, she was something.

The screech of an owl heralded Holly, with Chloe and Eagle on her tail feathers. Talons out, she stooped at Macon. He swung out, throwing her against a tree. She dropped to the ground. Growls erupted from Zachary and started a chain reaction in Garrett and then Asher. A solid kick from Zachary had Macon stumbling back. Garrett pulled his attacker by the arm and flipped him over his shoulder to land on some sharper rocks embedded in the forest floor. Asher surged with strategic punches, pushing his attacker back.

They'd gained a bit of ground, but the guards still outnumbered them unless they allowed the pairs to get involved. They lurked in the trees, waiting for the signal to attack. Since they didn't intend to kill the assholes, they needed to leave the strangeness to naked men and birds of prey.

The faint whistle of an arrow stilled all the shifters. They each took a step back as the arrow hit the ground between them and the guards. The explosive detonated, and Garrett turned to put his body between it and Nixie. But the guard was still in front of her. She swung hard at his chest when he turned to survey the fire.

Two more arrows hit the ground, detonating a short wall of fire.

Garrett lunged at the guard attacking Nixie. With an enhanced fury, he swung the guard over his shoulder, flipping him toward the flames. He skidded through the fire to the other side. Asher and Garrett hauled the unconscious men off the ground to throw them to the other side of the wall.

Margaret appeared, an ethereal being with her arms outstretched to the sides. White, auburn, silver, winds of many colours, fueled the flames stretching them along the forest, raising them higher to lick at the guards.

Zachary ran toward Holly, who'd perked up on the ground, and Garrett lifted Nixie in his arms. They all made a run for the vehicle, catching up with Nathan when he jumped down from a tree, bow in his hand.

"Good thinking." Asher shot out.

"I had some explosives left over."

"Good thing." Zachary lifted his arm in the air to allow Holly to take flight.

They reached the large SUV in minutes.

"You two take this one. Get lost long before you head to the meetup." Zachary opened the driver's door for them. Garrett set Nixie inside and waited for her to scoot over. "We'll still take the others, keep the guards from finding them later and hopefully make them split up if they still try to follow us."

"Thank you. All of you. I'll send word with the location." He'd let them know where he ended up. Just as he had contingency plans for escape vehicles, he had several locations to hide. All of them outside of Fort Vale.

Slamming his door, Garrett only waited long enough for the others to pile in his truck, with Nathan behind the wheel to drive them around to the other escape vehicles. He fished the keys out from under the seat and dropped them in the cup holder. With his bare foot on the brake, he pushed the button to start the car.

"There's a pack on the floor in the back. It has food, a blanket, socks, and sneakers for you."

Nixie reached for it the moment Garrett had said food. Her hands shook as she pulled out the food.

"Put the socks and shoes on first." In case they need to get out of the car and run.

Nixie nodded and did as he said. But as soon as her feet were secure, she dove back in for the food. Garrett focused on the road while she ate beside him. He wanted to roar into the night—they did it—but Macon was serious about finding out how Garrett evaded his system. It wasn't likely he'd stop searching for him. And Garrett still had to get his mate to safety while he searched for his sister, and hope Fate favoured them enough to keep the separation pain at bay.

SHE'D BEEN SLAPPED in the face. Left cheek, right cheek. A numbing sting spread through her body. Yet nothing touched her. Nixie shook with shock as they entered the motel. A motel. A real building outside of Keith's mansion. The guy at the front hadn't given them a second glance. The room was clean, but old and dingy. Stains rested beneath the burning scent of cleaner.

The others followed in only moments behind her and Garrett and the seventies-toned room burst with energy, breaking a dam that held her spine straight. She turned to Garrett.

"We're safe here?"

"For now."

"I'm safe? I'm free?" The words had to crawl over the knot in her throat. Garrett's eyes changed, thinned, and flashed with gold. The other faces in the room softened.

"Yes, little one. You're free."

Her knees buckled, hitting the tight-knit carpet with a

muted thud. The sandwich she'd eaten on the drive churned and boiled in her belly. Tears burned her eyes, hot drops of—she wanted to say relief, but it was so much more.

"Are you okay?" Garrett gripped her shoulders.

"Yes," she whispered. Nixie pushed the tears back and allowed Garrett to help her stand. Meeting the eyes of everyone in the room, she conveyed her thanks with an unspoken word. Garrett, Mr. Bright Blue, and Mr. Silver had all donned jeans. Two others she hadn't seen were also in the room. One she could easily name Grump and a petite brunette with a deep soul in her eyes. She straightened herself on the bed and winced.

"What is it with you and gouging out eyes?" Silver strode toward her, lifting the back of her shirt to inspect her back. "What the hell were you thinking? The last time you did that, you ended with a broken leg." Gouging eyes? An owl had swooped in and attacked Macon.

"And my happily ever after. I'm thinking of making it my signature move." She pushed Silver off her. "I'm fine, Zachary. The bruises will disappear soon."

"Nixie?" Garrett clasped her elbow. "I'd like you to meet my friends. Asher, Nathan, Zachary, and Holly." He pointed to Mr. Bright Blue, Grump, Mr. Silver, and the gouging owl.

A mellow chorus of nice-to-meet-you's moved down the line.

"Freedom is scary, isn't it?" Holly's lips pinched and her eyes watered.

"Yes, terrifying. How did you..."

"Holly was in the fighting ring I told you about." Garrett spoke low near her ear.

"So I understand how you're feeling. You're already handling it better than I did."

Nixie sat on the bed in front of Holly. She blurred in

front of her, and Holly's eyes glistened with unshed tears. "What did you do?"

"I shifted and stayed that way for a long time." Her lips twisted ruefully. "I flew, and I hid."

"I don't have that luxury. But hiding sounds nice." Creating her little homestead with her goats would be a great place to hide. Alone. She tried not to look over her shoulder at Garrett. "You're an owl?"

"I am. And I love it." Holly leaned forward like she was departing a secret.

"What about the rest of you? You're all shifters, right?" Showing up naked in the woods and standing here half naked was evidence enough, but the sheer size and muscle to each of them overwhelmed the room.

"Asher and Zachary are both wolves and Nathan is a bear." Garrett stood at the end of the bed, his golden eyes warm on her skin. "Nixie, how determined is Macon? What's he like?"

"I don't know. I'm surprised he hid and followed us to begin with." Keith's smart and dangerous lead lackey, but she hadn't thought he'd bother with her.

"He might still try to track you down." Asher tilted his chin down and glanced up as if he had glasses blocking his view on the tip of his nose. He settled himself in a chair.

"They found the burner phone you left me just before you started the fire."

Garrett shook his head. "Won't do them any good. But he's seen our faces and for some, that's more than enough to go on."

Nixie's sense of safety drained from her imaginary spout like molasses. But her freedom surged to fill the gap. She wouldn't let anyone take that from her again.

"Everyone here is from Alder Ridge. It's at least a two-day trip. You're going back with them where you'll be safe until I can come get you. I'm going after my sister."

Nixie stood and faced Garrett, cringing against his strict tone. With narrowed eyes, she stared, hoping he'd budge, twitch, blink, but nothing happened. "Oh, hell no."

"What do you mean, no?"

"I didn't say no. I said hell no. It has the same definition of no, but with even less chance of convincing me otherwise."

"Uh, we should all go check in with our mates." Asher stood.

"Wait. What did you just say? Mates?" Nixie turned on the other shifters at hearing the odd term.

"Ha." Holly yelled. Zachary whistled, and Nathan frowned.

"Good luck with that." Asher spread his hands and ushered everyone toward the door.

"Shifters have mates. A partner, a spouse, chosen by Fate." The door clicking closed followed Garrett's words.

"Fate? You don't have a say?" That sounded sad. What if Fate chose wrong? She'd force him into a life with someone he didn't like.

"No."

"Why didn't you tell me that before?" She'd asked for everything about shifters. They'd talked for hours.

Gold shone bright in his eyes until he blinked it away. It hit her. There was one reason he wouldn't tell her.

"Because I'm your mate." Nixie shared her realization with sickly glee. The smile on her lips felt twisted. Someone else, something else deciding for her.

"Yes, little one. You're my mate." Huskiness filtered through his already sexy voice.

"Don't *little one* me." No, no, no. Garrett had been the

first person she'd ever trusted. "Is this why you think you can order me off to safety?"

"I assumed safety would be your goal." His shoulders straightened like an edge.

"Whether it is or not doesn't matter. That's not for you to decide. I'm free, and I intend to stay that way."

"Nixie, you are my mate and I want you to be safe." Muscles heaved over his chest, drawing the attention of her gaze for a moment longer than she'd like. Nixie had begun to more than like him. "But I don't deserve the happiness they do." He pointed at the door his friends had left through. Nixie had recognized the guilt he carried a week ago. "Finding you was as much a surprise to me as this is to you."

"Wow, you know how to flatter a girl. Tuck her away for safekeeping, but make sure she knows she isn't worth it all in the same breath."

"That is not what I said." His growl carried a severe warning.

"Don't worry about it." She swung her hand across the empty air in front of her, imagining it was his face. Nixie didn't want to be with someone who didn't see her as worth getting over his own guilt. "I won't belong to anyone again."

"Nixie, it doesn't work that way." Garrett closed the distance, his hands sinking heat into her shoulders. Swinging her arms up and out, she broke his hold.

"I don't give flying hoot, or is it squawk? What sound does a hawk make? Whatever that is, I don't give a flying one of those. But you can't order me off to safety either. I didn't know Anya for long, but we were friends for the short time she was there. I'm going with you to find her. Then I'm buying my goats!" Her voice rose to an obnoxious cadence for her last five words. When they stopped echoing off the checkered walls, she stomped her foot to disturb the silence.

Garrett had become important to her, but what lay between them, his help and motives for getting her out, was all a lie. No different from when Keith first found her at the bar. Except Keith had never mattered to her. Keith hadn't made her feel and want for the first time in her life.

Nixie couldn't lie to herself. She'd had enough of that. Garrett was still important to her. The thought of not moving forward to find out what was between them hurt, but she wouldn't do it if it wasn't her choice. And he'd made it clear it wasn't his.

13

———

How could he deny her? Garrett wanted to hand her the world and wrap her up to tuck away to a safe corner. But not both. She deserved her freedom and the right to choose where she went. After the threat of Macon, Jeffreys, and the guys that had Anya were gone. He'd buy her the land and the home for her and her goats she seemed to want. Whether he'd stay out of her life remained to be seen. Fate hadn't allowed a couple to stay unmated yet. But he didn't deserve the same happiness and settled life as Nixie.

Yet here he was, standing in front of her with burning hands.

"You are important to me, Nixie." Honesty was the best foot forward.

"I'm important because Fate has told you so. That's not a true feeling that comes straight from you."

"Is that what you believe?" Garrett backed her to the bed until she stood an inch from the end, towering over her.

"You said Fate chose mates, and that you didn't have a choice." Her hair toppled around on her head, strands escaping in all directions. Her breasts overflowed the bright yellow bustier with shallow, angry breaths. Silence stretched, and the tension thickened. The need to answer her challenge, correct her assumptions, coursed through him. Warmth running through his veins and the wild side of him sprinting along the surface.

Tilting his head, he eyed the pins in her hair. Separating the strands with his fingers, he pulled them out one by one. "You're very wrong, little one."

"What are you doing?" She tried to duck her head away from him. He ignored her question.

"Fate didn't tell me I needed to visit you every night. Fate didn't tell me I enjoy your sass. Fate didn't tell me I needed to kiss you. Fate didn't tell me how proud I am of you." Garrett pulled the last pin and her hair tumbled down into a wavy mess. He applied pressure while pushing his fingers up from the base of her skull and through her hair, slowly fisting the strands.

Nixie's sexy, slim eyes widened, her pupils dilated to take over the soulful colour. Red infused her cheeks. Garrett pulled and tilted her head back.

"Fate only told me she chose you as my mate. She didn't tell me how I feel about you."

"You're proud of me?" Her breaths paused between each word.

"So fucking proud." He snaked his arm around her waist and settled her body against his. "I want you to go to Alder Ridge and stay safe because you're important to me, not because Fate has declared I need to protect my mate." Although the latter was also the truth, it wasn't at his core.

"No." Her hands flattened on his chest.

"No, what?" Muscles tensed, and he was losing his control. Danger didn't lurk near, at least for the moment.

The bed taunted him, but so did the shower. They both had soot and dirt smeared on their skin and on her clothes. Once she told him what it was she was refusing, he intended to kiss her.

"No to all of it. I won't be tucked away somewhere. And Fate has already taken my choices. She won't take this one too."

Garrett held her in place and lowered his head, his lips only brushing hers so he could still speak. "Fate isn't controlling this moment." He sealed the kiss, pleased when she didn't push back, but it took her a moment to melt into him.

She pulled back for air, and Garrett only gave the smallest space. "I won't belong to you." Her whimper caught him off guard. He loosened his grip on her hair and slid his hand down her back.

"That isn't my intention."

She sighed and let him kiss her again. Thankful for her outfit modifications, Garrett moved his hands around her ass and lifted. She wrapped her legs around his hips with no impediment from the skirt. Garrett turned away from the bed. They'd be back. If they were about to walk away from each other, he wasn't passing up this night that he'd promised for both of them.

Setting her on the counter in the bathroom, he turned the shower on.

"Garrett?" The fight and challenge had fled her voice, leaving uncertainty. He straightened, keeping his distance, waiting for what she needed to say. "What... How... How do you mate?"

Sure steps took him to her. Using his knuckle under her chin, Garrett lifted her head and turned it to the side. His other hand ran a line over the exact spot he'd intend to mark her if they mated. "Sex. And I'd have to bite you. Right here." Her skin pebbled beneath the pad of his finger. "Leaving a crescent mark on your skin."

"A mark? A permanent one?" Did her shaky tone hold arousal? She was aroused and ready for what he had planned, but he must have imagined the appeal in her voice about a permanent mark.

"Permanent."

"Don't do it." Nixie lifted her chin from his hand and stared into his eyes. "Don't bite. Please."

"I won't." Biting her wasn't in the cards tonight, yet her pleading for him to not sink his teeth into her gutted him. Garrett wanted her trust, even though he didn't deserve it. The trust of no other soul mattered. Only the person meant to be his mate.

"So, now what?"

Garrett pulled her from the counter and didn't use words to answer her. His fingers combed through the laces on her bustier and the back of her skirt. Her clothes fell to the floor. Shucking his jeans, he took her hand to pull her into the corner shower.

His cock nestled against her ass as he settled her back to his chest. Water beaded down their bodies as Garrett nudged them forward under the spray. He didn't have the control to keep himself from touching her everywhere, but he lingered. Lathering the bar of soap left by the motel between his hands, he covered her front, his hands and the bar sliding over her skin. Nixie sighed and leaned her head back against his chest. Garrett covered her abdomen before circling her breasts. Her breath hitched, the sound dropping straight to his balls.

Nixie writhed against him. She moved her head from side to side, exposing her neck. Garrett's teeth sharpened, a straight edge ready to pierce her skin. Leaning down, he let his breath trace down the smooth column, noticing a shiver that seemed to have a direct path down the side of her spine. A sweet spot he needed to remember for later. For now, Garrett had another mission.

He applied the soap to himself, rushing with his own wash, then used one set of fingers on her nipple, pulling and twisting with just enough pressure to bow her back. His other hand delved into her folds. Stroking her clit between his fingers, he drove her higher until she lost her breath and reached a silent plea. Garrett pulled back and Nixie cried out, dropping forward. Wrapping an arm around her, he turned her to dunk her hair beneath the water.

"You're mean." Even her whine held menace. Garrett didn't stop his grin from showing her how mean he could be. Now that he'd let go and had her body all to himself for tonight, she'd get all of him.

Despite wanting to drive her mad, he made quick work of washing her hair and rinsing them both off, then spun her back around. His hands returned to work to bring her to orgasm. His finger middle finger only circled her opening while he worked her clit to a hard nub. She panted, pushing her breasts up into his other hand.

"Garrett?"

"Now, little one. Come." His teeth still sharp, he nipped her ear.

Nixie's body exploded, waves cascading to crash with her hips reaching for more from his fingers.

She was amazing and all his. All his for tonight. He hoped Fate would understand.

HE SHATTERED HER. Nixie regained control of herself, her awareness sinking back into her. She quaked against him. Garrett only waited, unmoving, unyielding. The air in the shower thickened, both with steam and the tension coming from the shifter at her back. He had more planned for her. She felt it in his touch. But if she didn't want him ordering her around outside of this tiled stall, then she wouldn't let him have all the control inside it either.

She tried to turn around, but he gripped her shoulders to hold her in place. Shrugging from his hold, she spun and dropped to her knees before he stopped her.

"Nixie." His warning made her pause, delicious shivers igniting aftershocks to her climax.

"Too bad, fly boy."

"Fly boy?"

Nixie interrupted his growl by grasping the base of his cock and leaning forward and wrapping her lips around him.

"Fuck." The curse rumbled against the walls and his hand slapped hard against the tile to hold himself up. Triumph, a victory, if only for a moment. Nixie had control over him. For the first time in so long, she controlled something. And that something was a powerful man with a deep, protective, animalistic soul.

His taste exploded on her tongue and she wasted no time sucking him down. If she gave him any quarter, he'd wrench his control back.

"Damn it, little one. This is not what I had planned." His free hand smoothed over her wet hair.

Her smile was limited, but the corners of her eyes lifted too.

"I'll let you have your fun, but I won't come in your mouth. Not this time."

Nixie tried to pout. Garrett chuckled and palmed the back of her head. And true to his word, he let her have her fun. With every bob of her head, swipe of her tongue, and stroke of her hand, he tensed further, but never took over. Not until he couldn't take anymore.

Her scalp stung as he pulled her away and up to her feet. The kiss he gave her was more of a primitive possession as he turned the water off.

Garrett reached out of the shower for a towel. He vigorously rubbed it over her dripping hair, ignoring their bodies. Tossing the terrycloth to the floor, he gripped her thighs, lifting her high against him. His lips and teeth, sharper than normal, worked over her shoulder and upper chest.

Her core clenched, readying for another climax. His touch and each scrape of his teeth, knowing what they were meant to do, sent shocks through her system. She was climbing the peak with no direct stimulation, yet the pleasure shot to her clit as if by magic.

Lowering her to the bed, he sucked a nipple into his mouth. The powerful pulls threw her over the invisible edge. Garrett paused while she panted through the waves. Opening her eyes on a sigh, Nixie looked straight into glowing gold orbs staring down at her. They didn't blink, only flashed brighter, as he pushed hard into her, setting off another low climax. It vibrated along her body as he continued his harsh rhythm.

Nixie looked up at him above her. The change in his eyes was ethereal at this point. They not only glowed, but changed shape. She saw the sharper edge to his teeth. Part of her wanted to know what that felt like for him to bite her. To matter to someone as much as a mate would. But she had to stay true to herself. She needed to matter on her own, not because she belonged to someone.

The man above her would protect her and love her more than he thought possible of himself. One large hand cupped her hip, lifting her leg higher. She threw her head back with the new angle, breaking eye contact with him. He dropped to his other elbow and Nixie realized her mistake, exposing herself for his bite. His arm barred across her neck, so his hand covered the spot he'd traced in the bathroom, the exact line he'd said he'd bite when he mated her.

"Now, Nixie. Give me another one." His voice wasn't his own. Her body still thrummed from the after effects of the first three orgasms. His demand was all it needed to sprint forward. Nixie imagined herself running toward the edge of a cliff and spreading her arms wide. The climax ruled her body. Pleasure filled contractions wracked through her. Garrett thickened inside her, pulsing as he growled through his own peak.

He collapsed. Nixie enjoyed his weight as sleep danced with her eyelids. Long moments later, Garrett pulled from her with a moan, and tucked her against his chest.

"Sleep, little one." His normal tone still hadn't returned and Nixie expected his eyes hadn't either. The intensity of the night had been a shock to her system, one that kept her silent. Nixie felt as if she still hung in the air after leaping off the cliff, an updraft holding her there, swaying back and forth. She could either fly or fall. But no matter what her future held for her after this night, Nixie would be the one to choose. And she might just choose to fall.

GARRETT COULDN'T SLEEP. Nixie nestled against him, silent and limp, her breathing stretching as she slipped under a veil of dreams. But in Garrett's mind, the mating chant still rang strong and true. The room was sharp and clear, even in the dark. His eyes hadn't changed back to normal. Even now, his hands tensed on her hip to turn her over and take her again, but this time completing the mating. He stayed frozen behind her until he was sure she was in a deep sleep.

He pulled his arm free from beneath her head and slid from the bed. The mating chant in his head—*Mate, Mark, Mine*—faded the further he got from her. Snagging his phone from the nightstand, he called Zachary as he stepped outside and leaned against the door. Zachary didn't answer, but rounded the corner instead.

"I need you to watch over Nixie. From outside. She's sleeping." His voice rumbled deep, but no longer held the animal instinct.

"You okay?" Zachary stepped closer and paused, his nostrils flaring.

"No."

"Did you...?" He waved his finger between Garrett and the door that blocked Nixie in the room.

"No."

"But you smell like..."

"Sex, Zachary. I didn't mate her."

"Yet."

Garrett shook his head. "I need to blow off some steam. I'll be back." Zachary took his place outside the door and Garrett dashed into the shadows to shift. He lunged into the air, flapping his wings hard to get higher. And higher, until his strength waned and his lungs burned. The wind soothing over his feathers calmed the raging need to make Nixie permanently his. The strength of the bond surprised Garrett. His guilt wouldn't let him claim a mate. There had been so many he hadn't protected. How could he promise himself, promise his mate he would protect her?

The moment he sank his cock into her heat, it all crashed into him with the force of a stampede. It grew with a life of its own until he'd lost control. He'd had enough forethought to cover her neck with his hand, keeping himself from biting her.

Fate believed She had the right timing, but Garrett questioned her sanity. He needed to find his sister, not mate someone who hasn't had her own freedom for most of her adult life.

His wind caught up to him, flying beside him, around him. A sign of some sort. Oh, Garrett knew what it was trying to say, but it wasn't that simple. The golden swirls flattened alongside him, and Margaret appeared as if sitting on a ledge, her feet swinging and her hair flowing behind her as they flew.

Fate is wrong. Garrett assumed Margaret sought him out because of his mood.

"Fate is never wrong." Her eyes cast downward rather than meeting his.

After all you've been through, do you really believe that? Never wrong?

"I didn't say She was always right. But there is always more to it. She understands things we don't."

Nixie doesn't deserve the burden of me. That fact seemed obvious to him. If Fate was so all-knowing, then why didn't she see it?

"You are no burden, Garrett." Her motherly tone wasn't enough to change his mind. But he didn't need to argue that point with her.

Having a mate is a burden to her. She deserves to be free. If I mate her, that takes some of her freedom away.

"Why would it be? Why wouldn't she choose to stay with her mate?"

How could she ever trust me?

"How could she not?" The petite ghost growled. "You rescued her when you didn't have to. You're on a search for your sister despite not knowing if you'll find her. You protect with the best of your abilities, given any situation. She trusts you."

That wasn't enough for Garrett. *How do I tell Fate to wait? Nixie needs to be kept safe, and I need to find my sister.*

Margaret outright laughed, the sound fading in and out as if transparent like her. "Fate doesn't wait. She sees more than we do. You need to trust Her."

I've lost my trust in Her after the things I've seen. So many innocents have a fate they don't deserve.

"I can't argue with that." She sighed. "You deserve love and happiness, Garrett. Remember that." Margaret faded away and Garrett continued to fly until the unease in his chest faded away as well.

She's right. Eagle swooped in beside him, startling Garrett. He hadn't been expecting more company.

How long have you been nearby? Garrett hadn't sensed him.

Since you left the motel.

Garrett shook his head. He was glad Eagle and the others were around to keep watch.

Margaret is right. Let go of your guilt. Eagle matched Garrett's path in the air when he swerved to the side to avoid the treetops.

I'll deal with it later. For now, she needs to go somewhere safe, and I need to find Anya. This can all wait. Garrett swung away from Eagle, his *good luck with that* floating into the empty air space left behind.

Fate threw the mating at him with a vengeance, almost taking the choice from both of them. He needed the space between himself and Nixie before the urge was too strong. He landed in the same dark shadows and shifted before finding Zachary still standing outside his motel room. The sky turned orange and red on the horizon. It was time to get out of here.

14

A breeze blew her hair into her face, tickling her nose. Nixie jolted awake, her chest constricting, as she realized the motel door had opened. Garrett walked in, naked as the day she'd met him. She moved her hand under the sheets to his side of the bed. It was cold. He'd been gone a long time and with how tense his body was as he stared at her, waiting for her to calm, she wondered if he'd gone to sleep beside her at all.

With each breath in, another memory from the night before filtered through her mind. She hadn't expected freedom to carry weight. She'd expected light and airy, overwhelming space and possibilities. With the choices she'd always wanted to have, each one carried the weight of what if it was the wrong one. Trusting too easily had been her problem years ago. Could she even trust herself?

Nixie made two choices on her own the night before, ones that at the moment she didn't regret. Garrett wouldn't tell her where to go, and she wouldn't take back what they'd done.

"I didn't mean to scare you." Garrett moved further into the room, but kept his distance from her.

"Just startled. Where did you go?"

"I took flight for a little while."

"A little while?" Something in his voice, an almost indiscernible hitch, made Nixie call him out.

"I couldn't sleep." His lips twitched, then quickly straightened. Pulling clean clothes from a small duffel bag, he dressed. "It's time to go. I don't want to sit in one place for too long until you're safe in Alder Ridge."

"I told you…"

"Get dressed, Nixie." His harsh cut off, low and quick across the room, shocked her. That dominance was inside him, but up to now, he'd been gentle when exerting it over her. He never raised his voice, but he didn't need to. None of that would change her mind. Naked and vulnerable in bed wasn't the time to pick a fight.

With narrowed eyes at the shifter, who matched her glare, Nixie peeled the blankets off her body. The cool air pebbled her skin. The urge to cover her breasts was strong, but she kept her arms at her sides and her chin high. Garrett paused in pulling on his t-shirt, his eyes flashing bright. At least he wanted her, in some form.

Walking past him, his body heat warmed her side. She reached for the bag he'd brought for her and pulled out the first pair of jeans she'd seen in years. They were a true blue of soft, stretchy denim. Nixie found underwear and a bra, putting on the soft cotton first. So plain and a dream come true—she tried not to cry as she slipped her leg into the jeans. Garrett had continued getting dressed and packed up the room. He'd finished and had the bags by the door by the time she slipped on her shoes. Toe-covering supportive sneakers. She wanted more of them, and boots.

Garrett waited until she stood, then he opened the door and left with the two small bags. Nixie followed him, knowing he wouldn't come back inside to discuss her destination. The others stood around the parked vehicles, dressed and ready to hit the road. Garrett shut the back door to one of them, having thrown her bag inside. He loomed large as he stalked toward her, dropping his bag to the pavement without bending down.

Flutters of all colours swarmed in her core. Nerves, excitement, desire, fear. Not fear of him. Only of the choices she was about to make. The choices she'd already made in her short time of freedom. But Garrett didn't scare her. Despite her lack of trust in others and herself, she trusted him. A true soul. If only she were brave enough to mate him.

"I need you to go with the others. Please." His added please roughened as if forced. Standing only an inch from her, Nixie could see his muscles twitching. The man had yet to relax since he'd flown into her room to rescue her. When she didn't answer, his hands clenched into fists. Nixie took her time to study him, letting the tension grow. Piercing eyes cut into her the longer she waited.

Lifting her chin, she controlled her tone, clear and soft. "No."

"Nixie..." he started.

"I said no. I might not have known Anya for long, but I'm going with you to find her."

"I don't understand why you'd want to follow another path like this. Not when you can go with them where you'll be safe. And free." Garrett bent to line his face closer to hers. His constant calm cracked. Had been since he entered her the night before.

"I'm not the only one that deserves that."

"And if Anya is still alive, she will get it. I will get her out. You don't need to be there."

"But I'm choosing to be there." Now she growled, pushing forward to stick her nose toward his. Although she wasn't short, she still didn't quite line up to his. "You can't order me off somewhere safe to wait for your return."

Garrett closed his eyes and spoke through his teeth. "You don't have to stay there. Only until I know Macon isn't still searching for us, only until I get my sister. You'll be free to go wherever you want, even if it's without me."

Nixie pinched her lips together and the humourless laugh escaped as a jagged huff through her nose. "Without you. You're trying to send me off now without you. No. I'm going where I want to go. Now. Today. Not when you deem it safe." She pulled in a breath to steady herself. "I'm safe with you."

He broke. The crack spread, snapping his eyes to hers. Moving faster than she thought possible, his hand gripped her hip to push her back against the closed door. His other hand firmed around her chin and tilted her head. "You're not. You have no idea how close I came to biting you last night."

She'd wondered. There was nothing left for her to say. She wouldn't change her mind. His hand followed as she lifted her chin, unintentionally exposing herself further.

"I don't know how I stopped myself. I won't next time."

"Then you should keep your hands to yourself."

His fingers flexed even as his head lifted, struggling to let go. So many sharp needles of fear pricked her lungs, each with a different reason etched in the metal. Safety called, loud and bold in her ears. But it didn't compare to staying by Garrett's side. Nixie didn't want to mate him, but she wasn't ready to let go. And she needed to know what happened to Anya. She'd always done her best to help any woman that Keith had, and for those few weeks, Anya had felt like a kindred spirit.

A throat cleared behind Garrett, his shoulders blocking her entire view of the others. He let her go and turned his head over his shoulder.

"I'll go with you." Zachary grabbed Garrett's bag from where he'd dropped it and threw it in the same vehicle as Nixie's. Garrett looked back at her. While his body didn't relax, his face did. A single nod and he stepped to the side to let her pass.

Before getting in the vehicle, she turned to the others. "Thank you all for rescuing me. You risked yourselves and that's something I could never hope to repay."

Holly moved around Zachary and embraced Nixie in a hug. The other woman had to stand on her tiptoes to wrap her arms around Nixie's neck. "You'll be okay." She spoke low in her ear. "Come to Alder Ridge when this is all over, of your own choice. We might be a small group, but we're family, in a way."

"Thank you." Nixie didn't want to promise anything, but she squeezed the other woman back, holding onto the support. They let each other go, and after quick goodbyes from everyone else, they filed into the vehicles and hit the road.

Tucked in the backseat, Nixie chiseled at the uncertainty building itself into a boulder in her gut. She wondered if she'd ever trust her instincts and decisions again.

ZACHARY or one of the others should have punched Garrett to the ground when he'd grabbed hold of Nixie. Yet the woman had shown nothing less than the sass she'd held onto so tightly. She dug in her heels and stuck with her decision. She had to know he was right—Alder Ridge was the safest place for her right now. But no. She seemed determined not to back down.

Maybe he'd gone about it the wrong way. Who was he kidding? Of course, he went about it the wrong way. He'd thrown the order at her the moment they reached the safety of the motel. He should have discussed it and asked her, making her believe that going to Alder Ridge was her idea.

But now, the woman sat silent in the backseat while Garrett couldn't calm himself. Terror thrummed against his veins like wind against a tight tie-down strap. The droning vibrations grew louder in his ears.

"You know denying it doesn't go well." Zachary's murmur cut through the sound in his ears. Garrett blinked. They all had their own experiences with mating.

"Take the next exit." He ignored Zachary's comment. A discussion of mates and rejection wasn't one to have in front of said mate. It wasn't one he wanted to have at all. Hypocritical? Absolutely. Garrett pushed for his patients to talk—human or shifter. When it came down to it, Garrett would mate Nixie if it kept her from going through any pain, but all he was asking for from Fate was time. Time to keep Nixie safe and to find his sister. If, after all that, Nixie wanted him, he'd be there, but if she didn't, he didn't want Fate to punish her for that decision.

"Where are we going?"

"Following rumours. I don't even have names. Only nicknames for the vigilante group and there are a few of those. Absolution, The Family, Mortality."

"Run, before Mortality catches up to you," Zachary said darkly. "This could be a wild goose chase."

Garrett nodded. He didn't know what they'd find or where to lay his expectations. "Although sources assured me if I ask in the right places, I won't need to find them. They'll find me."

"Sounds like a lovely bunch."

"They also warned not to ask about them." At the same time he'd been told to head north. All of this information he'd gleaned while waiting for time to count down to Nixie's escape. It hadn't been easy while also staying under the radar, so he wasn't seen asking about Jeffreys by any of his guards or associates. The trail to the vigilante group started with asking what Jeffreys did with his cast offs. Garrett had paid others to make the initial inquiries. After that, he'd asked around himself. He found some that told the stories with glee and others that told the same stories with fear.

"Do you think they harmed the women?" Nixie leaned forward, her head poking between the two front seats.

"I don't know." Garrett didn't want to consider either possibility. "This old highway we're on should take us straight into town. But it will be a couple of hours." He leaned his head back and closed his eyes. The hum of the car tugged against his lack of sleep.

"So, Zachary." Nixie wiggled, bumping against Garrett's seat. "Are you from Alder Ridge?"

"No. I'm from Hull Creek."

"And?"

"And I moved to Alder Ridge when I found my mate. We stayed to be close to friends. And Holly."

"Then what makes Alder Ridge such a safe place?" She added extra emphasis and unnecessary inflections at every other word.

"The handful of shifters that live there," answered Zachary dryly. The exact reason Garrett had for sending her there. They would keep her safe.

"You guys are huge. Just one of you is a handful." The moment the last syllable drifted from her lips, she pounded her head against the side of Garrett's seat. He opened one eye to see the smirk on Zachary's face and the blush tinging Nixie's cheeks each time her head popped back up. Garrett felt his own lips twitch, and a small portion of him relaxed.

He couldn't be happier with the mate Fate chose for him. His problem was that Fate shouldn't have chosen one at all. This woman full of sass, no filter, and a beautiful blush eased his tortured soul. When he let her.

AFTER EMBARRASSING HERSELF, Nixie settled in the back and let herself rest. Despite having slept the best sleep in her life, she was still drained. She went from captive to free in the time it took to say those words. And then there was Garrett. Nixie didn't want to let him go. Leaving with his friends to Alder Ridge seemed lonely. But neither did she want to attach herself to him to the point of dependence or belonging.

Zachary drove with one hand on the top of the steering wheel and rested his other elbow on the door. He was Garrett's opposite in looks. She had a scrumptious amount of silver and gold sitting in front of her. They'd been kind. And Garrett trusted them.

Garrett's breathing slowed and his heavy chest lifted high. He hadn't slept at all the night before. It was no wonder he'd fallen asleep so fast on the drive.

Studying Zachary, she wondered if a different source of information might help her.

"Ask." He lowered his voice to an almost whisper. He must have felt her watching him.

"What is your mate like?" Start small with the questions. Zachary didn't seem the conversational type, but Nixie eased into it somehow and knowing what his mate was like would help her too.

"Beautiful, kind, strong." His granite face melted. Three words with so much pride and love. "Went through the same ordeal as Holly."

"The fighting ring?"

Zachary nodded once. Nixie connected the details of Garrett's story.

"You're the shifter who helped get everyone out. Garrett told me what happened."

"He did, did he?" Zachary met her gaze in the rear view mirror.

"Yes. He carries so much guilt." Enough to keep him from being happy.

"He told you that?"

"No. I can see it."

"We all see it." His eyes turned back to the road. Nixie leaned forward so she saw his face when she asked her next series of questions.

"Do all shifters boss their mates around?" They'd all seemed very alpha-like, but the situation they'd been in called for such personalities. What would they be like on a normal day?

Zachary's lips twitched. "Only when they ask."

"I'm enough of a smartass for the both of us." Nixie narrowed her eyes. "Just answer the question, Silver."

"If it means keeping them safe, we will." He adjusted his

grip on the wheel and leaned his head back against the headrest.

"What is the relationship like between mates?" If she'd listened to Garrett and gone to Alder Ridge, she could have seen the answer for herself.

"Just like any other, but more."

"There must be something different about it." Her night with Garrett had been all-consuming. That hadn't been just sex or a one-night stand, even if they'd only be together that one night. Power, strength, and a love unspoken. The relationship that followed wouldn't be just like any other.

Zachary tilted his head, pausing for a moment to think. "You feel it? The thing drawing you to him?" He didn't need to point to Garrett. She didn't have a word to describe her need to stay close to him.

Nixie nodded when he glanced in the mirror again.

"It's ten times worse for us. It will get that strong for you too, but it takes longer. Being mates is more than a relationship, more than a bond, more than marriage. Keeping you safe is our top priority. Don't be mad at him for trying to do that."

She understood that, but Nixie needed to hold on to her choices. And she hadn't been able to part from him. "If you agreed with him in sending me to Alder Ridge, why did you volunteer to come? Why didn't you or the others try to convince me to go?"

"Being away from our mates before we've mated never goes well." Zachary sighed. "If mates deny each other, they both go through severe pain, get sick, and for shifters, uncontrollable shifting. We wouldn't put either of you through that, and there is no way to know if that would have happened or not. It was an impossible choice for him to make."

Force her away into sickness and pain, but she'd be alive. Or keep her close while they chased down a murderous vigilante group. Not impossible. Nixie would have pushed him away, too. But he wouldn't have listened any better than she.

15

———

Garrett woke with Zachary's last words, but didn't alter his breathing. Zachary may have noticed the change in him, but Nixie wouldn't. She'd settled back again. Garrett waited until the town was in sight before straightening in his seat.

"This it?"

Garrett read the sign. *Welcome to North Falls*. "This is it. We'll grab lunch first." At the pub he needed to stake out and ask questions. He considered stashing Nixie somewhere first, but he doubted she'd follow that plan either. It was best to jump in and get this over with. After staking out the pub, he might change his mind.

"Alley Lounge, up the first right off the main drag." He used the same directions his informants gave him. Zachary threw him a side eye. Garrett wasn't just choosing lunch. His informants warned him if he started asking questions here, that word would reach the vigilante group.

Zachary found street parking near the pub. He gave the streets and area the same search as Garrett before getting out of the vehicle. Nixie reached for her door handle the moment the engine whirred to silence. Her spine straightened as Garrett set his hand on the small of her back. Not to get away from him, but a reaction to his touch. A gasp. She stayed within his reach, tilting her head over her shoulder. He hoped that whatever hers and Zachary's conversation had helped her to understand why he wanted her safe. There was still time for him to change her mind.

Opening the door, Zachary held it wide for them to walk through. Eyes followed them as they found an empty booth, but none lingered. Every surface was dark wood, casting warmth. Somehow, the place had the atmosphere of a pub, a bar, and restaurant at the same time. Small tables in the centre, large booths around the edges, a long bar, and a comfortable seating area next to a fireplace that cast its red and orange glow over half the room. There was something else about the place below the surface, but Garrett couldn't pinpoint it.

He nudged Nixie on the inside of the bench seat, then sat beside her. Zachary sat in the centre of the seat across from them. They'd tucked single sheet menus between the salt and pepper, laminated for their protection. He let Nixie look over hers while he chose the first burger to catch his eye, but he didn't put the menu down. His eyes scanned the room and the people in it.

His arm shook. Frowning, he glanced down at Nixie to see her trembling.

"What's wrong, little one?" Without thinking, Garrett wrapped his arm around her shoulders.

"Is ordering in a restaurant like riding a bike?" When he'd thought she'd followed along, she'd been scouting the place as much as him or Zachary. Not only with caution, but with excitement.

"I suppose. You're trembling."

"I'm not sure why." Her slim eyes widened, showing off their vibrant colour. "I haven't been in a public place in so long. Keith took me out in those early months, but once I figured out I couldn't leave, I became in-house arm candy only."

Garrett tensed. Twin growls whispered in the small space above the table. Garrett lifted his arm from her shoulders to lie across the back of the booth. He would have unintentionally hurt her from his clenching fist if he hadn't.

"I guess I'm a little out of my element."

"Understandable." Zachary set his menu down and made himself look relaxed against the seat.

"Nothing has changed about ordering in a restaurant. Server comes and asks what you want and you answer." Garrett smoothed her hair back from her face, sending the waves over her shoulder.

"I know." She sighed. "I think I'm just nervous to talk to people."

"You talked to me." Zachary reminded her. "And to Holly and the others."

"Yeah, I did. But these people are strangers." She lowered her head to drop a heavy whisper.

"Strangers can't see anything you don't want them to see. Your story isn't written on your face." He understood. When Tyrone first recruited him, he hated being out in public. Convinced people would see what he'd done, what he'd agreed to do.

"Feels like it is."

"Yeah, it does, little one." He turned his head to kiss her, but movement caught his attention. The waitress sidled up to the table.

"Hey, there. How is everyone today?"

"This place is great!" Nixie raised her voice, allowing a squeak to sound off in the middle.

"Uh, yeah. It is." The waitress smiled. "Can I start you guys off with some drinks?"

Instead, they ordered their full meals. Red-cheeked, Nixie kept her face toward her menu while she ordered. Once the waitress disappeared through the door to the kitchen behind the bar, Nixie backhanded his chest.

"Seriously, you'll order me off to some strange town, but won't order me to shut up when I need to."

Zachary hid his laugh behind his hand and Garrett outright chuckled. He cupped her cheek and lifted her face to his. Waiting for the red embarrassment to fade to pink, arousal dilating her pupils, Garrett kissed her. Despite their argument earlier and her edict that he should keep his hand to himself, she leaned toward him, opening up for his invasion. He showed his feelings hadn't gone away. He didn't want them to, but if he got his hands on her, they'd end up mated. Had her talk with Zachary changed her opinion?

Garrett ended the kiss, touching his nose to hers before straightening. Zachary had kept his gaze elsewhere, but a frown pulled his brows together.

"What is it?" Garrett kept himself from looking around the pub.

"Something feels off. Something smells off."

Garrett inhaled. "Something wild."

Zachary nodded.

"Wild?" Nixie nudged him for an answer.

"Shifters?" Zachary raised a dark brow.

"I think so. But I can't pinpoint them." The scent wasn't strong or even clear when mixed with so many other things. Other customers. Alcohol. The food. The building and furniture was old and carried a strong scent of its own.

"Could be we just missed them. If it is shifters we smell." Running into shifters wasn't something that happened often, but enough that it wasn't a concern. They were out there. And in a town like this close to deep wilderness, it made sense they'd cross paths.

"What's the plan? And what do you know?" Zachary spoke low enough that Nixie had to lean forward to hear them talk. Garrett explained what he'd found about his sister and the trail to follow.

"I've been warned against finding them in the same breath as them telling me how. All rumours, though. No one knows for certain who they are. This isn't the only direction people suspected, but it was the most common theory."

"A vigilante group we shouldn't mess with. Encouraging." Zachary followed his sarcasm with a nod. "The belief is they didn't hurt the women?"

"No one was sure, but either way, I'll find out what happened to my sister."

"Or you'll find another trail to follow."

It would have to end somewhere. He'd asked himself how far he'd go, but couldn't answer it. With no one to care for, he had all the time in the world. Until two weeks ago. Now he had a mate. Bonded or not, they were mates. Garrett wouldn't let anything happen to her. But that might mean abandoning his search for Anya.

⌖

"What is that?" Nixie leaned forward to peer around Garrett at the tall glass passing by on a tray. Bright red cherries and a rainbow umbrella topped the white creamy drink.

"Looks like a pina colada." Zachary followed her gaze.

"I used to like pina coladas."

"Used to?" Garrett had to lean out of the booth as she continued to watch the waitress walk by.

"I haven't had alcohol in years. Once I realized I was a captive, I wouldn't let myself have any. Had to keep these wits sharp." Her voice faded and her eyes didn't leave the drink until the waitress set it down on a table and it disappeared from sight. "But the moment I turned eighteen, I drank those things like my main food group. Always had extra cherries, so it counted."

The silence seemed a little weighted when Nixie leaned back against the booth. Across the table Zachary smirked, the corners of those silver eyes crinkling. She glanced up at Garrett, who held the complete opposite expression. His quirked brow created an authoritarian scowl.

"No need to ruffle your feathers." She patted his arm. Zachary snorted and cloaked the rest of his amusement with a drink of his beer. But Garrett didn't seem impressed with her placating. The waitress walked by their table and before she got too far away, Nixie's voice surged from her. "Excuse me?" More than just the waitress turned around. Several customers nearby silenced their conversations to look her way. Even a slow glance from the brute of a bartender. Nixie pinned her eyes on the waitress, ignoring her heating cheeks.

"Yes?" The waitress turned, uncertainty clear on her face. Nixie didn't blame the waitress for approaching their table cautiously.

"Was that a pina colada you just delivered over there?" She lowered her voice.

"It was."

"Could I have one of those, please?" Then, turning toward Garrett, she leaned forward to point at him with her nose. "Virgin."

Pale blue eyes bugged out of the waitress, and she opened her pinched lips to respond. "Sure. A virgin pina colada coming right up."

Nixie hadn't considered what the waitress would think of her virgin comment pointed at Garrett, but after seeing her bulged eyes, Nixie couldn't be happier.

The waitress turned around, but Garrett's deep call made her pause. "Extra cherries."

"Uh, absolutely." The waitress's smile shook as she tried not to laugh, at least until she'd turned her face away. Nixie busted. Her laugh, loud and true, drew the gazes of the other customers once again, but this time she didn't care. Zachary laughed along with her and Garrett's unamused doctor's frown transformed. His hazel eyes sparkled with their gold flecks, ready to flash bright. The dimple in his cheek appeared before his hand grasped the back of her neck to pull her toward him. Warm lips pressed a kiss against her temple.

Nixie looked up, her laughing settled. A future together stood on shaky ground, but moments like this made her crave for more out of her life. She'd be content with living in private and self-sufficient, but to have someone by her side to have that with might be nice. As long as he didn't control her. Garrett had been a touch demanding, but only in regards to her safety. Zachary's statement ran through her head as a question.

The low fire building between them crumbled when the waitress returned with her drink and their food. She set the sweet drink in front of her and Nixie squealed. She cut it off short by slapping a hand over her mouth.

"Calm down girlie. It's just a drink." Nixie's mumbled whisper didn't catch the attention of the waitress who set the plates of food on the table, but the two shifters eyed her.

Keep your mouth shut, woman! Her own voice screamed at her. She'd had enough embarrassment for one day.

They'd all thought they'd made their orders simple, but there was nothing simple about the loaded burgers sitting in front of them. Swiss cheese melted down the sides of the meat in front of her. Mushrooms overflowed and bacon ends stuck from two separate layers. Her mouth watered.

"Take it easy, little one."

Nixie snapped her eyes toward Garrett, disgruntled over his interruption. She was ready to devour the massive meat sandwich, trying to remember the taste of her favourite comfort food.

"You haven't eaten a full meal for a few days and before that, it was only soup and small sandwiches. Your stomach can't handle all of that." Garrett nodded at the burger. Nixie hated he was right. It made sense, but she was going to enjoy as much of that burger as possible.

Huffing, she turned back to her food and ignored Garrett and Zachary. Nixie wouldn't allow the reasonable doctor to hinder her enjoyment of the greasy goodness.

They all ate in silence and what she'd thought was content until she watched the two shifters more closely. Alert and cautious, their attention was on the people around them rather than on their food. The tension vibrating from them made her unconsciously eat faster. Until her stomach groaned with at least a quarter of her burger left.

Damn hawk. He'd been right.

Both men finished their beer to down the last of their meal while Nixie sipped at hers, twirling the umbrella between her fingers. Her stomach continued to groan, but she didn't want to waste the drink.

"It's time to go." Garrett signaled the waitress for the bill.

"There's something odd about this place." Zachary covered his plate with a napkin. Chills crawled down Nixie's spine. They didn't say another word while Garrett paid the waitress with cash. They left the pub with Garrett's hand persistent on Nixie's back until he settled her in the back of the vehicle.

"Now what?" She leaned forward between the seats.

"We find a place to lie low until we get back there this evening."

Why would they go back to the place they just rushed out of? But Nixie kept her comment to herself and settled in for the ride. She insisted she be a part of Garrett's search for his sister.

GARRETT SLID cash across the counter of the shady inn they'd found at the end of town. The clerk, a wiry bearded man wearing layers like it was forty below, looked skeptically at the cash and handed back Garrett's identification. A fake one. Since he'd started working for Tyrone, he'd gathered a few. They came in handy as he travelled when he should be in one place. It had kept Tyrone from tracking him, and they'd been useful in his search for Anya.

Nixie waited outside with Zachary. While it wouldn't be hard for someone to connect the two of them with the amount of attention they drew at the pub, Garrett didn't want her spotted here. Not when all they needed was a few hours to lie low.

The clerk slid an old metal key toward him. Garrett picked it up and nodded. Neither had said a word past asking for the room. Back outside, Zachary and Nixie pushed off the vehicle and followed in step behind him.

They stayed on the ground level and Garrett unlocked the second to last door.

"I'll scout around. I'll be back in time to go back to the pub." Zachary waited while Garrett let Nixie into the room, then walked off.

Shutting the door and closing them in seemed to stir everything unsaid like a cloud of dust. It settled when she turned to look at him, hovering and swaying in the air.

"How are you feeling?" Garrett grounded his feet, pushing them into the floor to keep from reaching for her.

Nixie frowned. "Fine?"

"In general. Not from the food. It's been overwhelming."

"I think I'm still processing." She sat down on the end of the bed. That was the last place he wanted to see her settle. His blood pounded.

"You should get some rest." Garrett turned his back on her and settled in a chair facing the window.

"Garrett?" Soft and uncertain—he didn't have the strength to ignore her.

"Yes?" He pulled in a breath to solidify his chest, guarding himself against her, then looked over his shoulder. Nothing prepared him for Nixie. He saw that now. Desire lapped at the blue in her narrow-set eyes. If that was all he saw, Garrett would have leapt across the room to push her back on the bed. But she mirrored his own thoughts and feelings back at him. The denial of their bond chipped away at his insides. He'd known other shifters who took their time to mate, as long as they spent enough time together. But Fate wasn't giving them that option. A storm brewed, ready to unleash. More time—that's all he asked for.

"Why don't you believe you deserve a mate?"

"I didn't do all I could to save the women in the fighting ring. I selfishly tried to protect my sister over them."

"Did you just use selfish and protect in the same sentence and didn't refer to yourself?"

He shot her a glare, and she threw it back at him—the force great enough to dent his next breath.

"You are so blind." She shook her head in disbelief.

"And why are you against mating, little one?" Garrett leaned forward, his elbows on his knees. Those few inches closer and his hardening cock stiffened further.

"Nope. You don't get to turn this around on me." She stabbed her finger in the air, aiming for his nose. "I have a damn good reason not to attach myself to a man."

"Yet, here you are." It wasn't fair to challenge her. She was right. She didn't deserve matehood forced on her when she hadn't had a free adult life.

"What do you mean *here you are*?" Muscles tensed, Nixie planted her fists on the bed beside her.

With slow movements, Garrett stood and stalked toward her, unable to contain himself any longer. "Why did you stay?"

"I told you." She pushed herself up to her knees. Her freckled nose didn't quite line up with his until she lifted her chin. "I want to help save Anya."

"That's not all, is it?" He stopped his advance when his knees hit the end of the bed. Her pulse throbbed in her neck and Garrett couldn't tear his eyes away from it.

"I told you not to turn this around on me." Her hands flew up and shoved against his chest with a weak effort to lengthen the four inches between them. Garrett didn't budge, but before she pulled her hands back, he wrapped his around her wrists. Her fingers on his chest snapped anything he had left. Being in public at the pub had been the only thing keeping his control contained, but now that they were alone, there was nothing left to stop him. He kept his eyes on her pulse, seeing the frequency increase. He let his eyes linger over her jaw. Her lips parted while she panted

"You shouldn't have done that. Answer my question, little one."

"No."

"No, what?" He waited to hear her tell him how much she wanted him, but that wasn't what came.

"No, I won't answer your question."

Garrett growled. A quick pull on her wrists upset her balance, so she fell against his chest. "At least you aren't trying to lie to me." He captured her lips with his, working hers apart with his tongue to lick and sup. Wrapping an arm around her waist, he brought her closer to the end of the bed so her front was flush with his.

Nixie moved her hands up his chest, but Garrett still kept the hold on one of her wrists. He knew the moment he touched her, it would be too late. He should let her go, but his fingers tightened.

"You don't need to answer me with words."

She leaned back enough to squeeze her free hand between them. "It hurts. Right here." Her hand pressed against her ribs.

"Me too, little one. It's too strong. I warned you what would happen."

"But neither of us wants this." Question pitched her words. She lacked confidence in her statement.

"I don't think that matters." He released her wrist, sliding his hand down her arm to settle against her waist. Keeping his touch gentle for the moment, he gave her a chance to pull away, to get away from him. She didn't take it. Licking her lips, her gaze landed on his mouth. The need to taste her tongue was the most important thing to him at that moment. He took her, claimed her with a kiss that was so much more. Heat and need surged between them, back and forth and growing with each pass.

His fingers played with the bottom of her shirt. Soft skin pebbled under his touch. Garrett wanted to see all of her pebble and shiver. Uncontrolled passion thrived. Her shirt hit the floor before he realized what he'd done.

Palms returning to her waist, he held her against him, so she had no doubt what was about to happen.

"Garrett?" She gasped against his mouth.

He released her lips and nibbled her jaw to allow to her speak.

"It hurts because we haven't mated, right?"

"Yes."

"Are you... Are you going to bite me?"

"Yes."

"Can we mate and go our separate ways?"

A growl worthy of a large predator, rather than the bird of prey he was, erupted. Nixie stiffened, her hands tense on his shoulders. The animal in him didn't like the idea. Neither did he. But he wouldn't force anymore on her than he already was. "Yes."

<h1 style="text-align:center">16</h1>

She'd had no choice but to suggest it. Neither of them wanted this, yet Fate forced it upon them, anyway. Nixie shivered as the heat rushed through her. Now that they touched, the ache in her abdomen receded. They each had their reasons for not wanting this, justified or not. Guilt blinded the man in front of her, believing he needed to be content with nothing because of his sins. His sins that weren't sins. He was human and cared too much for his sister. That wasn't a crime.

Fate threw Nixie from one set of hands to another. She needed to know that even if they mated, Garrett would still let her go. A few strides away, the bathroom beckoned her. The flimsy door and lock wouldn't stop a shifter. The idea of breaking the moment and hiding coursed through her mind, but it didn't take hold. Not when his teeth, sharper than normal, nipped her ear. Gasping, her breasts pressed against his chest. A weighted feeling surged, making her all too aware of their sensitivity.

"Is it going to hurt?"

He paused by her ear. "Is what going to hurt?"

"The bite?"

"A little." Garrett resumed, but moved his lips behind her ear.

Nixie whimpered. His hand gripped the back of her neck, fingers tightening, and she felt that kiss down to her core. A swirling thread that connected his lips to between her legs. All reason fled and acceptance of her future, of her mate, worked its way through her body. His hand slipped beneath the waist of her pants and hers reached for his shirt. She had to stop when he didn't let go of her neck. He took his time with the sensitive spot. As her hands lost their strength, his shirt loosened in her grasp. Garrett lifted his head and released her to rid himself of his clothes.

"You can't control this?" Nixie searched his eyes, trying to see past the glow. "You can't stop this?"

Garrett didn't look away from her while he pushed his jeans over his hips, baring himself to her. "Can you?"

She shook her head.

"Everything you're feeling, I'm feeling too, but a hell of a lot stronger. No, little one. I can't control this or stop it." He pushed her pants over her hips and lifted her off the bed, flipping her feet out from under her. She landed on the mattress with a bounce, the sound of the springs on the inside caving in. He pulled her pants the rest of the way off, tossing them to the floor.

Large hands gripped the insides of her knees. He slid them up her thighs, pushing them apart until her hips protested. His body followed until his mouth latched onto her clit. Strong sucks engorged the bundle. Cool air wafted over her when he let it go to lap at her entrance. No coaxing or gentleness. He deliberately placed each touch.

Garrett let go of one thigh. His fingers poised at her entrance. Nixie caught his eyes looking up at her.

"This time, I want to hear you scream." Filling her with his fingers, he latched on to her clit. No mercy or quarter as he thrust and sucked hard. Letting loose her screams wouldn't be a problem. She'd cried out the moment his fingers entered her and she moaned with every thrust that sent electrical quivers through her core.

"Garrett?"

He hummed against her and she erupted. Working her hard while she contracted on his fingers, Garrett brought her to the brink of another orgasm before lifting away. A smooth slide brought his body up along hers. That one movement was all he needed to enter her.

Nixie gasped as he filled her.

"Too quiet." He pulled out and slammed back in, eliciting a cry from her and a growl from himself. Tiny, bright lights obscured her vision. Nixie tried to grip his shoulders, needing something to ground her, but he took her wrists and pulled her arms above her head. "Don't move them." His true predatory nature came through. One hand slid down to her breast, and the other tangled in her hair, pulling her head back and to the side. He scraped his teeth up and down the column of her neck.

Everything inside her went taut, and she moved her hips to match his thrusts. Hooking her knees over his hips opened her further. She whimpered and moaned as she couldn't control the rioting sensations.

"Now, Nixie. Come now." He growled against her skin and his teeth stopped scraping.

Her body burst. Pulsing bliss shot from her core to numb her body. Pain pinched her neck as Garrett sank his teeth into her. While it hurt a little, it only increased the pulsing of her orgasm. She cried out, but not only with her voice. A tear tickled her cheek.

Garrett didn't pause, and he didn't release her neck. The quaking stopped, leaving only over-sensitized tissue where he continued to pound. He bit harder and growled. His cock swelled as he came, reigniting her sleepy pleasure. But she was immobile beneath his bite. Garrett didn't release her until he'd emptied.

She tried not to wince when he pulled his teeth and his cock from her. His wet, warm tongue soothed her neck. Her legs fell to the sides, and he pushed himself up, taking his weight onto an elbow.

"Nixie, I..." He swallowed and closed his eyes. When he opened them again, the glowing had dulled. Tilting his head, he kissed her. Hot, demanding, but like a calm after the storm. There wasn't anything for him to say. She'd made him promise they'd go their separate ways. It was only a matter of time until they found his sister and she wouldn't see him again.

GARRETT HELD Nixie against him while she slept, watching the faint crescent mark form. The sunlight in the room had shifted, indicating hours had passed. Hours that Nixie had slept and Garrett worried and wondered. He mated her. There had been no stopping it. Even now, he craved to roll her onto her back and have a repeat performance. Her taste still lingered on his tongue, and he wanted more. He'd never get enough.

But he'd have to.

He'd promised they'd go their separate ways. A plan that made his gut clench formed in his head. After they tracked down the vigilante group and had news of Anya, Garrett would set Nixie up wherever she wanted. He hoped she chose Alder Ridge. Because even though his promise included separate ways, Garrett could never leave her. He'd watch over her.

A light tap on the door pulled Garrett from his thoughts. The scent of a wolf drifted in. Sliding from the bed, he stood without disturbing Nixie. He threw on his pants and opened the door enough for him to slip out, holding his finger to his lips.

"She's sleeping."

"That would put anyone to sleep." Zachary inhaled, leaning in Garrett's direction. "You mated her."

"The pull was too strong, and we both ached."

"Fate isn't fucking around with you. I wonder why." Zachary leaned against the outside wall, his head turned toward Garrett, but his eyes ever roaming. His casual stance wasn't quite right for him. A tenseness in his shoulders flattened them against the building.

"What is it?" Garrett's senses kicked.

"We're being watched. I can't tell you from where or who or what. I wanted to go searching, but they'd see me leave. It's an instinct."

Garrett tuned in, seeing if he could find what Zachary was talking about. There it was. The hairs on the back of his neck and down his arms stood straight. No scent or sound. No direction to look, but eyes were on them. "Time to get out of here."

"I know you planned to leave her behind, but she has to come with us."

"I won't leave her here with someone watching. But there has to be somewhere safe for her."

"Garrett, you should know better by now. She's coming with us."

Garrett sighed, knowing Zachary was right. He hadn't

felt this torn since the first time he'd tended a fighter in the fighting ring. The need to protect his sister almost hadn't been strong enough not to help that poor woman. She'd been the smallest one in that group, even smaller than Holly, but she'd lacked the strength. Even giving it her all, she'd still come out of every fight beaten until her knees collapsed. Garrett had walked himself to the police station several times and every moment his hand wrapped around the door handle, an image of Anya flashed through his mind with the small hope that she was still alive and that he was making the right decision in lying low and trying to save her.

And now, that same guilt pulled. Protect his mate or find his sister. His mind had a difficult time allowing those things to coexist.

"I'll wake her."

Zachary walked away, easing himself into the shadows. Garrett locked the door behind him and sat on the side of the bed. Nixie's face had softened in sleep. The dark circles under her eyes had receded and a pretty flush infused her cheeks below her freckles. He ran a finger up and down her cheek, then behind her ear, tucking her hair.

"Nixie." Bending down, he kissed her head. She sighed. "Nixie." He tried again, this time kissing his mark.

She moaned and stretched her head back, but soon settled back into the mattress. They needed to leave, but Garrett decided they had a moment for him to wake her properly. He slid his hand down her neck and over her shoulder, pulling the covers with him. Following with his mouth, he stopped near her breast while his hand continued. Rolling her to her back, she moaned and stretched. Her back arced, jutting the pink nipple toward his mouth. When his fingers reached her clit, she woke.

"Garrett?"

"It's time to leave, little one." But he didn't pull back now that she was awake. He sucked her nipple into his mouth and circled her clit, applying more pressure. This needed to be quick, but he was going to enjoy it.

"Garrett." No more question, just a moan. He sank his hand further, moving his thumb to replace his fingers. Her folds were already wet, and he circled her entrance to spread it. The heat beckoned not only his fingers. His cock jumped beneath his jeans. But they didn't have enough time for that.

Her walls squeezed his fingers as he pushed them in. Curling them, he hit the sweet spot right away. He abandoned her breasts to see her face. Her eyes glazed. "Come for me, Nixie."

She tilted her hips to meet his hand, only increasing the pressure of his thumb. He'd leapt them straight to her peak, not allowing time for buildup. He sat on the edge with her, ready to burst at her cries of pleasure alone. With her head thrown back, her breath halted and her core clenched. A moment later, she broke. Her body crashing as her orgasm worked through her. Garrett slowed, but didn't stop, making it last. His jeans were painful against his cock. If he sank into her body, it would be quick, but he didn't want to rush. Not with someone watching them.

He kissed her, her chest heaving below him while she tried to catch her breath. Pulling his hand from between her legs, he braced it on the bed. If he touched her anywhere else, he wouldn't hold back.

"Get dressed." He sat up and pulled Nixie with him.

"Did I sleep that long?" She leaned her cheek against his shoulder.

"Yes." Cupping the back of her head, he kissed her hair. "You needed it."

"I guess I did."

"But we need to leave now."

"Why? It's still early to go back to the pub, isn't it?"

"We're being watched." Garrett didn't want to lie to her.

"By who?" Just as her spine straightened, filling with strength, her hand clutched the back of his arm. He couldn't let anything happen to her.

"We don't know. We can't pinpoint them, but they're there."

"I'll be ready in five minutes." She scooted around him on the bed to stand. Nixie didn't let go of his arm until the distance forced her. Grabbing clean clothes, she disappeared into the bathroom. Garrett kept track of her movements while he dressed and packed their bags. By the time she emerged, he was ready and waiting on the end of the bed.

She'd swept her hair into a high pony, yet the strands still reached to the centre of her back. She looked good in the soft sweater and jeans. He'd seen her clothes in Jeffreys' closet. They didn't suit her. This did. The colour he noted in her cheeks when she slept was still there. Her eyes glowed. Satiation settled her shoulders. Freedom looked good on her.

NIXIE'S BODY STILL HUMMED. It had been a bittersweet moment when Garrett pulled away rather than rejoining her in bed. She didn't want these moments to end, but carrying on would only make it harder when they parted ways.

Garrett held her hand as they left the motel. He slipped the key in an outside slot rather than going inside to check out. They felt it was safer if they'd find a different place to stay each night. Nixie concentrated on their surroundings, but nothing clicked. The instincts that drove the two shifters didn't register in her. Garrett had told her not to look at the trees or around the parking lot. That was difficult when all she wanted to do was search the area like a *Where's Waldo* book.

Again, Zachary drove, taking random turns and loops, exploring the small town before going back to the pub. The extra drive wasted enough time, as it had only been late afternoon when they'd left. Tension of all different types snapped at the air. Only a fool would think their ride had been full of comfortable silence. The shifters carried an alertness, waiting for someone to jump out at them. But the tension between herself and Garrett worried Nixie. Heat and need warred with an unreasonable sadness.

That drive gave her a moment to think. Without Garrett, where would she go? Not back to the same place Keith had found her, and Nixie hadn't travelled when she was younger. She'd choose a small town—not small enough that everyone knew how often you changed your toothbrush— but small enough that someone would notice if she went missing. Maybe even care that she was gone. Her goal of living self-sufficiently had been a beacon to her for years, but how to reach that dream had never appeared. A job and a lot of years saving money was her only choice. Maybe a place like Alder Ridge wouldn't be so bad. With or without Garrett.

They pulled up to the pub, parking close to the door. Inside, the atmosphere was similar to earlier, but more people gathered at the bar. They chose a table in the centre of the room rather than a booth. Nixie shivered, feeling exposed, until Garrett settled his arm on the back of her chair.

"Thank you."

He peered down at her, then pulled her closer to kiss her temple.

"What do we do?"

"We eat." Lifting her chin, he gave her a quick kiss. "Stop worrying."

"A little difficult when you two are strung so tight that if I poked you, you'd vibrate for hours."

Both shifters took a breath, relaxing against their seats. Neither had realized their stiffness. Which showed her how concerned they were.

The same waitress as earlier sidled up to their table. "You guys are back." She smiled at the guys for a moment, but then settled her gaze on Nixie. "Another virgin pina colada?"

"That would be amazing. Thank you."

"And what about you two?"

Garrett and Zachary both ordered beer. The waitress served another table after she'd given their drink order to the bartender. Setting the drinks in front of them, she also set down the menus.

"I'll be back in a bit to take your order." She bounced off to the next table.

"If your sources are right, it will only take one question to the wrong person and we'll have that vigilante group chasing us instead of us chasing them." Zachary leaned forward and spoke low.

"If my sources were correct about everything. Rumours have a lot of room for exaggeration." Garrett tailed his voice off as the waitress came back.

"All set to order?" She held her pen and paper in her hand and looked between the three of them.

"Sorry. We were too busy talking. Can you give us a couple more minutes?" Garrett lifted his menu off the table for the first time.

"Of course." She moved away, making her way around the tables, even the ones that didn't seem to be in her section. Touching and smiling at every waitress and even the menacing bartender, Nixie pegged her as the heart of the pub.

"Would it be terrible if I ordered the same thing I did at lunch?" Nixie peered down at her menu laying on the table. No matter how many times she looked it over, nothing registered as food except for that burger.

"I'll get that too." Zachary pushed his menu away and Garrett nodded, lifting her menu from the table and piling them all together to the side for the waitress to retrieve. She must have been watching because she came right over.

"What can I get you?" Her tone softened, and she stood relaxed beside the table. Garrett placed the order for all three of them. "It's one of our most popular burgers, but I don't think I've ever had anyone order it twice in one day."

Nixie shrugged and hoped the heat in her cheeks wasn't changing the colour.

"You guys aren't from here."

"What makes you say that?" Zachary leaned forward, resting his arms on the table.

"We're that small. We recognize faces."

"We're here hoping to meet up with someone." Nixie imagined Garrett with a fedora tipped forward and speaking in hushed tones. But he leaned further back and curled his arm around her shoulders. Now that the image was there, she couldn't banish it. Zachary with a similar hat and pinstriped suit and Garrett in brown tones with eyes that never stopped staring.

"Like I said, it's a small place. Who are you looking for?"

"We don't know their name." Garrett's lips twisted.

"Oh. A description?"

Garrett shook his head. "Don't worry about it. I'm sure we'll find them."

"Sorry I couldn't help. I'll get your order in right away." She waltzed straight to the kitchen and was out a moment later and talking to the bartender. Nixie still watched the entire scene with a 1920s filter.

"You're grinning." Garrett tilted to look her straight on.

"Sure am, Bugsy."

"Bugsy?"

Nixie shook her shoulders into character, leaned forward and darted her eyes between the two men. She spoke around an imaginary cigar between her lips. "We're looking for someone, see?" She straightened back to herself. "You're wearing a pinstripe suit and are the muscle, or the guns—whatever the term was back them. And you're wearing a brown suit and are the boss. And I can't forget the fedoras that tilt forward to hide your glowing eyes. I can't help but wonder what shifters would have been like back then."

"There weren't any." Garrett spoke low, the smile he'd given at her description fading.

"What do you mean?" Zachary leaned forward.

"Shifters died off during the time of the witch hunts. They went into hiding along with witches, and anyone else who had accusations against them. To protect them. Fate only recently restored the magic in shifters."

"Margaret tell you this?" Zachary lifted his beer. Nixie heard Garrett's answer before he spoke. He'd told her before that shifters hadn't been around for over three hundred years. Their purpose ruled every decision Garrett made and, from what she'd gleaned from the other shifters, it ruled them too.

"To protect."

17

———

The waitress had continued to chat them up each time she came over while they ate. Asking where they were from, what they did. They kept their answers as vague as possible.

After paying the bill, Garrett had opened a tab at the bar and suggested they play pool. He'd hoped everything would fall into place. They'd show up at the pub, find the vigilante group and therefore find his sister, or what happened to her, and he could take Nixie out of here. It would all be over. But nothing or no one stood out. While his senses stayed tuned into the atmosphere, he focused on sinking the eight ball. He straightened as the clunk and roll of the ball settled with the others.

"Sense anything?" Zachary asked low as he walked past to rack the balls for another game.

"No. You?"

"Someone is still watching us. But I can't tell if they're in here or not. It's weird." He pulled the triangle from its slot in the table.

"The staff checks on us now and then." He'd caught the

bartender, the waitress, and a couple others staring in their direction. A smile or nod ended their interest.

"Yeah, but I think it's someone else. I don't know, though." They all pulled the balls up and rolled them toward Zachary.

"Your turn to break, little one." Garrett bumped Nixie with the end of his stick.

"This is fun." Eyes wide, she bounced to the end of the table. Garrett eyed her form—back and left arm straight, jeans hugging her ass. He chuckled when he saw her tongue peeking out, concentration strong on her face.

Moving in behind her, he palmed her hip.

"Paws to yourself." She glared over her shoulder, keeping her arms in place to hit the ball.

Leaning over her back, he brushed her ear with his lips. "I don't have paws."

"Talons, then." Her voice softened as he'd hoped it would.

Zachary cleared his throat. Garrett nipped her ear, then stood, ignoring his raging erection. Nixie pulled back and hit the ball. The muted crack heralded her pout when the balls didn't move very far.

"Next time, try hitting the ball above its centre." The bald and tattooed bartender walked around the unused pool table and stopped next to theirs.

"Thanks." Nixie squeaked and took a step closer to Garrett, but not all the way. Garrett worked hard to keep himself relaxed. Zachary sat on a stool against the wall, sipping his beer and waiting his turn.

"How are you all for drinks?" He kept his attention between Garrett and Zachary.

"We're good, thanks."

"Good." He didn't leave, settling himself against the pool table. "Why are you looking for them?"

Garrett didn't pretend not to understand. The waitress had asked enough questions that she must have been relaying information to him. Better to get this over with and hiding their intentions would only prolong their search. "They have the answer to a question. I need to know what happened to someone important to me."

The bartender shook his head. "Let go and move on. That's the best advice anyone can give you."

"You're not the first to offer that." As each had told him how to find them, they'd also told him to move on.

"And you won't be the first to go missing after searching for them." He crossed his arms. "That won't stop you, will it?"

"No."

The bartender sighed and Garrett realized he was about to do the same as all the others—point him in the right direction after warning him away. "You just missed one of them. Should be able to catch up to him. I'll give you directions." He pushed off the table and stalked back to the bar. Garrett hesitated. That seemed too easy, just as it had with every other source of information. A glance at Zachary said he was thinking the same thing. His dark scowl followed the bartender before his feet hit the floor. He shrugged at Garrett and waited for him to go first.

Tucking Nixie behind him, Garrett trailed toward the bar. Zachary took up the rear behind Nixie. The bartender set their drink tab on the bar. After Garrett paid, he leaned forward to meet the bartender, realizing Nixie's gangster imaginative suited the situation better than he thought.

"North end of town, past resorts and straight into the

woods. About five kilometres in, you'll see a trail. It's faint, but there. That's where you'll find them."

"Can you tell us more about them?"

"No time. If you're going to catch up to him before he gets there, you need to leave now. And it's better to only come across one of them rather than all of them." He punctuated his warning with a slap to the bar, then turned away to the waitresses waiting to place drink orders.

Garrett cocked his head to the door, and they left.

"This screams set up. You know that, right?" Zachary stopped them before they could get into the vehicle.

"Yup."

"Okay. Let's go." Zachary put himself behind the wheel.

Garrett hesitated, wishing one more time that there was somewhere he could leave Nixie. Without the ability to pinpoint who was watching them, the safest place for her was between him and Zachary. Even if they were walking into a trap.

SNEAKERS WERE the best damn invention in the entire world, in Nixie's opinion. They kept her steady footed over roots and debris hidden in the dark canvas. Doing her best to stay quiet, she winced anytime she snapped a twig or crunched on a pile of leaves. It wasn't hard to see the twitch of the shifters' shoulders anytime she made a noise.

"Sorry, little one." Garrett whispered in her ear before he threw her onto his back.

"It's okay." She whispered back. Stealth was more important when walking into a trap without knowing what the trap was.

Both men often paused to listen to their surroundings.

Several times they'd tense, but continued moving. They'd tried to explain to her their sense of being watched. She could only imagine how frustrating that was when they couldn't find the person, especially with their superior senses. Nixie trusted them and their abilities.

They'd looked for signs of the man they were following, but found few. Enough to keep them moving forward. Each time they found one, Garrett and Zachary exchanged the same suspicious look. Even to Nixie, it all seemed a little laid out. Hansel's breadcrumbs. Or a trail of irresistible candy leading to the old lady with the waiting oven.

Nixie nipped Garrett's neck, sliding her teeth over the cord of muscle that connected to his shoulder. She couldn't blame an old hag for wanting a taste of him. Turning his head, he stared at her—the question *why now* written over his brow. She shrugged and did it again while he continued to hike.

They reached the narrow trail the bartender told them about. Setting her down, Garrett held her close to his side.

"Ambush." His voice didn't quite reach Nixie's ears, but Zachary nodded, hearing him well enough. "I understand if you don't want to go further. Ezaray is waiting for you at home and this is a setup."

Zachary seemed to consider his words, and in doing so, he also looked at Nixie. If he left, Garrett would ask her again to go with him.

"No, I'm good. Let's go."

Nixie sighed. She might have said yes. Understanding more of Garrett's motivations, she might have said yes this time. But she was glad she didn't have to choose.

Garrett went first, positioning Nixie behind him, and Zachary took up the rear. They hiked for another three kilometres based on Nixie's estimation, considering the five they'd already done to reach the trail. They wound through the trees, the trail barely visible in some places. Tall trunks narrowed the space for them to walk. Nixie wondered why they didn't spread out around the trail, but it was so faint in some places and changed direction suddenly, that if they didn't follow it, she feared they'd lose it.

The trees thinned and the dense foliage became sparse, allowing the moon to shed some light. Smoke formed in the air over Garrett's head. Both men tensed and stopped, forcing Nixie to bounce off Garrett's back. Without looking, she knew they'd found what they were looking for. Or what they'd been looking for had found them. They'd stepped on the trigger, swiped the stick from under the crate, pulled the wrong wire, sprung the trap.

Tilting to the right, she peeked around Garrett. Three small cabins created a V shape toward them, each with smoke twirling from their chimneys. And a row of men blocking the way to reach them. And blocking the way out from any other direction. Behind them, silhouetted figures stationed at different trees behind them. How had they passed that many men without Garrett or Zachary scenting them? Or had they passed them? Being a trap, they likely only just moved into position.

Nixie's fear awoke from where it had rested since escaping Keith. Alert and realizing they were in more danger than when against Keith's guards. And much more outnumbered. She'd place her money on the vigilantes.

"Don't tell me we tricked a couple shifters, did we?" One man stood ahead of the others. All of them wore some variation of black and grey, with fatigues and large boots. Knives strapped to their thighs and torsos drew Nixie's attention. "Well? You've found us." He spread his arms wide.

"At what point was this trap set? At the Alley Lounge or back in Fort Vale?"

The guy smirked. "Glad to know you're not as dumb as you seemed. So why the hunt for us other than to lead this man here?" He lifted his chin. Another of the vigilante group pull forward Macon, his arms tied behind his back.

"Macon?" Her fear doubled, choking her voice.

"You know him?"

"How the hell did you follow us?" Zachary growled.

"He didn't. You would have lost him soon after we caught up to him. Anyone following someone who's searching for us is of interest. As are the people searching for us." Warning seeped from the man. He shifted his feet, firming his stance. The others around him tensed, like a snap in the air.

Dizziness threatened Nixie as her head swiveled to see everyone. Garrett settled his hand on the back of her neck. His touch soothed the panic rising, but didn't abate her awareness of how bad their situation was.

The man holding Macon pushed him forward until they stood closer to the leader.

"I'll ask again. You know him?"

"He works for Keith Jeffreys. Didn't like how I got through his security." Garrett paid Macon no attention. His gaze stayed steady on the man questioning them.

"He works for Jeffreys? And you brought him here?" The man's growl would have been a bellow had the gravel in his voice hadn't given him his deadly tone.

"You told us you brought him here, not us." Garrett pulled Nixie a little closer, his hand settling on her waist.

The man gritted his teeth and looked away from them for the first time, casting his gaze to the ground. "Are you certain he works for Jeffreys?"

"One of his lead guards." Garrett confirmed.

"His lead guard." Nixie felt the need to add, but judging by the surrounding faces, the specific information wouldn't make a difference.

He lifted his head only enough to meet her eyes. Those three words must have confirmed her position with Keith, because those eyes softened. He nodded at the man holding Macon.

Tightening his hold on Macon, the man set his hand on the hilt of a knife attached to his thigh. He paused until he had Nixie's attention. "Might want to look away, love." Despite his warning, he didn't wait. Pulling the knife free, he moved in one smooth motion. It was done. Blank wide eyes stared into the trees and blood spurted from his neck, covering his front.

A scream caught in her chest. Garrett twisted her around until she buried her face against him. She heard the thump of the body hitting the ground and tightened her hold on Garrett's shirt.

"Where's Jeffreys?"

"Should be in custody, with his mansion burned to the ground." Garrett's voice echoed in her man-made cocoon.

"I'd prefer him dead."

"Sorry. Best option I had."

"You did it?" He paused, and she assumed Garrett had nodded.

"Reign, whatever you're doing out here is taking too long." Nixie recognized the tones in that voice, but it didn't sound the same as when she'd last heard it. Fear, worry, and fire had poured from every word. But now it spiked with cheerful serenity.

Garrett's arms loosened and Nixie turned to see the face she hoped for.

But she disappeared with a short scream, jumping away from the dead body still pooling dark blood on the ground.

"You promised I wouldn't have to see that again."

"I'm sorry, pet. It was necessary."

"Necessary, my ass! There are so many places for you to do that and hide the body. There's no need…" She stepped around to the other side of the man named Reign and stopped, wobbling enough she clutched Reign's arm. "Garrett?"

SQUEEZING HIS EYES SHUT TIGHT, Garrett hoped they'd see clearly when he reopened them. Even in the dark, he wouldn't mistake his sister's head of brunette curls that had emerged from the bunker-like cabin, chiding the cougar shifter leading the vigilante group. No wonder they'd had difficulty pinpointing who'd been watching them. It had been cougars.

Garrett opened his eyes again and blinked to make certain they'd adjusted.

"Garrett?" Anya's voice and the healthy glow to her skin almost brought him to his knees. If he hadn't been holding Nixie, he would have let gravity win. Hope had lived somewhere inside him, but he'd tried to suffocate it whenever he could. He didn't know if he could have handled being crushed in that way. This journey had always been about finding closure for him and his sister. But she stood in front of him, hale and beautiful.

With the vigilante.

Anya let go of Reign's arm and took a single step forward. Reign stopped her with a hand flat against her belly. An intimate hand. Garrett growled, the inaudible sound growing the longer Reign kept his sister from him.

Anya looked at his hand, then up at him. "I will make your life miserable if you don't let me go to my brother."

"That Garrett?"

"Have I told you of any other Garrett?"

Reign shook his head and let her go. She darted across the short distance. Garrett only had enough time to unwrap his arms from Nixie before his sister hit his chest. His sister. She was alive. He held her tight for fear it was all a dream. Breathing deep, he never wanted to forget this moment. Anya was alive.

And mated.

The scent he'd long missed mixed with the scent of a mate—not quite human and not quite shifter. But full of cougar. Garrett pulled her back and swept her hair away from her neck. A faint crescent marked her skin. Tilting to the other side, he saw its twin.

"You never told me your brother was a shifter, pet." Reign glared at Garrett over Anya's head.

"I didn't know. Until now." After mating, a mate's senses increased. Not to the full strength of a shifter, but more than enough to scent another shifter or mate. "Why didn't you ever tell me?"

"Stories for another time." He pulled her against him again.

"Nixie?" Anya's arms loosened, and she turned away.

"I'm so happy you're okay." Nixie stepped away from Zachary, who'd kept her close while Garrett hugged his sister.

"You are too." Anya embraced Nixie. She pulled back and looked over her shoulder at Garrett. "Another story you need to tell." She would have scented him on Nixie and the fresh mating.

Garrett nodded.

"Okay. They're going to clean that up." She pointed to two guys standing closest to Macon's body. "And you guys are coming back to the compound with us."

"I think you're forgetting something, pet." Reign crossed his arms and lowered his chin.

"I'm not forgetting a damn thing. You are." His sister squared off with the deadly cougar. Her mate. That fact alone kept Garrett from lashing out at the vigilantes and charging back through the woods with his sister over one shoulder and Nixie over the other. Anya was more than alive. She was healthy, vibrant, happy. And it was the vigilantes Garrett had to thank for that. He had to banish his roaring protectiveness over his baby sister being mated.

"Our compound is private."

Anya waited him out. The patience she always had baffled even Garrett. If she'd been the type of child to hold her breath to get her own way, she would have triumphed every time, turning every shade of blue imaginable. While she was patient, she wasn't manipulative.

"Fine. But only your brother."

Anya still didn't say a word. She stepped back to ensure the three of them circled her—her point clear. Garrett didn't understand the dynamics of the group, so he let his sister handle this. He wouldn't leave Nixie behind, and he'd feel much better with Zachary at his back.

"You're going to be the death of me, woman."

"Keep calling me woman and I will be."

"One more thing before we leave. Belanger." The instant and brutal killing of Macon and the certainty Reign had needed he worked for Jeffreys made sense. He was avenging his mate. Avenging Anya. Belanger was the man that started this, kidnapping Anya and using her to force Garrett to work for him.

"Dead." Zachary answered.

"You're sure."

"Very." The silver flash of his eyes left no question who killed him.

"Good. Let's go." Reign gave a circling hand signal to the others. Two stayed to deal with the body. Anya hooked her arm around Garrett's and walked alongside him. Cougar shifters flanked them on all sides, fading in and out of the night shadows as they hiked past the cabins.

"Anya." Reign called from up ahead.

"Or you could join us back here and meet my brother without any threats?"

Reign stopped and waited for them to catch up. His little sister wasn't afraid of the cougar. She was living proof that a few of the rumours regarding the vigilantes were true. Garrett didn't think they hurt anyone who didn't deserve it. The certainty of Macon's identity, Anya ordering around the group of deadly shifters. However, Garrett wasn't about to relax his guard.

"You saved my sister." Garrett stood at eye level with the other shifter.

"He did." Anya answered.

"Thank you." Garrett tried not to choke on the emotions that re-surged. Reign inclined his head.

"How did you get out, Nixie?" Anya leaned forward to see her around Garrett.

"Garrett and his friends got me out."

"I traced you to Jeffreys. When I got there, Nixie was the only one left." The trees thickened again, blocking the moonlight, as they left the cabins behind. Trails similar to the one they'd travelled wove through them, but were just as complicated. They didn't use them. They had a purpose for which only the cougars benefited.

"And the wolf is?"

Garrett looked at Zachary, giving him the choice to say his name.

"Zachary."

"He showed up at Belanger's fighting ring looking for someone. We ended up saving them all and deconstructed Belanger's organization."

"He took my cousin and when I got there, I found my mate." Zachary filled in his details.

"And that's when you killed him, right?" Reign asked.

"We couldn't do both, save the women and take down Belanger. But Belanger came after his own sister, and Zachary's cousin and his mate. He didn't make it out of that fight."

"At least I still have Jeffreys to kill."

"If you can get at him in custody."

"I can get at him."

The forest floor rose with a low incline, enough to have Nixie breathing harder by the time they reached the top. From the bottom and even while climbing, it looked like the top flattened and continued. But it opened up to a miniature village. A homestead with multiple homes to manage it.

"Welcome to my home." Anya passed him a sideways smile. And that's when Garrett realized that even though he'd found his sister alive and well, he wouldn't be taking her back with him.

18

———————

Nixie stayed close to Garrett as much as possible and close to Zachary whenever Anya wouldn't let him go. But her mate only seemed to tolerate that for so long. They'd arrived on what they'd called a compound, but it looked like paradise to Nixie. The self-sufficient rustic homes had been plucked from her dreams. Goats, sheep, chickens roamed the grounds. Their own source of energy powered everything they needed for all twelve homes.

They'd taken most of the night to hike here and now, with dawn soon approaching, they'd settled in Reign's home—Anya's home—next to a warm fire. They all had stories to tell, and neither Garrett nor Anya was willing to wait.

"Tyrone kept me for a little while, trying to find some other use for me other than blackmail." Anya sat on the floor between Reign's feet, his hand stroking her hair while she spoke. This was a tale he'd heard before. "He never told me I was blackmail. I overheard him talking to some employee of his. But I never cooperated. I fought against him with my every breath. So he sold me. I felt like a house being flipped for a while. Always sold for a higher profit until I reached Jeffreys."

"I admired your fight while you were there."

"You admired me? Hell, I admired you. I was terrified and acted like a cornered animal. You stared each of them in the eye and never let them see how much pain you were in."

"Keith became unstable after he got rid of you and the others with you. He didn't tolerate my defiance often."

"But you're alive. I wouldn't be if it weren't for Reign. Jeffreys sold us to Marks." Anya's jaw clenched. Nixie recognized the angry fire. The same fire that kept her fighting. She opened her lips to continue, but she looked away.

"We'd been tracking Marks for a long time, always missing him. We caught up to him after he'd taken Anya. You know the rest." Marks and company hadn't survived. "He'd had a dozen women with him at the time. We gave them all a choice. Stay with us or go home. Five of them chose to live here."

"We *all* had a choice?" Anya looked back at Reign.

"I gave you a lot of choices, pet." He leaned forward and nipped her jaw.

Nixie worried for Garrett. Finding Anya well, safe, and mated had to be as much of a shock as finding her gone. He carried such guilt that any outcome would cripple him. His eyes never wavered from the couple. And all the while, his hand rested on her thigh, circling his thumb, squeezing his fingers.

Zachary went next when Garrett didn't fill the silence. "Took me two years to find my cousin. I got lucky and sneaked inside. Garrett gave me a passkey. He offered to help me rescue Holly and Ezaray, my mate, but on one condition. We rescue them all and take down Belanger."

"I couldn't do anything to put you at risk, Anya. Even at

that point, I thought you were dead, but I never could have lived myself if I'd been wrong. I did the best I could to protect the fighters. It wasn't enough."

Nixie hurt for him. She wanted to take away his unnecessary guilt. Turning her gaze away, she looked toward his sister. Tears filled her eyes as she stared at Garrett. No blame or judgment. Looking at Nixie, they shared a moment of understanding, of feeling Garrett's pain. But Reign was scowling. Who knew what the leader of the vigilante group thought of Garrett's actions? Would they have risked others to save a loved one? What would Reign have done to protect Anya?

"How did you get into Jeffreys' mansion?" Reign leaned forward so his hands rested around Anya's shoulders.

"I was faster than their cameras and there were blind spots on either corner of her balcony. She carried me in, hiding me from the camera until we were in the room. Jeffreys was depriving her of food for a week and had sprained her ankle. I took her food and medicine until she'd healed and it was time to leave. He'd planned a meeting and a party, and that was when we made our move. I gave Nixie a couple of bugs to plant inside and she gave me a layout of the mansion. I called in a couple of friends, Zachary and a few others. Two of us shot explosives along one side of the house and toward the main gate, where party guests arrived. That kept most of the guards busy. But one followed Nixie back upstairs and Macon hid himself under her balcony to follow us after our escape. We had a bit of help getting away from him in the woods."

"He found you at the motel. Luckily, so did we."

Nixie yawned, exhaustion pulling it into a longer stretch than what she'd expected. Anya followed, yawning in tandem with her. She smiled as she leaned her head against her mate's knee.

"I haven't pulled an all-nighter in a while." There had been a couple of nights they'd spent together while she was at Keith's. Those were the nights they became friends, despite their circumstances or their brief time together.

"Time for bed." Reign pulled Anya to her feet.

"I suppose. I'll show you two to your room." Anya waited for them to stand.

"I'll make sure your brother finds his way." Reign nudged her toward Nixie and stared at Garrett. Garrett helped Nixie up from the couch and embraced Anya.

"Goodnight, Anya. I'm so happy you're safe." Her hair muffled his words.

"Goodnight." Then Anya turned toward Reign. "Behave."

"Now, Anya."

Garrett pulled Nixie close, and until his hand wrapped around the back of her neck, she hadn't realized how much she'd needed that contact. The entire night carried a heavy flow of adrenaline.

"I'll be right there, little one." He kissed her forward before he took her lips. Soft and warm, she soaked in the comfort. Letting him go, she followed Anya.

"Here it is. It's small, but it's comfortable. And the bed is plenty big. I don't think shifters come in size small." Anya turned in a circle and stood at the end of the bed.

"Unless they're female." Holly was about the size of Anya.

"Female?" Anya dropped to the bed. Nixie joined her.

"Zachary left out the part that Holly is also a shifter. I met her. She came to help rescue me. She's an owl."

"That's amazing. I can't wait to meet her."

"Are you allowed to meet her?" Nixie had no better way to ask how it was living with vigilantes.

"What do you mean?" Anya leaned back on her hands and frowned.

"Are you allowed to leave the compound?"

Her frown vanished and a soft smile took its place. "Not without Reign. And not often. But I'm not a prisoner, or captive."

"You're happy."

"I am."

Nixie's lips moved, but she struggled.

Anya giggled and nudged her shoulder. "Just say it. You never worried before."

"You live with vigilante shifters."

"Is that what they are?" Anya hitched herself up on the bed. "Yeah, okay, that's what they are. But I've never heard them call themselves that."

"How often do they—how should I say it—put on their anti-*Justice League* hats?" Nixie joined her by the pillows and they settled against them, staring at the ceiling while they talked.

"Not as often as people think. Their actions should bother me, but it doesn't. They saved me and have saved so many others. They aren't trying to fight crime outside of authorities. They only go after the ones the authorities can't or won't get to." Anya shivered, shimmying herself further into the pillows. "As long as I'm not walking over puddles of someone's blood like I did earlier, then I'm good."

"What was it like becoming a mate?" Had she struggled the way Nixie was?

"Well, you know. You're one now too." Anya yawned, covering it with the back of her hand.

"It's still new."

"Ah. Well, in my case, he was a possessive asshole who gave ultimatums and when that didn't work, he had to beg. I made him do it in front of all his people, too. I'm that kind of evil."

"You love him?" It was obvious, but she needed to ask. Needed to know that this was what Anya wanted.

"With all I have." Her whisper filled the room with emotion and her voice softened with sleep. "What about you and my brother?"

"I don't want to belong to someone again. But I'm not sure if I can say goodbye to him. We couldn't stop ourselves from mating." Nixie couldn't blame it all on Garrett. She'd had the opportunity to push him away and didn't.

"Maybe instead of Fate handing you over to another man, She's handing you a gift." Nixie hadn't needed to explain everything to Anya, not when the other woman had similar experiences and worse.

"Tell me about the compound." She still wasn't so sure about trusting Fate and her *gifts*. Now that they'd found Anya, her time with Garrett would be over soon.

Nixie fell asleep soaking in everything she'd need to live on her own. But no matter how hard she tried to imagine herself alone, Garrett was always there watching over her.

"You're not taking your sister away." The moment the bedroom door closed behind the women, Reign spoke low enough to contain their conversation between them. Both threat and demand.

"I don't intend to. Not unless that's what she wants." If he'd caught even a glimpse of her desire to leave when he'd first seen her run toward him, he would have bolted with both women. Damn the consequences.

"You think I'm keeping her against her will?" Reign's hands tensed into fists.

Garrett waited a beat before answering. "No." He sighed with his admission. "I've never seen her happier."

"She's pregnant." Reign lowered his tone further, despite the women wouldn't be able to hear them.

"I thought I smelled a babe." Just the faint touch of new life. Garrett had said nothing for fear Anya didn't want him to know.

"She doesn't know yet. But it won't be much longer and she'll sense it too."

"I want to see her. I can't just walk away and pretend she doesn't exist." The sink hole carrying the weight of everything he had collapsed. Like he soared in the sky and the air rushed through a gaping wound, trying to suck him through.

"We're private. We don't allow visitors."

Garrett readied himself for a fight. He wouldn't tear his sister away from her life, but he wouldn't give up seeing her and her child. His niece or nephew.

"But Anya will kill me if I keep you from her. She's worried daily about you. Has begged me to go find you. I couldn't, by the way."

"I didn't want to be found." Since working for Tyrone, Garrett had wiped all trace of himself. His true identity hadn't left a paper trail in years. "Being a hawk, I don't travel the conventional way. I didn't want Belanger to discover I wasn't where he thought I was. You didn't know who I was when you found us and led us here?"

"No. You're looking a little haggard compared to your

professional portraits. And I didn't first see you until you got here."

Garrett rubbed at his face. The scruff had turned into a beard and his hair wouldn't stay in one place. How he looked hadn't been a priority for him since he quit working at the hospital.

"I'll allow you to fly in." Reign leaned back in his chair and put his foot up on one knee.

"That's a start." Nixie came with him to find Anya. She'd want to see her too. And he couldn't fly in with her.

"A start? You're lucky I'm allowing that."

"Look, I.." Garrett settled his elbows on his knees, trying to hold himself together. "Do you treat her well?"

"Of course I do." His chin dropped, a sign to tell Garrett to tread carefully.

"Is she safe here?"

"Safer than anywhere."

"Good. Beyond your agreement to allow me to see her, I don't have energy for any fights. I appreciate you letting us come here now. And I'd appreciate some time to spend with my sister before we leave."

Reign relaxed, but he frowned at Garrett. "You really expected to find her dead."

"I didn't dare hope for more."

"You're welcome to stay for a few days. I give my word we will come up with a way to stay in contact."

"Thank you."

"Your room is the third on the right." Reign stood and walked down the hall of the small home. Garrett followed, picking up Nixie's scent. And Anya's. He nodded at Reign, who'd kept walking to his room and opened his door. Anya and Nixie were sound asleep on top of the covers, arms linked and heads together.

Reign stomped into the room behind Garrett.

"One of those is mine," he growled. He pulled Anya from the bed and settled her against his chest. Garrett couldn't pull his eyes from his sister. But when Reign paused beside him, Garrett met his gaze. "I love her."

Garrett nodded his understanding. Shutting the door behind them, he moved toward his own mate. He loved her. But was he willing to continue being selfish, denying her freedom, or would he be like Reign and demand they never part?

Nixie sighed when he brushed her back with his fingers. Gently, so as not to wake her, Garrett pulled her clothes from her body and tucked the blankets over her. He stripped and crawled in next to her. He would have pulled her against him, but she moaned and rolled toward him, throwing a leg over his and nuzzling his chest.

"I love you, Nixie." He tested the words aloud while she slept, fearing how they'd feel on his tongue. "I vow to set you free."

No. Don't go. Nixie's dream world darkened. The edges of her sight fading away, leaching closer as the darkness consumed one thing after another. Garrett stood next to a log fence, his golden eyes flashing. The darkness landed behind him and his form faded.

"I vow to set you free." He called out to her as he disappeared from sight.

No. This isn't free. Having all of this taken away from her isn't free. *Garrett!* She spun around, searching what was left of her dream world. It wasn't freedom if it came at a price.

And the currency hadn't ever crossed her mind. A man she loved.

This wasn't right. She wanted out. Closing her eyes, she pinched her arm until she was sure she'd have a bruise, but only numbness invaded in her wake. She opened her mouth to scream into the air for silence to fall back on her. *Wake up, damn it.* Swinging her arms, she searched for whatever bed she slept in.

"Nixie." Garrett's voice. He was back, but when she turned to search for him, she found the darkness inching closer. "Nixie."

She swung her arms harder. He had to be here.

"Nixie." His hands grabbed her shoulders.

She tried closing and opening her eyes. And there he was, his face above hers.

"Are you okay?"

"You're here." Nixie launched her arms around his neck, filling herself with his warmth.

"You were hitting me." He cradled the back of her head and settled them back against the mattress.

"I'm sorry." She squeezed him tighter.

"Don't be. Was it a nightmare?"

"No. Just a bad dream."

"Do you want to talk about it?"

"No." No way was she ready to analyze that. It was straightforward. Nixie didn't want Garrett to leave her. She reminded herself of the old adage parents tell their children —need and want are two different things. But that didn't matter right now and after watching him fade into nothing, she *needed* him.

Pulling back, she trailed her lips along his jaw until she reached his mouth. He met her every measure, growling when she wedged her hand between them to wrap around his length. He grew and throbbed in her grip.

"Now, Garrett. Please." But she didn't wait for him to roll over. Nixie shoved his chest, so he lay on his back. The moment, the need, her love for him, rode her hard. It wouldn't stop until she was connected to him the only way possible. She straddled his hips, keeping her hand on him to angle him at her core.

"Nixie, wait."

Her ringing ears muffled his warning. With the tip poised at her centre, she slammed down. She cried out. The sudden fullness and angle carried a pinch of pain.

"Damn it, Nixie. You weren't ready."

"I was plenty ready. I just need to move." She tried to rise and winced.

Garrett sat up and wrapped his hands around her thighs. He slid them to the backs of her knees and pulled. She wrapped her legs around him, sinking further onto him.

She held her breath.

"Easy, little one." He ran his hands back up her legs to settle on her hips. His fingers tightened, rocking her against him. "I've got you."

Nixie held onto his shoulders and his slow movements eased her rushed decision. Her core softened. Pleasure built like small pebbles being thrown into a well. Small splashes and ripples.

"That must have been some bad dream." Garrett pulled her hair to the side and nibbled her shoulder. Refusing to talk about it hadn't kept her from giving it away. Her need to have him had superseded everything. He'd recognized the ruling urgency.

Her leg muscles tensed, matching the rhythm of the hand still on her hip.

"That's better," he crooned in her ear while he found her breast. She tried to move faster, needing more to reach her climax, but he wouldn't let her. "This is all you get." His hips undulated with hers, applying pressure and friction to her clit.

It was enough to drive her mad and curse his name, but he never caved and let her move faster. With such a slow and gentle build, Nixie hadn't seen it coming. Her orgasm burst, sending tingles through her body. And as Garrett exploded after her, he struck her neck, sharp teeth sinking in. He wrapped his arms around her and she collapsed against his chest. Garrett lapped at her neck, his tongue smooth and warm. When he finished, he flipped her over to lay her on the bed.

Nixie didn't let go of him. The grip she'd had on his shoulders moved, so she wrapped her arm around his torso. A toddler-like version of herself threw a tantrum in her head, stomping her feet to get what she wanted, not what she needed. And what she wanted was a life with Garrett.

19

Garrett grew accustomed to stares from Anya's small community. Outright suspicion from the cougar shifters and severe nervousness from everyone else. Neither lessened as the days passed.

Anya proudly showed him around, introducing him to everyone and never fazed by the cold shoulders they'd turned on him. But every single person looked at his sister with fondness. She belonged here. Her eyes alight with satisfaction and warmth.

Reign had agreed to let them stay until Anya discovered she was pregnant. Garrett wanted to be here for that moment. And he hadn't let Reign dictate when he could and couldn't visit. When Anya walked in on the conversation, it ended with her finger on the end of Reign's nose. Garrett would be here as often as possible and wouldn't miss the birth of his niece or nephew.

Zachary had left two days earlier and Garrett asked for a favour of him when he returned to Alder Ridge.

A few of the homes on the compound still needed work before winter settled in. Garrett pitched in, earning nods of gratitude if not verbal ones. Nixie hung on every word Anya said while they finished the harvest and worked in the greenhouse. This was her dream. Self-sufficiency. She was like a sponge, soaking in everything she needed to live this way herself. How to care for the animals, what to plant and when, and what plants had medicinal properties. Garrett had been investigating their herb garden when Nixie and Anya walked in. Those slim eyes focused between his lips and the garden.

Until she'd asked, "how do I begin?" Garrett had worried she'd want to stay here. The community gave her the same warmth they gave Anya, but Garrett doubted they'd allow another shifter to stay. Maybe with time, they'd accept him, but despite being near his sister, this wasn't where he wanted to settle.

Garrett had given up everything when Belanger took Anya. His home, his friends. He didn't think he'd had friends either. Yet the shifters from Alder Ridge had helped him save his mate and Zachary covered his back while they followed a rumour and walked into a trap. There was a home waiting for Garrett.

Climbing down from the last roof that needed repairs, Garrett collapsed the ladder. "That's it for shingling. Anything else before we move on?" The woman living here had been a victim of Marks that stayed. He'd worked next to cougar named Callahan who'd said that despite being here for over two years, Esa was still shy around all of them.

"I don't think so. Thank you." Esa smiled and cast her gaze downward.

"Then how do you plan on moving that new wood stove inside?" Callahan only spared a second to glance at the stove sitting at the side of her house, covered with a tarp, before he narrowed his gaze on her.

Pink tinged her cheeks, and she shuffled her feet. Despite the way Esa carried herself, Garrett saw the pinch to her lips and smelled the irritation that flared. "It would be great if you two could take my wood stove inside."

"That's better, love. But you forgot to tell us to install it, too." Callahan tapped her nose with his index finger.

"Careful, Cal. One of these days the kitten is going to bite that finger." Reign strode past, pushing a cart of wood.

The more Garrett saw in this community, the more content he felt about leaving Anya here. Despite their choice of pastimes, the cougar shifters cared for each other and their people.

Esa spun around and walked toward the garden. Callahan's gaze lingered on her ass before he stalked past Garrett to pull the tarp off the stove.

"Is she your mate?" Garrett shouldn't have asked, but their interaction made him wonder.

"Does she smell like a mate?" He circled the stove, looking for the best place to lift.

"If she did, I wouldn't have asked." Garrett found his side and settled his hands in place. Callahan crouched to get his grip.

"It's none of your damn business, Tweety."

"I only ask because I'm wondering how you two handle the pain and sickness." They'd started to lift, but Callahan dropped the stove the half an inch back to the ground.

"Keep chirping. Sylvester's getting hungry." His eyes flashed and his shoulders squared.

"Never mind." Garrett held the other shifter's gaze. He crouched back into place, ready to lift the stove. Another moment and Callahan did the same. Garrett didn't speak again unless it related to installing the stove. But the time left him to wonder if there had been a way to avoid the pain, would he have still mated Nixie?

Yes. It hadn't only been about the pain growing in his chest. The urge had been too strong to deny.

They finished the installation and took the old one outside in time for Anya and Nixie to come find him.

"We're about to head home to start supper and were wondering if you're done?" Anya hooked her arm around Nixie's.

"Take him." Callahan growled. Anya winced.

"Guess I'm free to go." Garrett wanted to pull Nixie from Anya's grip, but settled with holding her free hand. It wouldn't be much longer before Anya sensed her own pregnancy. He refused to take away a single moment either of them had with her.

They passed Reign and Anya called to him to say they finished for the day and going home to cook. In the small kitchen, Anya started pulling everything from the fridge.

"Do you mind if I take a quick shower before I help?" Nixie's hair was falling out in several places and she'd smeared dirt over her cheeks. Her knee poked through a hold in the borrowed jeans she wore.

"Of course not!" Anya shooed her out of the kitchen. Garrett snagged Nixie's wrist and pulled her back against his chest. He kissed her, tasting the oncoming winter on her tongue. She flushed when he let her go.

"I'll be quick." Nixie left and Anya handed Garrett a pile of carrots.

"Start peeling."

He found a spot at the counter and did as he was told. "If you hadn't been happy here, I would have gotten you out."

"You could have tried. But, I know." She finished scrubbing the potatoes and put them into a pot with the skins still on. "I've missed you. And I'm going to miss you when you leave. But this is home. I struggled with that for a long time. That this place felt like home when it shouldn't. Silly."

"It's not. And I've missed you too, and will."

"You guys could stay." She set the pot down on the stove, her back to Garrett.

"I considered, but this isn't our home."

"I understand." Anya turned around and threw herself at Garrett. He only had time to free one arm to wrap around her. "I'm so glad you found me."

"Me too." He kissed the top of her head. She stepped back and blew out from rounded lips.

"I have something I need to talk to you about before Nixie comes back or before Reign gets home."

"What is it?"

"If there was another doctor or nurse or something in the compound, I'd ask them, because, well, you're my brother. But something is off."

Each day, the babe grew stronger. They'd known she'd sense it soon. Knowing where she was going with this, he didn't bother warning her that Nixie turned off the shower a few minutes ago and that Reign walked through the front door. Damn cougars were quieter than other shifters.

"I've been having dizzy spells. And I sense there is something wrong with me. But that's it."

"There's nothing wrong with you."

Anya frowned.

"Come here, pet." Reign leaned against the door to the kitchen. Nixie hovered behind him and Garrett motioned her closer. She excused herself past Reign.

"Damn it, Reign. Don't sneak up like that. I thought I was supposed to have increased hearing too, yet I can never hear you! Now, go away."

"Come. Here." He dropped his chin.

Garrett wrapped an arm across Nixie's shoulders and watched for when his sister would realize she was going to be a mom.

"Dizzy spells, huh?" Reign tilted her chin up.

"I didn't want you to worry until I knew what it was."

"I already know what it is."

"You do?"

Reign slid a hand down to her belly and flattened it over her womb. "Focus on what you think is wrong. Really focus, pet."

Garrett watched his sister's face cross the whole spectrum of emotions before her hands covered Reign's on her abdomen. Reign nodded when she looked up and Garrett did the same when she looked at him for confirmation. Her mate pulled her from the kitchen and they disappeared somewhere in the house.

"What's going on?" Nixie turned around to face him.

"Anya's pregnant."

"That's wonderful. Congratulations, uncle." Her eyes glistened, but the smile on her lips didn't reach them to make the tears she shed happy ones. If he was to be an uncle, then Nixie was to be an aunt. And now that the news was out, it was time for them to leave and face what future they chose for themselves.

🪶

THE GOODBYE at the compound had been painful. They'd spent the last night there celebrating with Anya and Reign. Nixie hadn't understood why, but the news had made her cry. She convinced herself they were happy tears, and some of them were. But part of her saw something else she wanted instead of needed.

They'd left the next morning, Garrett and Reign getting along enough that Reign gave him a way to contact them, and Nixie had a notebook full of information to go through. Everyone had been beyond kind to her, answering all of her questions and more.

The hike through the woods hadn't been as bad in the daylight, and they reached the vehicle Zachary had left for them. Before starting the engine, Garrett had asked where she wanted to go. That was it. Everything was over and she'd had to choose.

"Alder Ridge." If for no other reason than to see Holly again and meet the other mates. Alder Ridge would make a good starting point. Maybe even her ending point.

Garrett asked if she wanted to stop for the night about halfway there, but as the tension grew taut with their continued silence, Nixie said no, unless he needed to. They stopped long enough for him to get a couple hours of sleep and they hit the road again. They'd promised to go their separate ways and neither of them could forget that. But Nixie's dream of him fading from existence in front of her still plagued her thoughts. She'd woken from the same dream each night at the compound and turned to him each time, taking him into her body. But he was what she wanted, not what she needed.

Nixie had slept most of the second half of the drive until dawn peered through the windows and Garrett slowed as they entered Alder Ridge. Trees and foliage spread throughout the town as they drove down the main centre and forests seemed to surround it on all sides. Very few houses were the same, all having some unique aspect to them.

"It's beautiful here." Her head swiveled while trying to get the best look at everything they passed.

"It is," Garrett clipped, his voice low. Nixie kept her gaze out the window.

On the other end of town, homes were further apart. Garrett parked in front of one with two colours of siding. One blue, bright and fresh, and the other white and dingy. They parked beside a motorcycle with a large black truck on the other side.

"Wait here." Garrett got out and strode toward the front door. Zachary emerged from the house, a small dark-haired woman at his side. She must be Ezaray, Zachary's mate. She met Nixie's stare through the windshield and waved. Feeling a little awkward, Nixie waved back. She'd wanted to meet the other mates and considered getting out, but Garrett was on his way back with a white envelope in his hand. Zachary nodded at her, then ushered his mate back inside the house.

"What's that?" She pointed at the envelope he'd set on the dash with a light clunk.

"You'll see." He drove back toward town, but turned left not long after leaving Zachary's. The lane was narrow, with small gravel kicking up behind them. They stopped in front of a house about the same size as Zachary's. Nixie followed Garrett from the vehicle. "It's clean. Everything inside works, and it will survive a few winters. There's ten acres of land to go with it. You can have more if you want it."

"What is this, Garrett?"

"Yours, little one. It's all yours. If you don't want to live in Alder Ridge, that's fine. But here's a place to start."

"A place for who to start?"

"You. Just you." Garrett pulled her close and slipped the envelope into her front pocket. His hands wouldn't settle.

They traced her hips and up her sides. His chest heaved and his body shook. "I vowed to set you free, Nixie."

Those words. Her dream. They'd sounded so real. As real as they did right now. Her vision blurred as she watched the dream take hold of reality. He was fading away and just as in her dream when she opened her mouth to call him back, silence followed.

"There's food and cash inside for more groceries and for anything you need to get started. To get your goats." His lips tried to smile. "I paid all utilities for the first six months, so you have time to get your feet under you. But promise me you'll call me if you need help."

Her lips moved, but she couldn't make that promise. Didn't want to make that promise.

"Well, Zachary is nearby too. As are the others."

Her hands clasped his forearms when he tried to step back. It was enough to make him hesitate. He lowered his head. The kiss was soft, sad, stilted, and so very wrong.

"I made you a promise and I have to leave now if I'm going to keep it."

Stay, please. But only her eyes pleaded.

He didn't say another word. He backed up until he reached the vehicle. Nixie stood, numbness filling her body like lead. This time, as the dream finished and Garrett disappeared, Nixie couldn't reach out and find him there to comfort her. He'd left her alone with exactly what she'd needed. With no one to belong to.

◞

GARRETT HID in the same tree he had every day since he left Nixie in front of her house. The house and property had been the favour he'd asked of Zachary. Nixie had only needed to sign the paperwork. Garrett's name wasn't attached to any of it. He paid for it, but other than that, he stayed out of it.

He watched over Nixie, with Eagle by his side, never staying more than an hour to a time for fear he'd break his promise and go to her. She'd spent the first week inside the house, sometimes walking her property or sitting on the porch with coffee and her notebook she had from the compound. Sunset and sunrise were his favourite times to come. The times he got to watch her glow in the golden hours.

Nixie waved goodbye to the delivery truck who'd just dropped off materials for what looked to be a greenhouse plus extra lumber. The logo on the trailer matched the company Nathan worked for. He'd dropped it all off in her front yard and drove away, leaving Nixie to move it on her own. Struggling, she tried to lift the first bundle.

Before you got here, she told the driver to put it all right there and nowhere else. Eagle explained from his perch beside him.

Why would she do that? Garrett's wings flexed. He wanted to help her.

Good question.

Garrett wouldn't break his vow and go to her for the answer. *I'll be back later.* To watch her at the end of the day. While she continued to pull, yank, lift, and fall on her ass, Garrett flew off toward Zachary's. He shifted before he landed at their front door. He waited for Zachary to let him in.

"Why is no one helping her?" Garrett strode past Zachary and grabbed a pair of jeans by the door. Ezaray set down the book she held and stood.

"Where the hell have you been?" Zachary slammed the front door.

Garrett winced. He'd told no one he was sticking around. "In the trees or at Asher's safe house."

"He's looked for you there."

"I don't stay when he comes. Haven't felt like talking." Any other time, or about any other shifter, and Garrett enjoyed his discussions with Asher. But not about him and his mate. "Why is no one helping her?"

"She won't let us. We've tried. Nathan even said he'd make her delivery today himself. But she said no. She wanted a stranger. At the end of her first week, we caught her hiking through town with groceries on her back. I offered a ride, but she wouldn't take it. So I stole her groceries and put them away before she got home. And since then one of has been supplying her with food when she isn't looking. She changed her lock one day. Didn't work."

"I don't understand."

"She's trying to prove something to herself." Ezaray moved in front of Zachary.

"Accepting help isn't not being self-sufficient."

Ezaray set her hand on Garrett's arm and spoke slow. "She only needs herself." She glared at him, willing him to understand.

Maybe he understood her reasoning, but that didn't mean it wasn't, "Bullshit. She's trying to haul bundles of lumber."

"Ah, damn." Zachary grabbed his truck keys and slipped on his boots. Ezaray reached for her jacket, but paused when her phone trilled.

"That's my mom."

Zachary closed the distance and gripped her chin. "Small."

"I'm trying."

"What's small?" Garrett asked.

"Our wedding." Zachary grumbled like the event was an annoyance rather than a celebration. "Might be next year, though. We wanted to have it before this winter, but we can't get her family to agree to come without an argument."

"It's about time."

"Keep your peanuts in your own gallery or I'll give you my opinion of how you're handling your mate."

"I'll just say Congratulations then."

"Hey, Mom." Ezaray answered. "We already decided on the date. I know it's soon, but we want to beat the winter. No, we don't want a winter wedding, or a big one." She swung her hand at the door in the motion for them to leave.

Zachary paused before leaving the porch. "I'll send Asher, Nathan, and Anthony a message to meet us there." He tucked his phone back in his pocket and strode to his truck, but Garrett stayed where he was. "Aren't you coming?"

"No."

"Why the fuck not?"

"You guys are friends, neighbors. I'm the one she belongs to. I need to stay away. She deserves that much."

"Were we all that fucking stupid with our mates?" Zachary mumbled as he swung open the door, not expecting an answer from Garrett. He waited until Zachary peeled off before stripping and placing the jeans over the railing. Shifting, he flew back to the tree to watch over her until help arrived. She'd dragged the first bundle to the side of the house and still struggled with the second when four trucks drove up her lane.

Ezaray's words echoed in his head. *She only needs herself.* She might not need him, but he needed her. He missed her touch, her scent, and her sass. Garrett wanted to help her build her greenhouse, tend her goats. He'd considered opening his own clinic in Alder Ridge, but that didn't hold his attention long enough to plan it out. Not without Nixie. Not without a home.

If only she would trust him enough not to hold her back. He'd break his vow and be by her side for her next heartbeat.

20

———

"**W**hat are..."

"Not pushing us away this time." Zachary stormed past Nixie and lifted the bundle that inflicted the latest blister stinging her palm.

"You don't have to do that." Nixie ran to stand in front of Zachary, but she was too late. She stood in front of Nathan, Asher, and Anthony, blocking their way.

"Of course we don't. But you don't have to do it alone either."

"I want to do it alone."

Zachary grabbed her shoulders and turned her around. "Having help now and then doesn't mean you haven't done this on your own. Now grab an end." He waited for her brain to catch up and for her to grab an end of a bundle, then he took the other. Even though he could carry one on his own with ease, he included her.

She'd thank them later, although her blisters were thanking them now. The others grabbed bundles and followed behind to stack against the house. But they didn't stop at that. They'd made her show them her plans for the greenhouse and sheds. And started the frames for each of them, ensuring she did everything correctly so that she could work without them. Which she would.

Nixie thanked them all daily when they offered to help, but always turned them down. Why would she deserve what she wants if she couldn't provide herself with what she needs? And that meant doing everything on her own.

Garrett hadn't waited for her to find her voice before leaving. That hurt. But it had been the right thing to do. Nixie hadn't asked about him.

Her dream still plagued her, but now sound escaped her throat when she tried to scream at him. Too little, too late.

Holly had shown up a few hours after Garrett left. Nixie splashed her face in the bathroom, denying she'd been crying. She hadn't fooled Holly or Ezaray, who she'd brought to introduce, and when they'd tried to ask about what happened with Garrett, Nixie refused to talk. Over the first week, Holly brought the other mates, Gwen and Shaye, to visit. They'd tried to help her settle in, but Nixie took them to the porch to become acquainted, to become friends. But each tidbit of information, on shifters, mates, or even about gardening and managing a home, she stored away. It was the company she'd needed. People to talk to, friendships to build.

"There. The bottom frames for three buildings are done." Anthony, Holly's mate, packed away the tools he'd used with the lumber. Nixie had ordered everything she'd need, including the tools.

"The plan for your greenhouse should be easy for you too, but if you need a hand getting the sides up, call someone." Nathan patted her shoulder.

"But when it comes time to do the walls of the sheds, call one of us whether or not you think you need the help."

Zachary stood in front of her until she nodded her agreement.

"Thank you. I don't want any of you to think I'm ungrateful. I just need to take care of myself."

"And when you've proved your point? Then what?" Zachary crossed his arms. What came next in her life if all she ever had was herself?

"Have you talked to Garrett?" Asher frowned.

"I haven't seen him since he dropped me off. But that's for the best. We said we'd go our separate ways." But she'd expected him to at least check up on her. All four men looked at each other and then toward the trees on the south side of her house. Following their gaze, she saw nothing.

"How have you been feeling?" Asher stepped closer.

"Fine. Why?"

"I wondered if you'd still be ill with the separation despite that you've mated." She'd worried if Fate would go that far to take that last choice, but no odd pains or ailments bothered her.

"I'm fine."

"Stop suffering and call for help. Call any of us. Or call Garrett." Zachary's eyes floated to the south one more time before he squeezed her shoulder and followed the others back to their trucks.

Was she suffering? This had been a lot of hard work and stressful when worrying if she was doing it right. Was help such a bad thing? Remembering Anya and the compound, there was no way they set up even one of those homes without a handful of people. If she wanted that, she was foolish to attempt it alone.

But there was that word again. Want. This wasn't what she needed, either. She didn't need this homestead to prove to herself she could be self-sufficient. She'd shown she could take care of herself ten times over in these past weeks. What was she waiting for then?

She was suffering without Garrett.

Her gaze flying to the trees, she searched the branches for glowing gold eyes. Nothing.

"Garrett!" Leaves rustled, but it was in the low bushes. She tried again. "Garrett!"

Had the others been wrong and only looked at the trees for the same reason she searched the low branches?

"I know you're up there." She didn't. "Flap those wings, fly boy."

There. Nixie spun around to catch the gold from her peripheral vision. Two bright dots shone through high branches from one of the thickest trees. The branch bounced as he took off. She saw him, gliding down at a steep angle. Gold wind swirled around him in the air until his bare feet touched the ground.

"It's fly boy again, is it?"

"Had to say something to get you to show yourself. You sent them, didn't you?" She'd thought it had been Nathan who called everyone in to help, figuring the delivery driver must have told him she wouldn't let him move it closer.

"I didn't mean to, but I wanted to know why no one was helping you."

"Because being self-sufficient and answering to no one doesn't mean what I thought it did. I've been so focused on caring for myself and worrying about what I need versus what I want, so I didn't end up in the same position as before. Chasing desires into captivity and danger. I forgot I trust you."

"I've set you free, and I intend to make sure you stay that way." As if uncertain of himself, he took shaky steps to bring himself within reaching distance. The moment the tips of his fingers touched her jaw, she stepped back. She may feel foolish, but she hadn't been the only one blinded. Garrett couldn't get past his guilt enough to realize he should have stayed and showed her how wrong she was. He loved her. Although he hadn't said it more than in her dreams. But his guilt had a stronger hold on him than she did. And that was her fault, too.

"You never should have left."

GARRETT RETURNED to the tree in time to see them pack up the tools and materials for the day. And she'd called out to him. His heart leapt out of his chest. To hear she trusted him was a balm to his battered soul.

"You never should have left." Her voice turned hoarse as she stepped back from him. She closed her arms around herself, looking like the injured animal lashing out.

"If I hadn't left when I did, I never would have." He'd thought he'd experienced the worst in his life, but walking away from her had nearly torn him apart.

"But you felt you had to."

"Of course I had to. You deserve the choice."

"And I'm choosing now! What are you choosing?"

Garrett stumbled, his knees weak and his words caught in his throat.

"Are you choosing to hold on to your guilt or am I worth letting it go?"

And there it was. His guilt had been a living part of him for so long, it blended inside him, stretching and taking over. But he had nothing left. No fighting ring. No search for his sister. It was over. Holding on to the past would deprive him of his future. Was Nixie worth letting go and forgiving himself?

Hell, yes.

Garrett dropped to his knee—just one—and straightened his shoulders. "Nixie, I can't get enough of you. I left to give you freedom, but we were both wrong. If you can forgive me for my past and forgive me for walking away, then I can forgive myself. And you will always know your worth."

"I thought I needed to be alone, but what kind of life would I have without someone in it? There is nothing about your past that needs forgiving. And you need to see that too."

He nodded. He understood, but standing by while others killed women would take him a long time to get over.

"I love you." Her voice rose to a question. She still didn't come closer. He'd said the words aloud to her once while she slept. But not since despite how many times he thought them whenever he watched over her.

"Come here, little one." Garrett held out a hand for her to take. When he touched her, his soul sighed. "I love you, Nixie. I have since the moment I first touched you. Let me stay. Let me live with you. I want to be part of this homestead dream you have. Please."

"You do love me?"

"I'm sorry I gave you any reason to doubt that."

Nixie wrapped her arms around his neck and tumbled them to the ground. He held in a wince as the twigs and dry leaves scratched at his back. Burying his face in her neck, he held her close.

"I love you, Nixie."

"I love you, too. Stay. Please stay."

Garrett sat up and pulled them from the ground. Wrapping his hands around her thighs, he lifted her. "I'm moving in." He strode to the house and maneuvered the door open enough he could send it swinging with his foot. The house was small, and he'd only seen a couple pictures, but he made his way to the master bedroom easy enough.

Urgency grew between them. The weeks apart adding fuel to the already needy situation. Her skin felt like silk, and her scent was the purest he'd ever inhaled. Her hands worked as hard as his to rid herself of her clothes. Mouths, teeth, fingers, took over their bodies and demanded they reach their peak. After ringing her of the last quivers, he sank into her heat.

She arched to meet every thrust. Sweat beaded on the back of his neck and a sheen covered her forehead. "Nixie." Her name sounded like a sweet prayer from outside his own body. Her core squeezed him, and the pressure of his climax increased. He brought her to the edge and shoved them over at the same time. Burying his face in her neck, Garrett bit down, pulling in her taste and vowing to never walk away from her again.

EPILOGUE

John Boy bleated and rammed at the door for the third time.

"Shh." Nixie tried to hush him. It was silly to hide goats from a shifter. Even she could scent the new animals now that all her new senses had kicked in since the mating.

Before the snow had fallen, they'd finished both sheds and the greenhouse and had a successful first winter with fruits and vegetables. Winter gardens in Alberta were tough, but they'd worked hard at building a greenhouse that could withstand the cold enough to keep their produce growing strong. With not much else to take care of over the winter, Garrett had used the time to start his own clinic. Months of paperwork, renovations, and shipping equipment, and he finally opened last month. Just in time for spring when Nixie wanted to start all of her projects. And she meant all of them. Prioritizing wasn't her strong suit.

Goats weren't supposed to the be the first thing she got, but here they were, hiding in their shed while she blocked the door and waited for Garrett to get home.

The past few months had been peaceful. And Nixie needed that time. She started seeing a councilor and grew her friendships with the other shifters and mates. Having similar experiences helped her cope better than the councilor. Or maybe the two things worked in tandem. But she looked forward to the weekly coffee dates the most.

"Don't you start too, Marry Ellen." Double the bleating and double the ramming. As long as the rest of them didn't start in, too. "Damn." There was a third. Garrett better get home soon.

Gravel crunched and Garrett's truck came around the corner in the narrow lane.

"Okay. Shh, everyone. He's here." The goats froze for only a moment but then rammed harder at the door. "This was a good idea. This was a good idea. This was a good idea."

"What are you doing?" Garrett came around the side of the house and crossed his arms.

"Trying to surprise you."

He raised a brow that repeated her earlier thought. One can't surprise a shifter.

"Ta-da!" Nixie jumped to the side of the shed, pulling the door open with her. All seven goats charged, John Boy in the lead and heading straight for Garrett. He leaped and bounced, planting his hooves right into Garrett's groin. "Oh, no! Bad John Boy."

Garrett groaned and kneed the goat in the chest.

"Surprise?" Nixie covered her mouth with both hands, unsure if she should laugh or chase after John Boy. Garrett recovered, but his voice was strained.

"Seven? Didn't want to just start with two?"

"Well, no. There aren't only two Waltons."

"Ever thought of spreading them out like age gaps in the siblings?"

"Oh." Nixie gasped. "You're right. I should have spread them out."

Garrett chuckled, then eyed the goats.

"They're cute though, right?"

He adjusted himself and winced. "Yeah, real cute. Time to finish that fence."

"Both fences. We have chickens coming next week."

"Of course we do." Garret pulled her close and tipped her head back with a knuckle beneath her chin. He captured her lips with his and Nixie leaned into him. He was her freedom. And she was his. "But the fence will have to wait until later. Asher and Gwen invited us for dinner."

"Oh, good. I have a basket for Gwen." Nixie stepped away from Garrett. The goats had a partial fence, of which they'd steered clear and were wandering in and out of the trees.

"A basket of what?" Garrett clicked his tongue as he went after John Boy. Nixie gathered Mary Ellen to the shed and turned to get the others. She giggled as Garrett continued to struggle with John Boy.

"She asked for some of the herbs you've been growing. I cut some for her, but also propagated a few into her own pots."

John Boy faked a left turn, then bolted right. Garrett growled. A chortled laugh blurted from Nixie before she could choke it back.

"Think this is funny?"

"It is funny."

"You better get your goat before I get you." His seductive tone was her favourite. It pulled a yelp from her core and kick started her adrenaline. She herded John Boy into the shed with a treat. Garrett hadn't moved. His eyes only narrowed further, and the smirk on his groomed face made her belly flip flop and her feet twitch. "Run, little one."

He listened to the tiny, rapid heartbeat in her womb. They'd known for two months now, but Gwen had wanted to wait to tell anyone and to make the big announcement. He'd tried to tell her everyone except their parents already knew, but she insisted on hosting a party to tell their friends. They'd had their parents and his sister over the night before.

Maggie and Caiden should arrive from Firebrook soon. And he'd sent a message to everyone else in town. They all knew what the evening was about.

"Everything looks great, Gwen." Asher held her shoulders and pressed her back against his chest. And because he was as excited as a little boy at Christmas, he slid a hand down to cover their babe. Gwen tilted her head up and smiled.

"Think they'll go along with my planned announcement, even though they already know?"

"They will. They're here to celebrate." He turned her around, so she leaned against the railing and used the few minutes they had left until guests arrived to kiss her senseless. Senseless enough to lift the front of her dress and slip his hand beneath her panties.

"Asher, no." She followed her weak objection by gripping his wrist to hold him in place.

"Yes." He worked her nub until her body tightened. Asher pushed his fingers inside her warmth. "Quick. They're on their way up the lane. Give it to me, Gwen."

Holding herself up by his arms, she crashed, convulsing around his fingers. She panted as her oversensitive body returned to normal. Asher licked his fingers clean as the first truck door shut behind her. Gwen slapped his chest, straightened her dress, and turned to face their guests.

Caiden's eyes shot to the sky as he approached the porch. Asher nodded while Gwen embraced Maggie. "I'm so glad you two could come."

"Of course. I've missed you all so much." Maggie smiled at Gwen. She reared back, but recovered while Gwen gave Caiden a quick hug. Gwen was far enough along that even mates could scent the pregnancy.

Three more trucks pulled up, only staggered by a few minutes. Gwen ushered everyone inside after they'd reunited with Maggie and Caiden. Asher helped her pour drinks and get everyone seated, who all did so obediently with patient smiles waiting for the good news. He stood behind his mate, waiting for her to make her announcement.

Gwen tried to start a few times, then gave up and sighed. "Okay, everyone. Just say it."

They all laughed and yelled congratulations while lifting their drinks. His mate beamed up at him. She glowed with so much happiness it hurt. Asher looked around at all their friends. There had been a time when he'd felt the need to search for more of his kind. But Fate had brought them all to him, giving him not only friends but another family.

That family was growing, and by the scents in the room, it was growing by more than one.

❧

NATHAN FOLLOWED Shaye into their house. A house that he'd thought was perfect was about to be too small. He sat down on the couch and pulled his mate onto his lap.

"When were you going to tell me?" He gripped the back of her neck and held her so she couldn't hide from him.

"How did you know?" she whispered. "I only found out this morning."

"The same way we all knew Gwen has been pregnant for two months." Although Shaye's had only been detectable for the past week. Tonight had been the first time they'd seen any of the others for them to notice. They'd respectfully kept the attention on Asher and Gwen.

"We weren't ready. Are you upset?" Shaye turned herself so she straddled his hips, her centre settling against his groin.

"No, sweetness. I'll never be ready, but I'm not upset."

"I'm not sure how I feel about it." She twisted her fingers together between them. Nathan pried her hands apart and pulled her down to kiss her. He coaxed her open and slid his hands over her body, curious to see how it would change in the coming months. What he'd wanted to be a conversation escalated into more. Her hands fumbled with his jeans, pulling and tugging until he sprang free. Laying her along the couch, he bared her and entered her in one quick motion.

Locking his mouth onto hers, he dueled with her tongue while he set a steady pace that brought them both to the peak.

"I love you, Shaye. You're allowed to feel whatever you want about the baby. And I'll be right beside you the whole way."

"I love you, too."

Nathan moved down, his legs hanging off the end of the couch and his face lined with her belly. He traced her womb with his fingers until she giggled. Placing a kiss over his child, he met her eyes.

"If it's a girl, I'd like to name her after my mother. If it's a boy, after your father."

Tears glistened in her eyes. "I think that sounds lovely." She palmed his head, running her fingers through his hair as he kissed her belly. "But I'm not putting my baby to sleep in a dresser drawer."

"Guess we should plan some renovations, then. We might have a newborn by Christmas." Nathan pulled his mate from the couch and carried her to bed. Plans for an added nursery filled his head, as well as the first Christmas he looked forward to since before he could remember.

⤙

"I'M SO glad we're finally allowed to know." Ezaray flopped onto the couch. She sighed when her phone trilled for the fourth time that day with her mother's ringtone.

"Ignore it." Zachary plucked the phone from her hand and set it on the end table. He'd changed a lot since finding his mate. The bitter bad boy still lingered inside him, but finding people that accepted him made settling down easier. Finding his mate kept him alive.

"She'll keep calling."

"Then we turn the phone off."

"Then she'll start calling you."

"Good."

"No!" Ezaray reached around him and answered the phone. "Hi, Mom."

Zachary listened to the other end of the line. "How was the dinner party?"

"It was great. One of our friends is having a baby."

Two were, but it smelled recent enough that Shaye may not have yet realized.

"Oh, that's wonderful news. Anyway, I was talking to your cousins back east and they would love a chance to see you. They think being able to watch you get married would be a lovely way to spend a trip."

"Mom, no." Ezaray's voice firmed for the first time. Until now, she'd pleaded and coaxed her mother to understand. Zachary didn't blame her parents for wanting a beautiful event. Having missed two years of their daughter's life after someone had kidnapped her, they'd want to capture as much joy with her as possible. As did her extended family.

Zachary squeezed her knee in support.

"We don't want a big wedding. Neither of us wants that many people around at one time. Please understand. We only want our families and close friends, but if you won't agree, we're going to elope."

His brows hit his hairline. Damn, he never thought his mate would go that far. Eloping sounded like a fine idea to him, but deep down that wasn't what Ezaray wanted. They'd talked of a wedding with only close friends and family. White lights lining the trees and the lake in the background. Fall colours filling the trees and covering the ground. Zachary wouldn't deny Ezaray anything that made her sound as wistful as she did when describing that scene.

Silence stretched on the other end of the phone, faint breathing faded in and out.

"Don't elope, sweetheart." Her father's voice replaced her mother's. "We want to be there. We're sad to miss out on something your mother has been planning her whole life."

"I know, Dad. I'm sorry."

Zachary took her chin. Scowling, he shook his head. "Don't you dare apologize." He only spoke loud enough for her to hear and not her father. No way would he allow her to feel guilty over wanting a small wedding after what she'd been through.

Ezaray leaned against his side while she finished talking to her parents, planning for them to come visit so her mother could help plan their small and perfect wedding. She yawned once she set down her phone.

"Time for bed, Little Red."

Ezaray stretched up and swung her leg over his lap. "I have a better idea."

"Mmm, I like the way you think." He stood and lifted her over his shoulder. Screaming, she clutched the waist of his jeans. He palmed her ass while he held one arm tight around her thighs. "Careful what you ask for."

She laughed while he carted her through their home, the home they'd renovated together to house their future. Tossing her on the bed, Zachary looked down at his mate, eager to lose himself in her body.

"I love you."

"I love you, too."

HOLLY TWIRLED the rings around her finger. She'd added the band behind her engagement ring after they'd made their announcement. They'd known what the evening was about and held off telling everyone as long as possible, not wanting to steal the spotlight from Gwen, who had planned a special evening to celebrate.

Sitting on the porch as the sun finished setting, Anthony had stood and told everyone their news. They'd eloped the week before. It hadn't been easy telling their families that and it took a promised celebration in the summer to appease them all, but Holly hadn't wanted a big show. A party long after the fact she could handle, but being the centre of attention wasn't for her. Their friends had understood and only showed genuine congratulations.

Anthony settled himself in bed beside her, pulling her against him.

"It's wonderful seeing everyone so happy." Holly ran her fingers through the hair on his chest.

"But are you happy?" He cupped her cheek and tilted her face up.

"Extremely." She kissed him, nipping at his bottom lip. "Did you notice Shaye is pregnant, too?"

"I thought I sensed another one, but wasn't sure who or if I'd imagined it."

"It's still very new, I think."

"And what about you, little owl?" Anthony rolled her over, pinning her to the bed. "Do you want to have kids someday?"

She thought about it often, never sure if she was ready or would be any good as a mother. But Anthony? He would be an amazing father. Any child would be lucky to have him in their lives. His patience and kindness would ensure their child would want for nothing.

"Holly?" He touched his nose to hers when she didn't answer.

"Someday."

"I agree. Someday." He smiled before he kissed her,

settling his weight over her. "But there's something we need to do before that happens."

"Oh? What's that?"

Anthony rolled away from her and pulled an envelope from his nightstand. "Here. Open it."

She sat up against the headboard and broke the seal. Inside was a brochure. An Alaskan resort spread across the front cover. Opening it, she scanned the contents, seeing a spa, wildlife tours, hiking, and a magnificent picture of the northern lights. She blinked and looked back at Anthony, wondering if he was trying to ask her a question.

"Our honeymoon, little owl. We leave next week."

"What? Really?"

"Yes. I've had it planned for two months."

"But we didn't even decide to elope until last week."

Anthony shrugged. "There is no order of operations to life."

She kissed him and rolled on top of him, crinkling the brochure against the bed. "It looks beautiful, Anthony. Thank you. I can't wait to go."

"And I can't wait to take you there." His hands landed on her hips and he pressed her down on him. Holly moaned, unable to hold back as long as he had his hands on her.

"We might not be ready to start a family, but we need a little more practice." She ground her centre against his length, her wetness already coating him.

"We're a little rusty."

Holly pushed herself up on her knees.

"Not so fast, little owl." Anthony pulled her further up on the bed while he scooted down. "I'm hungry."

Holly caught herself on the headboard while her mate lapped at her core. She fell to the side when she reached her climax. Pulling Anthony closer, she took him into her body and realized for the hundredth time she was exactly where she was meant to be.

❧

CAIDEN DROVE into Firebrook by noon the next day. Maggie had insisted on staying in Alder Ridge long enough to have breakfast and coffee with Holly and Ezaray. Irish coffee. Which helped his little mate sleep for the drive home.

It had taken time, but Maggie gained her confidence enough to reach out to her friends on her own, staying in touch and getting to know the others. When Gwen had issued the invite, Maggie beamed with excitement. It wasn't the best timing with the spring thaw, but it was better than summer with tourists. At least it only been one night.

And today was a special day.

Caiden and Maggie had taken their time when designing their house. Maggie wanted it to be right, and Caiden didn't want unfinished projects when they moved in. They were going to break ground today.

Their plans hadn't changed in the last month, always coming back to the same design. It was time. And it was the right season.

Caiden slowed as they entered Firebrook. Maggie stirred, lifting her head from her shoulder. "That was fast."

"Sleeping helps with that."

"Sorry."

"Don't be, nymph." He reached over and gripped her hand.

"You passed the turn." Maggie's red curls swung. Caiden drove past the entrance to the lodge and the cabin they'd been living in. "Is there something you need to do at the restaurant today?"

"No." He'd taken the two days off for the trip to Alder Ridge. Despite the short distance, he'd rather spend the time with his mate than work half days.

"Where are we going?"

"You'll see."

Maggie frowned, watching his hands on the wheel. Reaching the other side of the lake, he turned up the road to his restaurant. The parking lot was full. It made him happy knowing his restaurant and the lodge were thriving. He and his brother had put their heart and soul into reviving it.

He kept driving, veering onto a fresh muddy road.

"This wasn't here a few days ago."

"No, it wasn't."

"Caiden, what's going on?"

He got out of the truck and walked around to her side to pull her out while she stared wide-eyed at the sight in front of her. "We're breaking ground on our house today."

"But we haven't finalized our plan." She gripped his arms in panic.

"Yes, we have. For the past month, we keep coming back to the same one."

"We have, haven't we?" She scrunched her nose.

Caiden nodded and pulled her in front of him, so she faced the spot of their future home. The longer she looked, the more she vibrated. She twitched and soon turned around, throwing her arms around his shoulders.

"This is really it."

He let her hug him, but couldn't stand it for much longer. Tangling his fingers in her hair, he pulled her head back. "Still think you can live with me?"

"Definitely, grizzly."

Caiden covered her mouth, sliding his tongue inside. His hold on her hair held her where he wanted her.

"Caiden," she whispered against his lips.

"Crew will be here in an hour. I asked them to wait until I brought you here."

"An hour is a long time."

"That's my girl." Caiden threw her over his shoulder and tossed her back in the truck. He had to admit, the idea of his own home was exciting. Living in the small cabin wasn't easy for a bear shifter. He'd lost count of how many times he'd hit his head on the ceiling when making love with Maggie. His tiny mate didn't have the same problem.

The locals waved as they drove past on their way back to their cabin at the lodge. Bonnie and Bella Boone stood outside the bakery with a cookie stand for the school's kindergarten class. Bonnie waved them down, swinging her arm into the street, then crossing it when they pulled to the curb on the other side.

"That was a short trip." One hand rested on the truck door where the window had disappeared.

"Just a dinner with friends." Caiden had a hard on that twitched to get moving. One hour, he'd said.

"That sounds lovely. You'll need to convince them to visit Firebrook someday."

"How's the cookie stand going?" His mate, while arousal leaked from her, didn't seem to be in as much of a rush as him.

"It's going great. Those little ones are so adorable. We split up the process for them. We had one group come in to bake, another to decorate, and the last to package. Then they're all taking turns selling at the stands. Thank you again, Caiden, for building them to size for the kids."

"No problem."

"And here's an extra thank you from the class." Bonnie held up a wicker basket filled to the brim with cookies.

"You didn't have to do that."

"I didn't. The kids did." She smiled and handed the basket through the open window to Maggie. Waving, she checked the street, then ran across.

"These look great." Maggie fingered the contents.

"Later, nymph." Caiden pulled out into the traffic. Two others had tried to wave him down, but he'd pretended he hadn't seen them. Even his brother waved at him from the front of the lodge as he'd pulled up the lane. When Wyatt slapped the back of his truck as Caiden tried to keep driving, he slammed on the brakes. He rolled down his window and hollered. "It can wait."

"I'd rather it didn't."

"Then it can wait." Tourist season would hit soon and he and his brother would see way too much of each other.

Caiden hit the gas, leaving Wyatt to scowl in his rearview mirror.

"Maybe you should talk to him."

"That hour I said we had? It's forty-five minutes now."

"Let's go!"

"Good girl."

Inside their cabin, Caiden started stripping as soon as he shut the door. He pulled at Maggie's clothes before she reached the ladder. He climbed up after her and found her already laying on the bed.

Focused on her body, her dusky nipples and her knees that couldn't decide which way to go—open or closed—Caiden hit the centre beam across the ceiling. The same damn beam as every other time.

"Fuck," he growled.

Maggie slapped her hand over her mouth, but she'd made no sound. Glaring down at her, he waited. The laugh would come.

There it was. Her laugh sputtered forth between her fingers. He smiled, and she froze. He knew how he looked. Payback for a laugh was a fun time. Even better with the clock ticking down. How many orgasms could he force from his little mate in—he looked at the clock on the nightstand —thirty-five minutes?

Join my newsletter to receive special content, the most up to date information on releases, and special promotions.
http://bit.ly/sarahurquhart

Also, visit my website at...
http://www.authorsarahurquhart.com
... to see my full book list.

The next paranormal romance series by Sarah, Firebrook Bears, begins with **Wild Rescue.**
https://books2read.com/firebrookbears1
For a look into the town of Firebrook, join Bonnie and Easton in this free novella.
https://books2read.com/firebrooknovella

www.ingramcontent.com/pod-product-compliance
Lightning Source LLC
Chambersburg PA
CBHW020343220726
48290CB00013B/541